Keith's People

KEITH'S PEOPLE

A NOVEL

ELLEN PERRY BERKELEY

ELDERBERRY PRESS, LLC

All characters and incidents in this novel are products of the author's imagination, and any resemblance to persons living or dead is purely coincidental. Vietnam during and after the war, however, is represented accurately, to the best of the author's ability, according to material from many sources.

Cover design by Jim Nicolai at youralbum@aol.com

ELDERBERRY PRESS, LLC
1393 Old Homestead Drive, Second floor
Oakland, Oregon 97462—9506.
http://elderberrypress.com
E-MAIL: editor@elderberrypress.com
TEL/FAX: 541.459.6043

All Elderberry books are available from your favorite bookstore, amazon.com, or from our 24 hour order line: 1.800.431.1579

Library of Congress Control Number: 2002112790
Publisher's Catalog-in-Publication Data
Keith's People/Ellen Perry Berkeley
ISBN 1-930859-44-9
1. Vietnam——Fiction.
2. Vietnam War——Fiction.
3. Communism——Fiction.
4. Viet Cong——Fiction.
5. Mystery——Fiction.
6. Suspense——Fiction.
7. Murder——Fiction.
I. Title

This book was written, printed, and bound in the United States of America.

part one

chapter one

In the middle of the afternoon on the last day of his life, Bernie Novinsky chuckled. Some days were just gooooooooood. He was back in his cubbyhole after taping his weekly program, an interview with a middle-aged relic of the Sixties' counterculture who had made a name for himself in all the predictable ways and was still miraculously holding it all together. Patric Curtin had leaned into the camera at the start of the hour, full of confidence, his thick dark hair uncombed, his shirt open at the neck, describing breathlessly, intimately, how his recent two-week trip to the Socialist Republic of Vietnam had been the peak experience of his life.

Still predictable, Bernie clucked to himself. For decades, these people have swarmed to every new "socialist experiment" in order to bring back "the truth" (never less than glowing) about a place that any fool could see was an economic disaster, repressive, and a hell-on-earth for the people who *couldn't* leave after two weeks. How did these people have the nerve to "rejoice" in the change under Gorbachev when they had never even hinted that any change might be welcome? Bernie had no use for them, and not much use for Gorbachev either — the guy's playing us for a fool, he wrote recently in an article that was still, he was happy to see, being hailed and blasted in all the predictable places.

But here was Patric Curtin, fresh from his latest travels, smiling, confident, pleased to say on TV that Vietnam has had its own Gorbachev for four years now (since 1986) —"he is sometimes called the 'little Gorbachev,'" Curtin purred — and pleased *not* to say that Vietnam remains just about as dismal and repressive as it has been for all the years (fifteen and counting) since the North Vietnamese rolled into Saigon in 1975. Here was Pat Curtin clinging to his upside-down vision of utopia as to a dream of eternal youth. Oddly, it kept him young. Pat Curtin had a body without flab, a face without lines, a compelling voice, eyes clear and sparkling. To Bernie, he was a Perfect Guest: high on sex appeal, low on honesty and integrity, easily demolished. Most of Bernie's guests (and Bernie, too, he would be the first to admit) were the opposite in all respects.

Pat Curtin had lost more and more of his cool as the studio began to heat up. And, near the end, were those *jowls* discernible below the corners of his down-turned mouth? Bernie smiled now at the memory.

In the final few moments, Curtin had pulled what he probably considered his trump card, laying the blame for every problem in Vietnamese life on the war — on the American war, long over, Bernie pointed out, not on the years of war afterward in Vietnam, against Cambodia, and not, surely, on the vast portion of the Vietnamese budget currently going into the military. ("Somewhere between 40 and 50 per cent, isn't it?" Bernie had asked pleasantly. Pat Curtin had blinked.) "Is it," Bernie then asked, "that America should feel so guilty, so responsible for Hanoi's every brutality, every rigidity, every mismanagement, that we will grant immediate diplomatic recognition, to be followed by reparations *and* foreign aid *and* trade *and* investment *and* — what else? Did I leave anything out? Delegations of unpaid experts? Planeloads of privileged college kids, eager to play at work they know they can always stop doing?" Curtin's mouth had tightened and Bernie, a veteran debater, had smelled the panic of a cornered animal.

"Isn't it," Bernie followed, "that there are people who would like to attract hard currency to Vietnam not simply to save the Vietnamese economy but to save Vietnamese communism, at whatever price to the Vietnamese people, and to save it without requiring the Soviet Union to pour in a whole lot more money — which the Soviet Union no longer wants to do anyway?" It was too bad that this question came so close to the end of the hour, giving Pat Curtin little time to organize and deliver his reply, but that's the breaks, chuckled Bernie. Being a guest on Bernie Novinsky's program was always chancy. As a television critic had quipped recently, Novinsky's guests got exposure all right, but some of them also got exposed.

The post-program pleasantries were minimal. Pat Curtin had extended his hand to meet Bernie's and the hand was hot and damp. He had mopped his face with a boldly printed handkerchief from his back pocket. He regretted the need to leave immediately — some important engagement involving a good number of people, he hinted — but what could he do? His constituency awaited him "out there," was the unspoken message. And because Bernie saw that the man was embarrassed and shaken, he didn't prolong the departure. Bernie was not an unkind person. He didn't live for other people's humiliation. He lived for *ideas*, he liked to say, and thus could be well satisfied that the past hour was an intellectual triumph, not a personal one. Still, as he sometimes said to friends (very close friends), it was great to see one of these bastards squirm.

Back at his tiny desk, a little more than an hour after he had left it, Bernie was smiling in what he hoped looked like intellectual triumph. His eye caught a telephone message folded into a near relative of an origami beast and he silently complimented the artist. He was still smiling when he read the name on the slip; apparently Ho Chi Minh had called Bernie Novinsky at precisely 3:22 p.m., leaving no message.

"Gimme a break," Bernie said to himself in mock despair and went looking for Adam Willner.

Adam wasn't your typical "go-fer." For one thing, he was working at the public television station where his father was considered one of the hottest executive producers in a decade. For another, he wasn't precisely *working*. He was taking time off from college (whether by his choice or theirs wasn't clear) and was spending his days at the station during more or less the same hours as everyone else. But he wasn't trusted with much; people soon found that Adam Willner did his work slowly and sloppily: the worst combination.

Still, he was likable and he had connections.

Bernie Novinsky was willing to give him the benefit of the doubt since Adam was "dating" his daughter (whatever *that* meant). Bernie didn't think it an altogether promising match, she from Columbia and he from Bennington. But youth was a time for experimentation, or so he had been told — and so he could still remember.

He found Adam's lanky height folded with great skill onto a tiny rolling secretarial chair.

"Is this your handiwork?" Bernie asked, gesturing with the origami message.

"Yeah," said Adam, rising and smiling.

"Ho Chi Minh? The man's been dead for twenty-one years."

"Actually, Ho Chi Minh is only a rough approximation," said Adam. Bernie was momentarily silent. Then he said, not unkindly, "The point is to write down the name the way the person gives it to you." Good grief, what was his daughter *doing* with this turkey? No, he'd rather not know what she was doing with him.

"I would have, but I couldn't find a pen that worked," said Adam. He warmed to his subject. "You know, when you do a pledge week here, you shouldn't tell people to get out a pen and write the station a check, you should tell them to get out a pen and send it in. You'd get hundreds of pens. Hundreds of working pens. All colors. All kinds. What a fantastic scene!" Bernie chuckled. He was impressed. He had long ago decided that you can't count on the basic skills of the young, but occasionally you ran across one who had a certain style. Adam hurtled on.

"The real trouble is that it's not the real world in this place. You know? Nobody steals the supplies. The pens just stay here and run dry. Any other office, the stuff walks out the door so fast it doesn't get a chance to go bad. You know what I mean? There was a guy at Bennington could have opened a stationery store with what he got on just a three-month job. He spread it all out on his bookshelves. He didn't have that many books, which is how he had the shelf space, you know? Anyway, he spread it all out, and it looked like an aisle at Woolworth's. Impressive. And he left it there, and used it little by little, until some *reptile* suddenly began *stealing* it from him. Can you believe, some guy from our own *house*? It was the biggest thing at school all term. We had a house meeting that went on until practically—"

"Adam," Bernie interrupted, "did Ho Chi Minh say what he wanted?"

"Well, we had a bit of a problem understanding each other." He smiled. "Yes, yes," he added, in a passable W.C. Fields imitation.

"I suppose he'll call again," Bernie said, not wanting to press the point. Ever since his own trip to Vietnam he had been getting letters and calls from Vietnamese refugees resettled in the U.S., asking whether he had seen this brother, that father, who hadn't been heard from since the unfortunate one had been taken to his second or third re-education camp.

Adam was slouching uneasily against a low partition. "He didn't want to leave a number. Which was OK, since I couldn't find a pen to write it down anyway. But I think he'll call again. He said he wants to talk to you about the spies coming out with the new boat people — from Vietnam, you know."

"Of course I know," said Bernie. "He said *spies*? And *new* boat people?"

Adam nodded.

"His exact words?"

Adam nodded again.

"Then why didn't you write it down? On this — message?"

"I didn't have to write it down. I could remember it."

Bernie turned away, thinking that life was either immensely funny or immensely sad. He felt very middle-aged. It had been a long time since he had said anything so dumb, or even thought it. And then he wondered whether Adam might be pulling his leg, saying something absurd to test the absurdity of a world that hears something absurd and goes right on. He looked up to read Adam's face, but Adam was gone. Bernie Novinsky was left with the sense that life was terribly funny *and* terribly sad — both, and simultaneously.

• • •

In the living room of a seedy two-room apartment on Manhattan's Upper West Side, Bernie Novinsky's picture lay on a worn coffee table from which coffee had never been served (at least not here). It was a small picture, smiling out from the *Times*. It was the only picture on a five-week-old page of television listings.

Nothing in the sparsely furnished apartment looked untidy, and a visitor might wonder why an outdated television page hadn't been thrown out. But the thin gray man who lived here had no visitors; he knew no one he might have asked in and no one he might have been surprised by. He and he alone looked upon these four yellowed walls.

He looked around the place now, more intent on what he was doing than on anything he was seeing. He went over to the door and picked up the paper shopping bag that was beside it, inspecting the outside of the satchel and poking at the towels inside. He was frowning slightly.

He took a grayish coat from the small closet near the door and placed it decisively over the back of one of the kitchen chairs. There was no kitchen, of course, just the ancient necessary appliances along a wall of the living room. He took the chipped coffee mug from the dish drain and put it back on its shelf above, then took the Horn and Hardart spoon and put it back in the utensil drawer below. His furniture was as drab as he was, not with a lack of color but with the mismatched colors of things acquired on the cheap and by chance over the years — a table with an edging of pitted chrome and a top of faded blue laminate; a permanently depressed easy chair in a fabric that was once probably red; and a pair of straight-backed chairs (not precisely a pair), one painted green, with a dirty yellow cushion on it, and the other, with his coat over the back of it, stained a blotchy schoolroom brown.

He reached onto the shelf of the closet for his gloves. Yes, gloves would be important. He placed them on the table near his coat.

From the pocket of his shapeless gray pants, he took out a piece of paper, unfolded it to read it, then carefully folded it again and put it back. He looked around the room, his eye passing over walls that — to anyone else — would look desperately bare: no mirrors, no pictures, not even a calendar. But he was not seeing the walls; he was running down a mental checklist, nodding to himself the way people do when they are accustomed to having only themselves for companionship.

Now he went over to the coffee table, picked up the picture of

Bernie Novinsky and opened the folded page to its full dimensions. He looked at the picture for a long moment, only the slightest trail of an emotion pulling at the deep wrinkles of his gray face. A friend might have noticed the gradual graying of his skin, the steady leaching out of his substance. But he had no friends. No one, until Keith, had ever reached out to him, made connection with him. Keith wasn't exactly a friend. But he was the only one who did some of what a friend was supposed to do.

Suddenly, in a movement unusual for the still room and in a display of feeling unusual for him, he crumpled the page into a tight ball and pressed it even tighter. He walked over to the shopping bag beside the door and dropped the wadded newsprint into it. Very carefully, then, very thoughtfully, he put on his coat and buttoned it, pulled on his gloves, picked up the shopping bag, and left the apartment. He would discard the picture of Bernie Novinsky as soon as he saw a trash can.

• • •

Bernie had a few things to do before he left the station. Look over the mail that accumulated from one weekly visit to the next. Exchange some office gossip. Make some quick phone calls. He tried Hallie at her office. No answer after seven rings. He tried her at home and got the answering machine. "You gotta catch the program this week," he said to the machine. "This guy's friends are gonna be lining up to shoot me. Let's hope they stand in a circle and give me a chance to duck. How's everything? See ya soon?"

Towering suddenly over the entrance to his cubbyhole was Adam. "I forgot to say, Mr. Novinsky, that was a really interesting show." And then he added, "I've just about decided not to go to Vietnam," in the same way he might have said he wouldn't be watching the day's rerun of "Star Trek."

"I didn't know you were considering it," Bernie said.

"Well sure. I mean it's the place to go, before too many people do it. The thing is, I've heard about tourists getting pig liver three meals in a row. I wouldn't be able to choke it down *one* meal in a row."

"You'd be surprised what you can choke down," Bernie laughed.

"Oh yeah?" And then, when no examples were forthcoming, "Still, pig liver must be the worst." He nodded solemnly to himself. "I wonder if that means breakfast too."

Bernie was also solemn. "I didn't know you were especially interested in Vietnam."

"Well, I've talked to a few people who've been. Friends of my parents. They'd be more like the man you interviewed today. You know? People you wouldn't think very highly of."

"I think highly of anyone who uses his brains and is honest about what he knows. My beef against these people is that they are either deliberately lying to themselves about what these places are like or are deliberately lying to the rest of us. It's been going on for sixty, seventy, years now: the Soviet Union, Cuba, China, Nicaragua, now Vietnam. The same story, for seventy years."

"I guess you've been around a long time, Mr. Novinsky," said Adam.

The weight of that observation made Bernie feel rather older than he liked. "Long enough to know a few things," he replied, smiling.

"Hey, I gotta go do a delivery. Catch you later." And he was gone.

Bernie thought of calling his wife, but decided against it. He would soon be home. He tucked the origami message into his bookshelf, stuffed a few things into his briefcase, swept up his coat, and left his cubbyhole. Near the elevator, he passed three or four women coming in for a volunteers' meeting. They recognized him and smiled shyly, seeming to expect no greeting in return. "Nice to see you here," Bernie boomed out. He thought it likely that at least one of them had recently been to Vietnam, returning with stories about how friendly the people were, not at all what she expected, and how generous, even though they had nothing.

• • •

During all of the gray time of day, on this gray street, the thin gray man had stood without moving in the doorway, part of the scenery, waiting. When the street lights came on, his head jerked up involuntarily, as if he'd been dozing in a streetcar and been awakened by the weight of his own head falling onto his chest. Keith had said this would be the hardest part. Staying alert. Fixing his attention on the building opposite. Waiting. Keith was right.

He moved only occasionally, shifting his weight. Now, barely moving, he eased back his coat sleeve and cast a glance at the watch sliding down his bony wrist. Ten of six. Shouldn't be long now.

Manhattan's side-streets may look the same, to the unobservant. But to this aging man, his lifetime spent in New York City, every street had memories. He had been to organizing meetings on this very street, in the townhouse of a machinist whose wife had inherited money. . . . Or perhaps it was in the next block. The townhouse was gone, if it had been here at all; in its place was the large apartment building opposite, a dark and heavy masonry pile that had probably been on this street for decades.

He was up a few steps from the sidewalk and back from it, alongside one of the two squat columns holding up a portico around a stone doorway.

Immobile and silent as a gargoyle, he watched the few people hurrying home. "Why don't you see me?" he could have shouted. But he was not the shouting kind. Even when his wife left him. Even when his son left him. Even now, when he was old and ill and his own self — his only real friend — was about to leave him.

At his feet, leaning into his leg like an affectionate cat, was the shopping bag with the gun in it. He had planned to carry the gun in his coat pocket — this was Keith's advice — but he'd had a rush of worries at the last minute. Couldn't the gun be seen there? Couldn't it slip out? Or, if he kept his hand around it, in his pocket, couldn't it go off accidentally? He'd always been a worrier, and all of this was new to him. In the end, he'd taken a shopping bag.

A chill was sweeping into the side-street from Riverside Drive, but the chill was already deep inside him. It was late October, and this was not an easy night to be out. He forced his eyes to scan the street.

Maybe this wasn't the right night after all. Always the worrier. He should call again.

He could use the phone down the street and still keep an eye on the entrance to the apartment building. Yes, he'd call again. Keith hadn't said he shouldn't. He walked to the phone near the corner.

The same woman answered.

"Hello? Mr. Novinsky there?" he asked.

The woman's voice was pleasant. "No, but I expect him shortly. Would you like to leave a message?"

"When will he be home?"

"My guess isn't any better now than it was then," she laughed briefly. "He was taping a show this afternoon. He usually calls if he's going to be very much delayed." Then, after a pause, "May I give him a number where he can reach you?"

"You think soon now?"

"Yes, within the next half hour, I'd say. He'd be glad to call you if—"

The thin gray man brought his waiting finger down on the telephone hook. He thought of making another call, to Keith. But he didn't. Keith had said he shouldn't.

• • •

Inside the Novinsky apartment, the woman moved languidly to the window and looked absent-mindedly through a slat in the Venetian blind to the empty street below. Sometimes she could see Bernie approaching. And sometimes after she had seen him, she went back to her desk, letting him think he had surprised her there. She had only recently taken to doing this. She wouldn't have liked trying to explain it.

• • •

Bernie smiled as he walked the two blocks between the subway and his corner. He didn't usually get such a high from his interviews. And now he was getting a name for them too. It wasn't that he was unfair in his arguments (well, maybe a little unfair in his timing) or that people were watching just for the show of it. No, his *ideas* were what was winning him a following. His ideas and his fearlessness. He'd always been combative. And he'd always *cared.* Not just another pretty face.

Why, he might even become a television "personality." He'd been a serious writer for all these years, of books and tracts and articles.

Could he stand the notoriety? Stand it? He'd *love* it. Was he recognizable already? Rose Novinsky's plain little boy — his wiry hair still in Brillo ringlets and his serious brown eyes too close together — looked expectantly at the small man hurrying across the street toward him.

"You're Bernie Novinsky?" asked the man in the gray coat, his face only partly illumined by the street light. Something in his constricted voice suggested he hoped — just a little — that he was wrong.

• • •

The black kid rearranging grocery bags on his delivery bike saw it all. A kid who thought he'd seen everything saw one white man ask another white man for his wallet — nicely, as though he was asking for some directions, but he had a gun, which made it not so nice — then saw the man with the gun jerk away at it, firing three, four, five times, recovering with difficulty each time from the recoil, but firing as though it was the most natural thing in the world, as though he'd done it thousands of times before. Or maybe he'd never done it before.

The black kid saw the gunman look at the body on the sidewalk, one leg twisted under it and a look of surprise fixed on the bloody face. He saw the gunman back away from the blood gushing toward his feet, a look of surprise on *his* face. And the boy with the delivery bike, a boy who had acquired his knowledge of the world very young and wasn't shocked by much of anything any more, had a look on *his* face (for just a moment) of utter surprise.

The boy watched, his mouth open, as the man in the gray coat ran to the corner. Then, wheeling his bike around quickly, the boy followed. Bernie Novinsky did not move. He lay dead in a puddle in front of his apartment building. The puddle was dark and wet and glistening from the reflected light of the street lamp. It could have been a puddle of rainwater, or of something spilled. But it was Bernie Novinsky's life-blood and it would stain the sidewalk for days afterward.

chapter two

Hallie Cooper looked up at the vintage wall clock — for the third time in as many minutes — and rose with determination.

"Look," she said. "I've been waiting for Sergeant Zinck more than an hour. Can you give me some idea how much longer he'll be?" She raised her voice against the hubbub.

The clerk looked up blandly and blinked several times. "I really don't know, ma'am." He bent down again over his work, on good behavior in front of a visitor.

"Is there some way of finding out?" Hallie asked, not bothering to keep the edge out of her voice.

"Well, he's got a fresh D.B. and he's pretty busy." He paused long enough to be sure of Hallie's blank look. "That's a dead body," he added generously.

"I know the case," said Hallie, making a point of not thanking him. "I — knew — the victim."

"Oh, I thought you were a reporter," said the young man, released from his work by the demands of this new situation.

"I *am* a reporter," said Hallie briskly. "But I also knew the man who was killed. . . . Can you find out when Sergeant Zinck can see me?"

"You don't *have* to know him, I mean the deceased," said the young man.

"Of course I don't have to," said Hallie heatedly; "I just do." She bit her lip for an instant and winced. "Did."

"But you might get in quicker if you know him. *Knew* him, I mean." The young man's tone was respectful.

"Fine," said Hallie. "I knew him. Now when can I get in to see Sergeant Zinck?" Her voice was sharp, commanding.

"I really don't know, ma'am. Uh, did you know him well?"

"Look, I just want to see Sergeant Zinck. You and I could spend the whole afternoon talking about this, and I'd be happy to mention your name in the newspaper — let your superiors know how hard you work, how much time you spend talking to visitors, that sort of thing. Or you could get me in to see Sergeant Zinck."

"I'll see what I can do, ma'am. I'll tell him you knew the deceased, if that's what you'd like."

"Yes. That's what I'd like."

"Instead of your being a reporter."

"Look," said Hallie with some severity. "I'm a reporter. I also knew the deceased. You may include both of these facts in whatever proceedings you are undertaking. Please let us not discuss this further." She sank back onto the bench, exhausted by her failure to move this day along and to keep her grief and anger under control. The clerk jumped up and departed on his errand. Emotional outbursts made him nervous. He came back to his desk and glanced at her only long enough to be sure she wasn't turning violent. She was dabbing a handkerchief at her eyes. He kept an uneasy watch on her until Charlie Zinck bolted out of his office a moment later, his hair rumpled.

Not that Zinck's hair was especially long. But like certain men of a certain age, Zinck was pleased that he still had hair at all, and was glad he had enough of it to look rumpled. No gray hairs yet for him — well, maybe a few — just a messy dark mane suggesting that he'd been out in a November gale instead of stuck in an overheated office. Hallie Cooper saw an athletic man, a man no longer young but a man determined not to be old before his time. For an instant she imagined him at the helm of a sailboat, a stiff breeze tangling his dark hair, the sun tanning his strong arms.

"Sorry to keep you waiting, Ms. Cooper. I've been behind all day." He moved quickly, motioning her toward the tiny cubicle that was his office. "You'll want to take your coat too."

"I thought . . . in a police station," she stammered.

"Even here. Maybe especially here." He smiled perfunctorily and motioned her to a chair. Unhinged. The lady was definitely unhinged. Handsome but coming apart. He looked at her steadily, pleasantly, waiting for her to speak. She had probably been breathtakingly pretty at twenty and would probably be strikingly beautiful at sixty — the gray eyes, the delicate nose — but here she was somewhere in between and no longer pretty and not yet striking. She was real, though, and even her hesitation drew him in. He knew about her, as did anyone who read the best afternoon paper in New York. She was tough and strong and a pro. And here she was, in his office in the middle of the afternoon, coming apart.

"I want to talk to you about Bernie Novinsky," she said, after a long moment, and the squeak in her voice surprised them both.

"Yes. What about him?"

"He was killed. Yesterday. . . ." She paused and he waited. "I want to tell you that it *wasn't* just a robbery. I don't care *what* it looks like, that man was *not* killed for the money in his wallet. He was killed because he made enemies with everything he did, everything he wrote, and it would be a travesty to pretend otherwise. He *loved* making enemies. He *lived* for it. And he surely died for it." Her face was flushed, her eyes moist.

Again the detective waited. Then, "You knew him?"

"Very well. His wife and I have been close friends since college."

Then she wasn't sleeping with him, thought Zinck. Or maybe she was.

"I want you to find out who killed him," she said, her voice like a little girl's, trusting, pleading.

"That's what we're here for," Charlie Zinck answered. He regretted the lilt in his voice. Why had she really come?

"How did you learn about his death?" he asked.

"I was covering a meeting last night, until about nine. When I got home I listened to my answering machine. There was a message from — him. And one from Joan. 'Right in front of our apartment building,' she kept saying. 'Right in front of our building.' I couldn't make it out. I must have called her back a dozen times. The line was always busy. Finally, she had sounded so odd, I just went over there. I stayed the night. . . . She said you'd been there earlier." Then almost hesitantly, as if tattling on someone who has told a small lie, Hallie Cooper said, "She wants to think it was just a robbery."

"What would she get out of that?" Zinck had been wondering about Joan Novinsky himself, since last night, wondering about a lot of things about her.

"What indeed?"

Zinck waited. "What would she get out of that?" he repeated.

Hallie Cooper took a deep breath, using the time to decide how far she could trust this man into whose care she had brought all of this. She exhaled slowly. She would trust him, a little. "What she would get is just some ease from the terrible anger she feels toward him. Some relief from the idea that he brought it on himself. That he asked for it somehow, by being the kind of person he is — was. That he didn't care enough about her to be different. Do you know what I mean?"

"I think so." He knew exactly what she meant. It could have been a description of his own marriage, except that he hadn't stayed married and hadn't gotten killed. He ran into his ex-wife every few years. She was probably the age of the woman facing him now. But the ex had developed mean lines around the mouth and frown lines between the eyes during the past five years, and Charlie Zinck was beginning to understand finally (nothing to do with the lines) that she had never loved him the way he wanted to be loved.

He looked at the woman facing him and asked quietly, "What was the message he left on your machine?" He saw her flinch very slightly: just a flickering of the eyes.

"Nothing of any consequence, really. He thought the program had gone very well — the taping — and he wanted me to be sure to watch it. The person he interviewed would hate it, he said, and would probably want to get a bunch of people together to . . . do him in."

"Those were his words?"

"No, I don't think so. But that was the general idea. He was joking, of course."

"Of course. I'd like to hear that message, if you haven't erased it."

"I haven't."

"Will you bring it in tomorrow?"

"I will."

He was struck by the earnestness of her promise, a little girl's promise. In all her years of growing tough and worldly and capable, some part of her had never grown older. Possibly never grown up.

"Tell me about you and Bernie Novinsky."

"He was . . . very important to me." She said no more.

"Were you intimate?"

"We were very close." Her face contorted briefly with things unspoken, and he felt an urge to cradle her head against his shoulder, to draw her grief from her. But urges were for people not on the public payroll.

"Were you sexually intimate?" There were other ways to ask it but this would do.

"No," she whispered, and he saw the sudden tears on the tightly closed eyelids.

At this point you either believed the person or you didn't. Charlie Zinck thought it was probably fifty-fifty on this one. But it wasn't worth belaboring, for now anyway. It certainly wasn't worth grilling her about, for the next twenty-four or thirty-six hours, which is what the outside world might have suggested. Why did the outside world think that intimidation was every cop's favorite recreation? Second only to fornication, maybe, but right up there with getting drunk and —

"Who do you think wanted to kill him?" Zinck asked.

She opened her eyes and spoke very calmly. "It would be a long list, the people who wanted him out of the way. He had very firm views and he made a very strong case for them. I can imagine some people feeling quite glad they don't have to contend with Bernie Novinsky any more. The gadfly swatted. But that's different from actually going out and *doing* something about it, doing it *themselves.*" She paused and he waited. "I can't think of anyone like that. It would have to be someone pretty crazy."

"Any candidates?"

"No. Truly."

Some people, when they said "truly," really meant it. And some didn't. Charlie Zinck thought it was probably better than fifty-fifty that she meant it. But he had been lied to by pros, in this job. Which reminded him. Time to go over to Novinsky's apartment building again and get lied to by amateurs — by the people who didn't want to get involved — and perhaps by the people who were already involved and understandably wanted to keep that information to themselves.

"Well, thank you, Ms. Cooper." He rose. "It was good of you to come." He wasn't just sure *why* she had come, and whether it was good or not, but the job required numerous such harmless flatteries.

"You'll think about what I've said, that it couldn't have been just a robbery." Her voice, her look, made it a question.

He nodded firmly and she nodded in return.

"And you'll bring that tape to me, from your answering machine," he reminded her.

She nodded again and left. Looking at her as she walked quickly past the clerk and over to the elevator, he suddenly saw the limp. How had he missed seeing it when she came in? He remembered a little girl in grade school with him. They had called her "Cripple" until she cried, and then until she learned not to cry any more.

• • •

If you were lucky, you got a few hints from every witness, the reluctant ones as well as the eager ones. If you weren't lucky, you just got a headache. Charlie Zinck was beginning to get a headache.

He had been to see the only two people that Steve Marino had been able to unearth all day and last night, who had seen *anything*. Did all the people in this building live in their bathrooms? A whole apartment building, twelve floors of old-style grandeur, of people living in their large, old-timey black-and-white-tiled bathrooms: telephoning their mothers, pissing, bathing, eating, reading, fucking, watching TV, riding exercise bikes, crying, writing poetry, in their bathrooms, while the world went to hell outside.

It wasn't that he'd gotten nothing from the two people he'd just talked to. They'd each seen *something*. But when you added it up it wasn't much. Or it was too much. Try asking your Identikit cop to work up someone who's a cross between a little old guy, white, and an adolescent boy, black. Even Identikit cops have their problems.

Anthony Perrone in apartment 3A, who'd been sure he'd seen the black kid who'd done it, was a certifiable racist. Not that this was illegal, or even uncommon, but it put his observations into a certain light. He had raved on to Zinck about the black kid who'd held him up at knife-point three years ago. "And this kid with the bike was the spitting image of him, lemme tell you. And he was there when I heard the shots. I don't know what other proof you need. Hell, if you'da put him in jail three years ago, none of this woulda happened. But you never even picked him up. It's like he never even existed, except in my mind. Christ, maybe I'm the one doesn't exist. Nah, I exist, all right. I was robbed. I exist."

Perrone had mopped his damp forehead with a handkerchief gone gray, bewildered by a world that did not take him seriously. *His* world was insurance, and the detective complimented him on what Perrone proudly called his "rogues' gallery" — signed portraits of all the presidents since Eisenhower. "I write to 'em and ask if I can serve 'em in their insurance needs," Perrone smiled conspiratorially. "I never get a policy out of 'em, but I always get a photo." Zinck nodded his approval of a thorough job and asked Perrone to come down to the station to work with the Identikit cop. "But you guys have it all already," said Perrone, his stress level rising again. "You drew a picture three years ago, coulda been done by one of those street artists it was so perfect." Zinck explained that it was routine to do a new one for any new investigation — if it wasn't, it was now — and left. In the corridor he mopped his own brow.

Caroline Gottschalk in 4C, who'd peeked out at the old guy last night for a good two hours, wasn't any more help.

"I don't want to get him into trouble. It's a free country, after all. We can't go arresting people just for *standing* there, can we? He certainly didn't look like a *killer*, if you know what I mean, and I'm sure you don't want us calling 911 whenever we see anything the least bit peculiar. Heavens, in a city like this, you wouldn't have time to do anything but answer the phone, now, would you?"

She was exceedingly vague about the man's appearance — not *too* old, not *too* short — considering that she'd kept a close watch on him through a lengthy phone call with her elderly mother, through the evening news on several channels, through the meticulous preparation of a gourmet feast for one. Overweight and under-appreciated, Caroline Gottschalk had been a junior high school teacher for too many years; all her sentences ended in questions. So when Zinck asked her whether she'd seen a black teenager hanging around at the time, she took the opportunity to place Zinck irrevocably among the dumb kids: "Not all our criminals are black, now, are they, Officer?" At the end of this unproductive interview in her vastly overheated apartment, dumb-kid Zinck wiped his moist palms on the flowered slipcover of her sofa before rising to meet the dismissive handshake of the teacher.

And now, going to meet Steve Marino at apartment 2D, Charlie Zinck definitely had a headache.

Marino had beeped him that he'd found one more person Zinck ought to talk to, an elderly man whose wife thought he'd seen something. Zinck opined that women didn't usually know what their husbands had seen, even when they were both looking at the same thing. Marino informed him that the elderly man would be just getting back from his day-care program by now. Zinck said he was ready for a day-care program himself. "Yeah," Marino answered agreeably, "I know what you mean."

Steve Marino was waiting outside 2D when Zinck came out of the elevator. Marino was a chunky kid, a big blond kid with an easy grin. You wouldn't think he was much of a cop if all you knew about was the pigeons. But Zinck knew him better than that — and trusted him, more or less. Zinck smiled broadly now, recalling the pigeon incident. Marino smiled back in greeting.

The white-haired woman who answered the door seemed distracted, and she glanced over her shoulder at the man sitting in the living room with his back to the door. The apartment was dimly lit, the shades still up, and the deepening twilight was visible outside.

"My husband likes to sit by the window," she said. She talked about him as though he couldn't hear.

"It was your husband who saw something yesterday, Mrs. Korngold?" Zinck asked. "He was here alone?"

"No, I don't leave him alone any more. I was here, but I was setting the table, fixing supper. I was in and out of this room."

"And your husband?"

"He was just sitting there. I check on him every so often, but otherwise I can leave him alone in a room. I should tell you that his memory isn't what it used to be." She looked at Steve Marino. "Perhaps I shouldn't have let you come back. But because of the murder . . ." She walked to her husband. "Dear, these people want to talk to you. . . . Dear?" She put her hand on the old man's arm, and he finally turned to look at her. It was a blank look, as trusting as a child's but without a child's expectation.

"Sir, could you tell us what you saw yesterday?" Zinck began. "From this window?"

The old man made no answer.

"Did you see something unusual yesterday?"

"Yes."

"What did you see, sir?"

"I was looking out this window." He spoke slowly, every word delivered with difficulty.

"You saw something unusual yesterday," Zinck prompted.

"Yes."

"Did you see some*one*? Someone *special*?"

"I always look out this window." He didn't continue.

"Did you see something special, yesterday, from this window?" Zinck pressed.

"Yes." Again the old man was silent.

"Could you tell me what you saw?"

"When I was a little boy, my sisters and I looked out this same window."

"What did you see yesterday? What happened yesterday, Mr. Korngold?"

"I've lived here since I was a little boy," he said. He smiled gently.

Zinck exhaled in frustration and turned to the man's wife. "You didn't see anything yourself?"

"No," she said limply. "I wish I could help."

"What makes you think your husband saw something? We won't keep you long, Mrs. Korngold. Just a few more questions."

"That's quite all right. As I said to this young man, my husband became quite excited. That's not usual for him."

"What did he say to you? His exact words, if you can remember them."

"He called to me: 'Alice, Alice.' So I came running in. I don't think he said anything else. He . . . doesn't talk very much these days. . . . I didn't even connect it with anything until the police drove up a few minutes later."

Marino turned to Zinck. "Excuse me, but I . . . know this." He knelt down next to the old man and spoke clearly, intensely. "You looked out this same window when you were a little boy."

"Yes," said the old man. He was searching Marino's face, trying to recognize him.

"And your sisters looked out this same window with you."

"Yes."

Steve Marino put his hand on the old man's arm. "Tell me about your sisters."

"I had two sisters, Ida and Ruth."

"Were you the oldest?"

"No. Ida was the oldest, I think. Yes, she was. But I was next."

"You took good care of your sisters, didn't you?"

"Yes."

"Because you didn't want some man to hurt them?"

"Yes. A man in a doorway," said the old man.

"A man in a doorway," Marino repeatd.

"Yes," said the old man, nodding slowly, frowning slightly.

"A thin man waiting in a doorway," Marino prompted, fixing the old man's gaze with his own.

"Yes."

"Which doorway were you afraid of?" asked Marino. "Point it out to me."

A long moment passed, and then the old man raised a heavily veined hand to point to the stone doorway across the street. The doorway was back from the sidewalk and sheltered by a portico. Steve Marino inhaled slowly. One wrong move and the old man's tattered memory would be lost to them both, his frayed thoughts swept down another path entirely in his tangled brain.

"He came from the doorway . . ." Marino prompted.

"Yes," said the old man.

"And then . . ."

The old man was silent for a long moment. "I'll tell Ruthie not to play between the buildings." He leaned back in his chair.

"You'll tell Ruthie not to play between the buildings," Marino repeated.

"Ruthie was the pretty one, Ida was the smart one," the old man said, almost to himself, repeating an ancient truth as if to keep it alive — keep himself alive.

"And you took very good care of them, didn't you?" said Marino.

The man didn't answer. No one moved.

Steve Marino tried once more. "You told them to be careful of a thin man waiting in a doorway. Tell me about the thin man."

Still the old man was silent. He had turned to look out the window.

"Tell me about your sister Ruthie," Marino began again. The old man's face was like a death mask, without affect. His lips were closed, as if he had never spoken before, would never speak again. He was staring out the window.

Marino rose, disappointed and defeated.

Zinck turned to the old man's wife. "Maybe you can get something, just quietly, the two of you." The woman shrugged, her face pained. She shook her head. "If you should," Zinck continued, "please call me. Anything, even if it doesn't seem very important."

"There won't be anything, Officer. He has very little recall of recent events. I'm sure he saw something, but he simply isn't able to remember it."

"I'm sorry, ma'am."

"Thank you." She reached out a thin hand to shake Charlie Zinck's hand, to feel its warmth. The room was almost dark now. The old man was still staring out the window.

To Steve Marino, she extended both her hands. "Someone in your family too?" she asked.

"Yes," said Marino, and the old woman drew him quickly to her, giving him as much of a hug as Steve Marino had ever received in uniform from a member of the citizenry.

"Thank you, ma'am," said Marino. "It's my father. He's a lot younger. But it's the same."

In the corridor, waiting for the elevator, Steve was quiet. Then he said to Charlie Zinck, "Sometimes I can make contact with my father if I zero in on something long ago. We can talk then, sort of. . . . You know those hawks, coasting along on a thermal current? If they find that good warm air, they're home free. If they don't find it, they gotta do a lot more wing-flapping. I had this man on a thermal, sort of, but it didn't take him anywhere."

"Good try, though, Steve," said Zinck. He meant it, and he knew Steve knew he meant it. The guy took a lot of ribbing about those pigeons. "Say, how did you know the man in the doorway was thin?"

"The Gottschalk lady. The schoolteacher. She also said he looked cold."

"Wonderful," said Charlie Zinck in a fair imitation of Clint Eastwood.He liked Clint Eastwood. He liked a woman once who told him he looked like Clint Eastwood (suspecting, all along, that she said this to all the cops). "A man stands outside for two hours, at the tail end of October, and he looks cold. Wonderful."

"Well, what can I tell you?"

"At least she remembers what she saw." It was a mild observation, without sarcasm, but as soon as he heard it Zinck knew it sounded rotten. "Sorry."

"That's OK. You get used to it. I had to tie my Pa's shoelaces for him last Sunday. You get used to it."

"I guess so. What else did you get from the schoolteacher?"

"Some cookies." Marino grinned. "She said I looked thin."

"She thinks everyone looks thin. Except me," and he sucked in his gut. "I didn't get much of anything from her. She told me she didn't see the man's face. You too?"

"Yeah."

"Maybe someone over there saw him," said Zinck, gesturing to the building across the street. "Been over there yet?"

"Yeah. There's only a few apartments. Nobody home. I'll get back on it. And there's a few apartments left in this building. I feel like an Avon lady."

Zinck laughed. "Just don't start selling on the side. The department tends to frown on moonlighting."

They were in the elevator now. "What did you think of Perrone in 3A?"asked Steve. "I don't think it adds up. Kids change in three years. It's gotta be a completely different kid."

"That'd be my guess too. The guy's got an image of a kid pasted on the inside of his eyelids and suddenly he thinks he's got a match. I'd hate to go to court with him."

"And I don't know what he saw the kid *do*. He didn't see the kid do anything."

"Yeah. He just knows the kid *could*." Zinck sighed.

"Wonderful," said Marino.

They rode in silence a moment, and then the elevator door opened, closing off their thoughts.

In the lobby, the doorman was near the elevator, as far from the entrance as he could get.

"Have you thought about what I asked you earlier?" Zinck asked. "Whether anyone has been interested recently in Mr. Novinsky's comings and goings." Implicit in that question, and asked explicitly a short while ago, was whether Mr. Novinsky's comings and goings were anything special to be interested in.

"I've been wrackin' my brains, sir. . . . Truth to tell, sir, and may my sainted mother forgive me, I'm glad I wasn't on duty yesterday. There are only so many jolts a heart can take." He crossed himself. "You'll be wantin' to see Sam, the relief man, now. He spends most of his time restin' in the alcove, I'm told , but maybe he managed to catch somethin' out of the corner of his eye. And if you need someone to vouch for me, like I said, I was at my sister's place all day. My nephew was home on leave."

Zinck needed some air. So much helpfulness and no real help. Any doorman who wasn't deaf, doped out, or blind knew the comings and goings of everyone. But it would take a while. The deceased is always a saint, for three days at least. "I'll be back," he said to the doorman, and he hoped it sounded ominous.

Zinck and Marino then left this place where the unthinkable (which was always in everyone's thoughts) had become real.

• • •

The street was almost empty. A few people were hurrying home in the cold, heads down, collars up. In the summer there would be dozens of eyes on the street: people sitting on stoops, leaning out of windows, lounging on fire escapes. Only the large building in the middle of the block — Novinsky's building — would be shut tight, its air conditioners turning every room in on itself. But that would be summer, when the street would be alive with music and chatter and car-washing. Today, in late October, Zinck and Marino were virtually alone on the street. There seemed to be no eyes and ears on the street but theirs, no activity to be seen or heard but theirs.

They crossed the street and stood in the doorway across from Novinsky's apartment house.

"Good hiding place," said Charlie, nodding his approval. "No one's gonna see him here."

"*He* saw him," said Steve, gesturing to where the old man was sitting at his window, staring out at them with blank eyes.

"But what did he see? He's trying to keep his sisters from playing between the buildings. *Between* the buildings? What could he have seen there. Nothing *happened* there."

"I'll check it out anyway," said Steve. He wanted to believe in the old man, wanted to believe that this diminished shell of a man knew more than he seemed to know. Maybe the old man knew everything he once knew but was just tired of talking — tired of tying his shoelaces and telling time and all the rest of it. Tired of laughing. Tired of living.

"OK, let's give it a shot," said Charlie.

They crossed the street again to Novinsky's building. Between it and the brownstone next to it was a space perhaps ten feet wide, separated from the sidewalk by a heavy metal gate of elaborate scroll-work. This was the only such gate on the block, barricading the only such side yard in the block.

"Not one of your usual dump-heaps," said Steve. "It probably gets cleaned two, three, times a week." A few garbage cans stood inside the gate, their lids fastened. Fresh debris lay near them: a crumpled shopping bag, a towel. Further in, a concrete ramp led down to the basement. Steve leaned on the gate and it opened, to his surprise. "I'll just look around down there. Won't take me a minute." He was half-way down the ramp when his flashlight beam picked out the wallet. He crouched down and held it with one hand while easing it open with the other, held it as though it were a living thing, ready to spring away.

"Hey," he called to Zinck. "This is *his*. Novinsky's. The guy threw it away after he robbed him. No, *before* he robbed him. I mean he *didn't* rob him. Look at the bills in here."

Charlie Zinck ran down. "Now why the hell wouldn't the guy take the money, after he went to all that trouble getting it?"

"I dunno. Maybe he got distracted. There was a lot going on."

"Yeah," Charlie laughed. "Let's get all this stuff outa here. Good work."

Out on the sidewalk again, Steve Marino waved a salute to the old man sitting in his window. "*He* led us here, you know. He couldn't tell us, but he led us to it. He told us in his own way." Steve wanted to get the old man's attention, wanted to tell him somehow that he was proud of him. The old man didn't make a sign. He was looking out in Steve's direction. His face was placid. He was dreaming of long ago, perhaps, or of yesterday, or of no time.

Charlie Zinck was thinking it had all been too easy.

chapter three

Too early the next morning, Steve Marino was tapping excitedly on the door of Charlie Zinck's office. Even without a second cup of coffee in him, Zinck was aware that Steve had a woman with him, and the woman had red hair, and she looked excited too.

What does a woman wear to her local police station? That depends, surely, on whether she has been allowed to add to what she was wearing when the policeman surprised her.

The young woman who entered Zinck's office seems not to have been given that chance. Her coat was open, descending modestly to her ankles. From its style it might have dated from the Crimean War. From its condition it might have seen action in that very conflict. Under the coat she wore black jersey tights, and over the tights a small apron-like piece of cloth that fluttered demurely against what would otherwise have been called her private parts. Topping all this (in more ways than one) was a form-fitting sweater of an amazing pink, apparently shrink-wrapped to a free and massive bosom. And on this bosom, which needed no enhancement, reposed a world-class collection of beads in all shapes and colors, the tangle of beads alternately drawing the eye toward and away from what Zinck, in his younger days, would have called a world-class pair of lungs.

"This is Miss Kimberley Dayline. She met the guy in the doorway," said Steve Marino, as though that explained everything.

"I came to look at a line-up," said the young woman, seemingly unaware of the effect she was having as she eased her coat onto the back of her chair.

"Yes. Well. We can't have a line-up. We don't have a suspect."

"Oh." She was disappointed. "I could look at some mug-shots," she said.

Zinck sighed. Ah, TV. It was probably a good thing that people thought of their local police station as a place where they might meet a Don Johnson leaning against the water cooler. But when all they got was a C. J. Zinck, it could only reinforce the idea that life was unfair. And there were already enough angry people out there. Charlie Zinck worried about what people thought of the police.

"Why don't you tell us what you saw, and we'll see where we go from there." He kept his eyes on the young woman's face. But if his life had depended on it, he could have given a fairly accurate guess as to her dimensions. This was a spectacular woman: a Dolly Parton without the voice. Or maybe she had a voice. It didn't matter. He wondered whose idea it was — hers or Steve's — for her to come down here.

"I live across the street from that murder," she began. "The officer here told me you were interested in anyone who saw the little man in the doorway of my building. Well, I saw him. I talked to him. I wouldn't say he was a *murderer* or anything." She shrugged. The beads shrugged with her.

"How did you happen to speak to him?" asked Zinck.

"Well, I was going in my building. He was waiting outside. I didn't want him to come in too. But he didn't seem to want to. He was waiting for someone." She gave little mini-shrugs with every sentence. Steve Marino's mouth had fallen open.

"How do you know he was waiting for someone?" asked Zinck.

"He said so. I asked him if he was waiting for someone, and he said yes."

"Did he say who he was waiting for?"

"No. We were talking about other things."

"What things?"

"You're gonna think this is weird."

"We hear a lotta weird things here. Please go on."

"Well, I should tell you, first of all, that I believe in fortune cookies. I always have. They really work for me. OK? So, I had this big bowl of wonton soup about three o'clock, after my last class. I'm studying photography. Downtown. I don't eat much lunch. But I got this fortune cookie, probably because the waiter didn't remember I didn't have the whole lunch. Usually, you know, you get the fortune cookie only when you have the whole lunch. So I got this fortune cookie, and it said, 'An old friend will return.' So I was looking around for someone I knew, all the way uptown. And then I got to the doorway of my building, and there was Uncle Harry."

Zinck bolted forward in his chair. "This man is your uncle?"

"Not exactly. . . . Of course I don't know that he isn't." She caressed a few beads pensively.

Zinck took a deep breath and frowned slightly. "Please go on. You thought you recognized the man."

"I swear to God I thought it was Uncle Harry. But then I got right up close and saw it wasn't. At least not if you look at things in a certain way. But if you look at things in another way, he certainly *was* Uncle Harry." She was silent, pondering the imponderable.

"Please," said Zinck, struggling to keep his glance on her face. "Please do continue with what happened."

"I always had the feeling that Uncle Harry wouldn't go very far away. He'd be able to come back, you know? Actually, I don't know that he *hasn't*."

"Your Uncle Harry went away recently," Zinck summarized. "But not very far."

"Well, we can't know that for sure."

The penny dropped for Zinck. "You mean he *died*."

"I thought that was clear."

"Not quite. I thought he just moved away, like to Jersey."

The young woman gave Zinck a disgusted look. "Of course not. He *lived* in Jersey."

The room was still. Kimberley Dayline was looking through the glass in the door. Charlie Zinck was looking into his coffee cup. Steve Marino was looking at the girl, memorizing her mammaries.

Zinck tried again. "Uh, after he said he was waiting for someone, what happened then, Ms. uh Dayline?" His mind was clearly wandering.

"Well, I didn't think there was any harm in talking to him a little. He looked so much like Uncle Harry that it was a little like talking to Uncle Harry again. But easier. There were always things I couldn't ask Uncle Harry. But I could ask this man. I asked him if he was afraid. He said he wasn't, not really. I asked him if he was ready. He said he was, almost. It wasn't a whole lot of words. But I felt real good, afterward. It *was* like having an old friend return. Except I know this isn't the way it happens. I mean when a person comes back he doesn't *have* to look like what he used to."

"Uh, no," said Zinck, wondering how the hell *he* knew such a thing. "Did the man seem nervous?"

"He looked like he was concentrating. I was definitely picking up concentration. But maybe that was because he was in a lot of pain."

"How did you know he was in pain?"

"I just knew it. It isn't something I can explain."

"Did you notice what time it was?"

"No. I don't believe in spending a whole lot of energy checking on the time."

"Can you say how long you talked together?"

"A few minutes. Not long. He said he thought he'd been to a party once, across the street, for the Rosenbergs. I said, 'Oh, for Josh and Lisa? They're friends of mine too.' 'No,' he said, 'for Julius —' and I think he said Ethel. 'Oh,' I said, 'I don't know them.' And then I admired his shopping bag. I used to collect them, until something began eating the glue out of all the bottoms. I thought of pasting them back together again but then I got interested in photography. But you know what was really weird? He said he collected shopping bags too — the ones a judge or somebody gives away. And then if he doesn't like the person he fills their shopping bag full of disgusting garbage and leaves it on someone's front stoop or in a hallway. I think that's really juvenile." She looked at Zinck and Marino for confirmation.

"Did he say anything else?" Zinck asked.

"No. I did most of the talking." She smiled at Steve Marino, who closed his mouth and gave her a furtive smile in return.

"And then what?" asked Zinck.

"Then I went inside. I didn't see him again. I was in my darkroom. Actually, I was working on some portraits of Uncle Harry."

"You have good photos of your uncle?" Charles Zinck leaned forward eagerly again in his chair.

"They're pretty good," she answered. "I got a B on them."

"They'd look enough like the man in the doorway?"

"No. They wouldn't."

"I don't have a firm grip on this, Ms. Dayline. I thought you said the two men looked alike."

"The man in the doorway looked like Uncle Harry did *at the end*," the woman explained with exaggerated clarity, as if speaking to the simple-minded. "Uncle Harry didn't let me take pictures of him then."

"At the end of his life, you mean?"

"Well, of course."

"OK, let's grab the big picture," said Zinck. "You don't know what time it was when you saw him. You spoke for a few minutes. You didn't notice whether he was there after you went inside. He wasn't doing anything special, I gather." The woman shook her head.

"OK, let's grope our way toward a description," said Zinck.

"I don't know why you're spending all this time on a poor little man who'll be dead soon."

"What makes you think that?"

"Because he's dying."

"What makes you think that?"

"I don't *think* it, I *know* it. I don't know *how*." Her upper body added a comment of its own and the beads realigned themselves once more. Steve Marino nodded soberly, agreeing with something he had heard or thought.

"OK, let's get our hands on that description," Zinck said. "Officer Marino has a real feel for these things. He'll be handling it in another office."

"Yes, I can see you have a lot of people waiting for you," Kimberley Dayline said pleasantly. She stretched to remove her coat from the back of her chair and five pairs of eyes took in her every move: Zinck's, Marino's, and the eyes of three other policemen suddenly interested in the case. Don Johnson wouldn't have been at the water cooler for the past ten minutes; he'd have been walking up and down outside Charlie Zinck's office with his buddies, falling back to exchange views and then going in again for further investigation and corroboration. . . . Thorough. That's what a cop had to be.

• • •

And thorough is what Zinck was. Watchful that his gut wasn't getting flabby. Cynical. Not sure he was doing any real good. But hard-working, shrewd, caring, principled, thorough.

So, by the end of this day, with a little time out to review the important details of Ms. Dayline's visit, they had found the black kid. He hadn't been hard to find. Only a few grocery stores in the area made deliveries, and only one employed a young man of a size and complexion to meet the exacting specifications of Anthony Perrone in 3A. The boy was fourteen: a hard worker according to the manager of the supermarket on Broadway, and an honor student according to a clipping supplied by his grandmother.

A snapshot from three years ago showed him a foot-and-a-half shorter, struggling to keep the American flag from dragging on the ground in a Memorial Day parade. Perrone knew when he was licked but he was sore about it anyway. The cops were more gracious, taking the young man home in an unmarked police car driven by an unmarked policeman. "OK," said the cop when he pulled in at a hydrant to let the boy out; "this is it." Even the language was unmarked.

Back at the station, they now had an additional detail on the thin, cold, sick man who had stood in the doorway before gunning down Bernie Novinsky. Or did they? "White guy. Real old. Runnin' real fast for a guy couldn't walk so good. Like this. And the dude's coat flappin' away behind him. Probably stole it. It didn't fit him real good."

"Oldest trick in the book, a limp," Zinck said later to Marino and to the young policeperson named Liu who was now helping on the case (and who seemed to think she was earning her pay by giving the men dirty looks whenever the name of Kimberley Dayline came up. "Anything odd will do it," Zinck went on. "Remember the Pink Glove Bandit? Broad daylight and no one saw anything except those goddam gloves: Day-Glo pink, up to the elbows, and a likeness of Miss Piggy on the back of each hand. Whoever was wearing 'em coulda been Elvis Presley and no one woulda noticed. So maybe our man limps all the time and maybe he just limps after he shoots someone — to confuse any bystanders who may not be confused enough already."

"And maybe," interjected Joanne Liu, "Mrs. Novinsky is the grieving widow and maybe she isn't." Joan Novinsky was turning out to be a very busy woman, according to the doorman, the super, and a couple of public-spirited neighbors. Not that they really *knew* anything, but they wondered aloud to Officer Liu, in some detail, why the woman was so often in the company of men who were not her husband. The widow herself appeared to be too grief-stricken to be of much help. Zinck had been back to see her twice today, asking her all the usual personal stuff and getting nothing but tight-lipped monosyllables.

"Officer," Joan Novinsky had finally said to Charlie Zinck, "I fail to see that this sort of questioning is necessary to your investigation."

"Mrs. Novinsky, I wouldn't be asking you if it wasn't strictly routine. If I'm barking up the wrong tree, I'm sorry. It's not my wish or intention to get you agitated."

"I am agitated, Officer, let me remind you, because my husband has been *murdered*. On the *street*. By a common *thief*. We depend on the police to prevent this sort of thing. We do not need the police to inquire into our personal relationships." And then, with her mouth hard, she added, "I suppose you're allowed a certain amount of this to compensate for the difficulties of the job."

Understandably, this got Zinck to thinking there was definitely something *there* there. He asked Joanne Liu to keep at it: researching the friends and whereabouts of Mrs. Novinsky and exploring the possibility that the lady had arranged for the untimely departure of her husband herself — not *done* it herself, but gotten someone else to undertake the problem, as it were. Of course, this "someone else" could be anyone from the half-orphaned daughter (whose name was Sara) to her bean-pole college-kid companion (whose name was Adam) to anyone else in the entire goddam Tri-State metropolitan area.

Zinck also asked Joanne Liu to give them some peace about the female visitors who normally came to any precinct house. Come off it, he said to himself, there's nothing normal about the female visitors they were getting on this case. And because the black kid had talked about the old man's limp, Zinck suddenly remembered Hallie Cooper's limp. He winced slightly, with a sympathy that could find no other outlet. Get a grip on this, he said to himself. Sure, the woman was smart, and beautiful, and suffering. But he, Zinck, couldn't help her suffering, even if — by some miracle — she allowed him to comfort her. He imagined putting his arm around her, cradling her head against him. He imagined the scent of her hair. Hey, get a grip, he said again to himself.

So how does Hallie Cooper fit into all this anyway, he wondered. The deceased sounded real chummy with her in the one-sided conversation he'd had with her answering machine. Still, the woman brought the tape in today. She could have said she'd erased it. Instead, she was giving them information — the tape and more. She'd had a note from Bernie this morning, she said sadly, the last she'll ever get from him. It was about a woman named Anna Carr McElroy who'd been in Vietnam for the past couple of years. There was more. This woman McElroy had been a long-time anti-war activist, which was the only reason they'd let her live in one of the villages of North Vietnam, near the place where there'd been riots recently. She was a sociologist now, this Anna Carr McElroy. She'd gone Respectable Academic over the past fifteen years. Trouble was, the book she was working on was not the book the Vietnamese government expected from her. Her book was going to infuriate the entire Vietnamese government, maybe even topple a few Party leaders. They were into that, these days — blaming a few officials to keep from blaming the whole failing system, Bernie had said in his note.

"Bernie loved her, of course," Hallie Cooper rushed to sum up. "He'd had her on his program about a month ago and thought I should do a major story on her. He enclosed a couple of chapters of her book. . . . It's the last thing he'll ever send me." Her explanation finished, she dropped her eyes.

Again, Zinck had a brief urge to soothe her. But that was for other times, other places, and perhaps for other people. For now, for him, he welcomed the return of his cop's suspicion of anyone who volunteered too much information. He wanted to see those gray eyes again, open and honest. But Hallie Cooper mumbled a hasty good-bye, not quite meeting his eyes. Maybe the lady was just grieving, thought Cop Zinck. And maybe Ho ChiMinh is my uncle.

• • •

Kimberley Dayline didn't see the earliest editions of next morning's newspapers. She had worked in her darkroom most of the evening before, then gone out to the bar on the corner to see whether she knew anyone. There she met an old friend (reaffirming her faith in fortune cookies) — well, he was a *friend* of an old friend — and by the time one thing had led to another, it was three o'clock in the morning before Ms. Dayline was alone and wrapping up the day. She awoke closer to noon than she'd have liked, and she rushed out of her apartment and downtown to her photography class.

In the subway station, Uncle Harry was everywhere. Page one of every newspaper, clear across the newsstand. And she had put him there. For this deed whose consequences could not yet be seen, Kimberley Dayline made a silent apology to her departed uncle — "wherever you may be," she added aloud — and she reached into the waste-bin to get her personal copy of this story that had crowded out all world events. Never buy a newspaper if you can read someone else's, her mother had always said, and while there was much of her mother's teaching that Kimberley Dayline had already discarded, she was sensible enough to keep some basic points from her upbringing as a foundation upon which to build a stable life.

The newspaper she fished out of the waste-bin was virtually intact and she congratulated herself on a good omen. The story was fully contained in a single caption under the large drawing. She read it, nodding at the words "thin, middle-aged or older, pale-skinned, Caucasian," frowning at the words "possibly ill." What did these policemen know?

She folded the newspaper carefully and put it back just as the downtown express pulled in. She got into the subway car, decided to stand, and reached for the ceiling strap, aware that her coat had fallen open — aware, too, that the man sitting below her outstretched arm had suddenly folded his newspaper in order to stare straight ahead.

• • •

Zinck, Marino, and Liu were on the phone all morning. By noon they had a fistful of leads to follow.

Most of the calls would lead nowhere. The woman who thought there was a certain resemblance between her ex-husband and the man in the newspaper: she wanted him picked up for defaulting on his alimony. Or the man who was trying to find the driver of the car that side-swiped him late one night when they'd all had a snootful: he wasn't sure his guy was as old as the guy in the picture, but what the heck, that's what the police were for, wasn't it? Or the elderly woman whose son walked out of the house one day ten years ago and never came back: he'd probably look like this now.

By the time the phoning eased up, Zinck and the others had a small encyclopedia of modern woes — of love spurned and possessions ravaged, of spirits wounded and lives devastated.

By chance, Zinck caught the call from M. W. Dupree. No Miss or Mrs. or Ms. — just M. W. Dupree, a woman with no time for the extras. "The man you're looking for is a tenant in my building." Was she sure? She was sure. How so? Because the drawing was an exact likeness of Maurice Orlov in her building and because for weeks Orlov had had a picture of Bernie Novinsky on his coffee table. Case closed. "How do you know about the picture on his coffee table?" asked Zinck. "I'm the super," she said, quite rightly expecting no further questions about her knowledge of the man's apartment. She probably knew exactly which drawer Maurice Orlov kept his underwear in, and what he kept under his underwear. Cops had to go through all kinds of Mickey Mouse with search warrants, but supers could sniff around at will. One of the compensations for the difficulties of the job perhaps. . . . Zinck was off the phone and ready to roll in two minutes.

• • •

The city had thousands of buildings like the dark brick apartment house where M. W. Dupree lived, worked, and got to know her tenants. Eighty or a hundred people would tip her too little every Christmas, would be glad there were no elevator men any more, would put up with windows painted shut and brown water in the bathtub and a buzzer system that was usually on the fritz. Resignation would dog their days. There wasn't a tenant free of the certainty that someday they'd have a tragedy here and then they'd be sorry but then it'd be too late.

Charlie Zinck left two men in the lobby to cover the stairs and elevator. Two more went out to cover the fire escape. Two more came with him to find the super.

M. W. Dupree was a worn little woman. Life in the basement had not put roses in her cheeks. Her hair was thinning. "Apartment 5B, but he's not in now," she said flatly.

"You're sure?" Zinck asked.

The woman shrugged. "He wasn't in half an hour ago." She was a firm little woman who knew her own mind and trusted it. He didn't doubt her. "We'll check it out," he said to the two cops with him, and to M. W. Dupree he said, "Later, I might need to talk to you."

"Any time. I'm always here." Her voice had no trace of cordiality. She worked a long day and was on call for the rest of the day and night; she didn't have the time for graciousness, or the place for it. Her barred windows looked into the too-near windows (also barred) of the next building. For light from the heavens, she turned to her walls, which were lined with cheaply framed renditions of her Savior. "I'm always here," she repeated, and the three men ducked out of her dimly-lit burrow in the basement.

They rode wordlessly to the fifth floor and rang the doorbell of the apartment across from the elevator. The airless corridor smelled of trapped disinfectant. The men were sweating under their Kevlar vests. Another ring on the doorbell. Still no answer. Charlie muttered, "Gotta do this one by the book. I'll be back with a search warrant in twenty, thirty minutes. Try to make yourselves inconspicuous, OK?"

He returned in forty-three minutes, rushed down to M. W. Dupree for the keys, and rushed back to Orlov's apartment on the fifth floor. He worked the three locks as quietly as he could. Nobody spoke. They heard every noise in the building: an obstinate faucet complaining nearby, a door slamming somewhere, the elevator door opening above them.

When the third lock was opened, Charlie pushed the door in quickly and the three men sprang to what they'd been trained to do. They darted past doorways. They dropped behind furniture. They came up cautiously on any place large enough to conceal a person. But the small apartment was well and truly empty. And then each man took the few deep breaths he hadn't been able to take in the past minute. After the surge of adrenaline there was always this sudden relief (maybe a letdown?) that this time — *this* time — the danger hadn't materialized. Charlie Zinck holstered his weapon, mopped his brow, sat down, and then took a *real* look around.

The place looked only vaguely lived in, like a furnished room between tenants. Lacking a presence, somehow. What was it? The absence of newspapers on the tables? The lack of pictures on the walls? No, it went beyond that. The place didn't have any personal effects. No special trinkets. No treasures from a fondly remembered vacation. No photos of loved ones. No nothing. The place didn't look like it was anyone's *home.*

And then one of the cops found the shopping bags, stacked neatly on a shelf of the cheap bookcase. They were printed with a variety of the ethnic names to be found in this turbulent cauldron of a city (no longer a melting pot, more like the giant kettle in which savages boil their captives). Each shopping bag proclaimed its person to be "experienced" or "accessible" or "working for a better city." What these persons had been most earnestly working for, of course, was the privilege of becoming (or remaining) senators and councilmen and borough presidents and judges.

Charlie Zinck grinned at his colleagues. At that point he'd have said it was eighty-twenty they'd have Maurice Orlov of 5B in custody by nightfall. He'd have been wrong.

part two

chapter four

Anna Carr McElroy — author of a recent magazine article on Vietnamese women that had caused a national stir — was dressing for Bernie Novinsky's funeral.

No one ever looked twice at Anna Carr McElroy and she knew it. Her hair was the color of potato skins. She had no single feature that could be called beautiful, and she didn't make much of the qualities that could be called passable: a pert figure, a trim face, and eyes of a heartbreakingly pure blue. She concealed her innate plainness under layers of acquired plainness — her entire small wardrobe was suitable for funerals. Her mother often said peevishly, "Anna, I cannot see the sense to dressing the way you do." But Anna's mother couldn't see the sense to a lot of things about Anna. Anna's mother was dazzling — in the flesh if in no other way — and so, inevitably, Anna grew up determined to be dazzling in her intellect and in no other way. Unlike the good little girl who must be seen and not heard, Anna Carr grew up wanting to be heard and not seen.

And she *had* been heard. As a graduate student and then as a young instructor in sociology, Anna Carr had been celebrated among the anti-war activists for her keen debater's mind and her keener instinct for the jugular. Over the years she had produced a fair number of academic papers that were cited frequently "in the literature" (that is, by other people in *their* academic papers). Married, she had become Carr McElroy in other people's papers; she chose not to hyphenate the name.

Her book on the women of Socialist Vietnam, coming out next year, was already being discussed. One of the more respectable leftist magazines had editorialized briefly about Anna with an outrage it usually reserved for neo-Nazis and Republican presidents. And a long-time leader of the women's movement, interviewed by Barbara Walters, had deftly dismissed Anna's concern for women with a savagery she usually reserved for unrepentant pornographers and serial rapists. Anna's book was destined to reach a readership that would know what to think of her heresies.

Of course, Bernie Novinsky had done his part too, telling his audience a few weeks ago that his guest was writing "a brave and important book." Anna, who was still writing it, wanted simply to get on with it and move on to something else. The past few years had not been easy. In the small mirror over her bureau she noticed how tired she looked. And bewildered, somehow. Bernie Novinsky had been important to her, and the shock of his death had given her a wild-eyed look, a frown: eyes straining to see what couldn't be seen.

They hadn't known each other long, but in a very real sense Bernie had known her to the core — and Anna knew it. They'd met at a large party on the Upper West Side soon after her return from Vietnam. This most recent trip had left her disillusioned and depressed. She'd gone as a friend of the Socialist Republic of Vietnam, eager to bring back a positive report of the new women of the new Vietnam. But she'd seen both more and less than she'd expected, and she didn't know what to do with it: where to publish it, even *whether* to publish it. She found herself looking to Bernie Novinsky, a stranger, for answers to questions she could no longer ask her friends. And within the hour, on the evening they met, she found herself considering him a friend — out of the sure knowledge that soon she would have few others.

She'd been able to travel anywhere in Vietnam, city and countryside, South and North, she told him, and she'd made the most of it, staying for days at a time in mountain hamlets, coastal villages, provincial capitals. She'd been invited to spend a year but extended the year to two, not because she was getting a lot of assistance but because she wasn't. She'd spoken in their own language to hundreds of Vietnamese women. But different as all the women were — loggers and teachers, doctors and prostitutes, peasants and factory workers, women walking behind the tired water buffaloes of the impoverished countryside and women riding in the shiny imported cars of Party officials in Ho Chi Minh City — they were alike in describing their lives with the officially prescribed "joy and zeal." It didn't take long for Anna Carr McElroy to grow weary of all this "joy and zeal." But what lay underneath? She was not to find out, she told Bernie, until well into her second year in Vietnam, when the beautiful Tran Thi Hai had become Anna's friend and — in the single worst decision of her life — decided to trust Anna.

Anna told the whole story to Bernie on the night they met. Tran Thi Hai and Anna were already friends, able to sense without words when the other was worried or distressed. Anna spent a lot of time in Hai's part of Saigon, returning there once just as Hai was returning from a visit to her husband, the first she had been allowed in eighteen months. "He is well," Hai chattered gaily to all; "he is plump and busy and happy." But to Anna she said nothing, and when Anna stretched out her hand to caress the other woman's cheek in sympathy, Hai caught the hand in her own and held it tightly to her, her face contorted. Still, the tears came. And then the words, for Anna's ears only: "He is plump because he is swollen with beriberi. He is busy because the camps are no longer for re-education; they are prisons where the miserable inmates are worked until they die. And the guard who . . ." — a flicker of physical revulsion crossed her face — "the guard told me that if I do not speak of that place as a paradise created by the state in a spirit of humanitarian forgiveness, I will never see my husband again. But I will never see him free, I know that. Some people have been released, but he will not be free until he goes to his grave. He was with them in the beginning — they can never forgive his leaving them. But he is a civilized man. He was right to do what he did. And he is right to hate them. Ah, but I grieve so, for him. I grieve for us all." Her voice was barely audible as she finished. She dropped her face to Anna's shoulder.

Suddenly alarmed, Hai then said, "You will not tell," and Anna shook her head. "And yet you *must* tell," Hai said with quiet intensity. "We are all prisoners today in Vietnam. We are all frightened into submission. I will not speak of the camp because I fear what might be done to my husband — or my children. Their future would be ruined by such an 'incorrect' attitude on the part of their mother. But we are all held hostage. If our families are not already at peril, they are potentially at peril, depending on us to do our play-acting, attend our meetings, express our 'one-mindedness,' show our 'joy and zeal' for the great proletarian future. All of us must work hard and lie, and must encourage hard work and lies from everyone else. What I fear most is relocation to a New Economic Zone, which is nothing but a labor camp without the barbed wire. I am sure I would not survive there, yet I am expected to persuade other women to volunteer for these barbaric places. I have a quota to meet. Oh, no, 'renovation' has not affected this at all. . . . Anna my friend, I am sick to death of dissembling, of doing such violence to others to save myself."

To the look of horror on Anna's face, Hai gave no heed. "The collective spirit is a sham," she rushed on. "Everyone thinks only of himself, only of his duty to his own family, his own ancestors. All the rest is fear. We are frightened of every small-minded, ignorant, power-hungry cadre. And they, too, are afraid — of every Party bureaucrat above them who is more powerful. This is a prison, the whole country. I would flee with my children, if not for my husband. And I probably could not even get out now. They are watching more carefully now, and there are executions and jail sentences for those who are caught. . . . Oh, how weary I am of this prison. But they would kill my husband if we left." She wept heavily, then: a river of tears for herself and her husband and her children and her country.

Anna was sobbing as she told all this to Bernie on the terrace of someone's large apartment on the Upper West Side. He had his arm around her shoulders, and he was trying to comfort her merely with his presence; there were no words to comfort her. They were interrupted occasionally by other party-goers, who turned back into the apartment thinking they had interrupted a pair of lovers. But Anna was too shattered to respond to the maleness of the man next to her. And Bernie felt not the slightest attraction for this distraught and red-eyed woman.

Sobbing, Anna told Bernie of her shock at hearing such denunciation of Vietnam from a woman she had considered a model of Vietnam's new womanhood: a woman who had seemed selfless, hearty, dedicated to country, stoic in the face of hardship. Hai did not speak again to Anna in this way. She had said to Anna, on that emotional day, "I cannot tell my story. But *you* can. Please tell *all* our stories." The next day she was composed again; and the next week when Anna returned from a short trip she was gone. To a New Economic Zone, it was said. One of the most primitive. With her children. Even the one who had TB.

Over the next months in Vietnam, and very surreptitiously, Anna looked not at the surface facts of the lives of Vietnamese women — the long hours they put in, the difficult jobs they performed — but at the deeper truths of their lives. She asked new questions, very carefully, and she got new answers, received quick new confidences. And everywhere she looked she found verification of Hai's anguished words. Everywhere there was dissembling, depression, wariness, a desperate scrambling for survival, a massive reliance on anything illicit, and a constant fear of being found out. An entire country turned into prisoners, or mental patients — or children. She hadn't seen it earlier because she hadn't wanted to. Would she now tell what she knew? Should she? It was this wrenching dilemma that she poured out to Bernie. She could protect the women whose stories she would tell; she would change enough of the facts to keep their identities secret. But what of herself? She would be considered a sell-out, and worse, cut off from every group she had valued. Her work wouldn't even be considered decent social science. . . . But it would be *truth*, Anna knew, and with Bernie's encouragement on that first evening and in the weeks afterward she found the strength to begin to write it.

Now Bernie was gone. Gone, too, was Richard McElroy II, known to friends and media alike as Chip. He had always hated being second to anyone: second in name to his father, a well-respected businessman in Terre Haute, and second in status to Anna, to whom the Vietnamese originally extended their invitation. Hadn't he, too, been prominent in the anti-war movement? Hadn't he, too, made a break with his family over the war? Weren't his principles and his sacrifices as strong as Anna's? He went with her to Vietnam, but he felt as though his only purpose was to carry the duffelbags. He found it hard to understand the language. He would sit for long hours by himself, writing bad poetry.

When Anna first voiced her doubts to Chip about the new Vietnam, in the quiet of their tiny hut, he had argued with her. Surely, Hai was some sort of misfit, angry at the world. After all, her husband was still alive, wasn't he? Whose work would Anna be doing if she went public with stories like Hai's? "Whose work will I be doing if I don't?" Anna replied. "You've been co-opted," Chip hissed at her one day, hatred in his eyes. "Do you think I'm going to *get* something out of thinking what I think?" she shouted. "Don't you know what it's *costing* me?" Then they lowered their voices, knowing that they had very little privacy in this village that was their home base, even though these people spoke little or no English.

Anna's husband left Vietnam soon afterward, agreeing to save face for both by pretending that his father was terminally ill in Terre Haute and that Chip would return to Vietnam after his father had died. He did not return, of course, and his father did not die. Anna learned from a friend that Chip was in New York City working by night as a dishwasher in a fancy restaurant and working by day in the environmental movement.

Anna looked dully at her image in the small mirror. She was very much on her own, she knew. She and Chip had said too much to patch it up. She had accused him of being brutal and dishonest and hopelessly gutless. He had accused her of being bourgeois and short-sighted and hopelessly credulous. In the end, all she had left of their eleven-year relationship were a few trinkets they had picked up here and there, and a few press clippings about the two of them: one of the shining couples of the anti-war movement. (Chip had taken the scrapbook, leaving Anna with the small wad of duplicate clips from inside the back cover. Why had they saved these duplicates, Anna wondered. For this?)

Anna also had her memories. Mostly of meetings and rallies and victory parties. And of fierce discussions about the failings of the rest of the world.

Anna was dressed. She wore no make-up. She ran a comb through her hair and wished — not for the first time — that she had been born better-looking. She checked to see that she had the address of the funeral parlor. Then she left her apartment for the streets of Greenwich Village. She would take the subway uptown.

• • •

The subway station was not crowded on this early afternoon. The trains didn't run often on weekends, but only a sparse crowd was waiting for the next uptown local. It was a typical Village group: a few local residents dressed for the day off, and some late-rising actors or hustlers or dope dealers (who could tell?) rather more scruffily dressed. They might all have stepped out of *Vogue*. Anna was apparently the only person on her way to a funeral.

She walked half-way down the platform, to be away from the clot of travelers at the turnstiles. She was thinking about Chip, wondering when they would run into each other — she had no doubt they would — and she was imagining their first words. He would be smiling and tall and protective, possibly even friendly. Anna heard a train coming.

The man who approached her on the subway platform was tall and thin, like Chip, and for an instant she turned eagerly toward him. But he was no one she knew, and she composed her face again.

The man kept coming toward her and she looked impatiently down the track at the approaching train. Whoever this man was, whatever he might be demanding or offering or asking or selling, she'd be rid of him as soon as the train stopped. The train was charging toward them.

He was next to her now, crowding her toward the edge of the platform. She had a moment of panic — she didn't like to be crowded — but it didn't seem important enough to make a fuss over. The train was almost upon them. He wasn't the first rude person she had encountered in this city.

And then he rushed her, lunging at her, pushing her. Anna Carr McElroy lost her balance, tottered briefly at the edge of the subway platform and fell into the track-bed below. Her scream of indignation was drowned out by the clattering of the incoming car and by the reverberations of sound bouncing off the walls of the underground tunnel.

Too late, the train stopped. Anna's body had been carried thirty feet along the tracks. Somewhere along the way she had lost her shoes, and most of her face. Her ragdoll body was suspended upside-down from the forward edge of the forward car. By estimation of the Transit Police, she had died instantly from simultaneous impact to her head and upper torso.

"She coulda made it," said the first transit cop on the scene, "if she coulda stayed between the tracks, let the cars go over her, ya know. But she tried to get over to the side here, under the overhang of the platform. And she didn't make it. She took it head on. Jesus, what a mess."

It was only after the train moved on, Anna's body having been lifted from the bloodied track-bed, that the young man's body was found. He, too, had been hit by the first car, but he had fallen beneath the cars and he lay there in a growing pool of his blood.

Everyone was questioned, naturally, but almost no one had noticed the two. One woman thought they must have known each other; "I saw them standing near each other," she said. Someone else said he had seen Anna smile at the man. He remembered it, he said, because he couldn't see what the guy saw in her. Maybe they were brother and sister, he said.

As to whether Anna had fallen, or jumped, or been pushed, no one knew. As to whether the young man had preceded her or followed her, no one knew. It was similarly a matter of conjecture as to whether he had jumped in with her, in a suicide pact, or been pulled in after her. Perhaps he had lost his balance from pushing her, said a stout black woman who was thanked by the transit cops and who added shyly that she was glad to help. In sum, nobody saw. Nobody knew.

And within an hour nobody was left at the scene. The next train had rumbled in, picking up everyone from the station and from the accident train (that train having slowly moved off, empty, to the yards). Only the long smear of red remained in the track-bed, linking the place where Anna had come to rest with the place where the young man had fallen. If people saw the dark smear, they probably didn't identify it as blood. Only after seeing the evening papers did a couple of people realize they had been at the very scene of an accident. Or a suicide. Or a murder.

chapter five

Six days after Bernie Novinsky had been shot and three days after the likely suspect had been fingered by his super, Charlie Zinck's stomach went sour. Too much coffee and not enough to show for it. "I mean, we've *got* the guy, we've got him cold," he said to Marino. They'd been in frequent contact with M. W. Dupree, who'd been in frequent contact with apartment 5B. But there was nobody there, nobody for several days now.

"Yeah, we've got him, we just don't got him *yet*." Marino was on automatic pilot, working his way through a pile of paperwork.

"Guy might never come home," said Zinck, belching.

"Yeah."

The phone rang and Zinck reached for his Gaviscon tablets before answering.

The voice was a woman's. "Sergeant Zinck?"

"Yes, ma'am, what can I do for you?" He was chewing noisily.

"This is Hallie Cooper, Sergeant. I thought you should know . . . I wanted to ask . . . did you hear about Anna Carr McElroy?"

"No, who's that?"

"I mentioned her to you. Bernie Novinsky thought I should do a story on her. Sergeant, she's *dead.* On *Saturday.*"

"How did she die?" Not from natural causes, he would bet. There was something in Hallie Cooper's voice.

"No one knows. I mean, she died in the subway. That's what the television story said. She was pushed, or she fell. Or she jumped. Just as the train was —"

"Yes, I saw that too, on TV. And?"

The pause on the other end told him that his caller was taken aback.

"*And,* Sergeant, I think it could be the same person who killed Bernie Novinsky," she said briskly.

Charlie Zinck belched quietly. Christ, everybody's a detective. "Would you happen to have any evidence to support that?"

"No," she answered surprised. "I'm only suggesting that you might want to look into her death. You might find some connection to the murder of Bernie Novinsky." Her tone was beginning to verge on the unpleasant, Zinck thought. Why was she bringing this to him anyway? He hadn't ruled out a love triangle, or a quadrangle, or an even more interesting diagram in the Novinsky case. Was she somehow part of the geometry?

"Where did it happen?" He took a swig of coffee as a chaser for the Gaviscon, knowing it was a bad idea. This whole day was a bad idea.

"In the subway. I told you."

"Where? What part of town?" He knew it wasn't *his* precinct, but he'd forgotten just where it had happened.

"In the Village. Christopher Street station of the IRT."

"And what makes you think this is connected to the Novinsky murder?"

"It's just a hunch — that the person who killed *him* could also have killed *her.*" She paused, perhaps for effect. "Uh, the young man was found with her."

Zinck was silent for a long moment. The thin gray man they were seeking in the Novinsky case could not be described as young. "Ms. Cooper, we like to have a little more evidence before we jump to conclusions. We don't even know the woman was a homicide. Didn't they say it was possible they both jumped?" Even as he said it, he knew it sounded amateurish and beneath him.

"No, we can't be certain of anything at this point. But you'll be investigating it, I hope."

"Ms. Cooper, let *us* figure out what we'll be investigating. I appreciate your calling." Yes, she had a decided limp, and there was undoubtedly some suffering there, but he didn't give a damn.

"If you don't mind my saying so, Sergeant, I would have expected a little more interest in something that seems to me a rather remarkable coincidence. I wouldn't want to tell you how to do your job . . ." — Charlie Zinck rolled his eyes heavenward and suppressed a belch — "but I think you should see whether there's any connection between these two deaths." She stopped. That about wrapped up her thoughts on the subject.

Christ, she was beginning to sound like his ex-wife. More like his ex-brother-in-law actually. Now *there* was a winner. . . . "Like I said, *we* decide how to do our jobs here." Then, mindful of her protected status as a member of both the second sex and the Fourth Estate, he added, "But thank you very much, Ms. Cooper, for bringing this to our attention."

Hallie Cooper said only, "Thank *you*, Sergeant," in an icy tone, before hanging up on him and almost cutting off her own words.

Zinck put the receiver down slowly and reached for the Gaviscon bottle. He had been thinking of the Novinsky case as practically solved. All they needed was the Perp — and it was just a matter of time before they found him, or before someone clear across the country found him. Why complicate things? He took a moment to convince himself it was *not* amateurish to suggest a double suicide at the Christopher Street station. That kind of thing happens all the time in the Sixth Precinct, he told himself.

Chewing heavily on his acid-relief, Zinck also told himself that he did not need any more unsolved murders today. They had two more cases that had come in since Bernie Novinsky, neither of them even remotely a double suicide. One involved a woman whose hands (and feet!) had been crudely removed, probably by the person who had been with her when she O.D.'d in an abandoned building. The police had located her by olfactory means, as their report delicately put it; her decomposing body had been diminished somewhat further by the varied wildlife of that habitat. The other murder involved a man whose stiffened body had been propped up on a dilapidated La-Z-Boy that was discarded at the curb on a side-street off Columbus Avenue; no one had given him a thought until one of the Sanitation Department workers asked him if he wouldn't mind please getting up and letting them get on with their job. ("I *thought* there was something peculiar about him," J. D. Williams of the D.S.N.Y. said later to reporters; "he didn't match the chair, ya know? Musta been two thousand dollars worth of threads on him." Naturally both of these corpses were members of the Doe family and required a lot of police work, most of it boring and unproductive and interminable.

"Steve," Zinck called over to Marino, "how'd ya like to check out something that's someone *else's* problem? Down in the Village, a woman dead on Saturday in the subway, Christopher Street IRT, name of Anna McElroy, acquaintance of the deceased Mr. Novinsky. Find out what they're working on, and what they think it amounts to."

"Telephone OK? I'm up to my ass in paper here."

"Sure." He had a lot of deskwork and telephone work himself — nothing more on the Novinsky case, but plenty more on the precinct's two homicides since Novinsky and on the vast number of still-unsolved homicides before Novinsky.

In this job you had to live with a gut-destroying sense of falling ever further behind. That, and a large bottle of Gaviscon.

• • •

By the time Charlie Zinck reached the legal limit of Gaviscon for the day — big warning on the bottle: no more than sixteen tablets unless prescribed by a doctor, and who had time for a doctor? — he was feeling better. He wasn't tasting his stomach any more, for one thing. And the day was almost over, for another. Not that you left your problems at the office, in this line of work. Some day, he promised himself, he'd get a nice simple job as a toll-taker on a bridge somewhere. But the problems you took away with you could be diluted or even drowned by creative recreation. He had something along these lines planned for this evening, a casual date with an old girlfriend — emphasis on the old, he had to admit — by the name of Jackie O. (No, not *that* Jackie O. This one was

Jackie *Olshavski.*)

"I thought you two rubbed each other the wrong way," said Marino, hearing that the lady in question was still in the picture.

"We do," answered Zinck. "For any length of time, that is. But we like to get together for shorter takes, sorta rub each other the right way and say goodbye again." They would be saying hello within the hour.

And then Hallie Cooper called again. "Sergeant Zinck?"

"Yes, ma'am, what can I do for you?"

"Sergeant, it's Hallie Cooper. What you can do," she said (a smile in her voice), "is forgive me for my behavior on the phone this morning. I think your job is probably tough enough without having to deal with hunches from the public. I'm sorry to have made your day any more difficult than it probably already was. I was rude and overbearing and I'm very sorry."

Zinck took a deep breath, raised his eyebrows and leaned back in his chair. "Well, that's really very decent of you. The apology is accepted. But it wasn't really necessary. We like to think we're open to ideas from outside. As a matter of fact, I've got a man looking into the McElroy death, even as we speak." He didn't mention Marino's two-word report to him, earlier in the day, on the verdict brought in by the transit cops — double suicide. Zinck hadn't given the case another thought. Nor, he suspected, had Marino. And the transit cops? Forget it.

"I've been looking into it myself," said Hallie Cooper.

"Oh?" said Zinck, leaning forward in his chair.

"Yes. I had some time to kill today and so I began to track people down. The transit police were very helpful. This sort of thing isn't exactly my specialty but I thought that if I want to deliver any wild speculations, like the ones I came up with on the phone with you this morning, I ought to go out and get some evidence, as you put it."

"And?"

"Well, there's evidence and there's *evidence*. I don't really know what to call it, what I've got. But I'd be willing to bet real money that these two people did not jump in front of that train together. They weren't the type. They might have been, separately. But not together. They were *not*, as the gossip columns say, 'an item.' She was straight; he was gay. She was political; he never watched a news program. I'd bet real money they didn't jump in front of that train together."

Zinck was impressed. He liked a woman who talked a good wager. "Look, lemme clear outa here, meet you somewhere and buy you a drink, and we'll talk about what you've got." Goddam transit cops. What kind of asshole would stick a label of double suicide on a completely mismatched couple? "You got some more time for this today? Like now? Or, better, half an hour from now?" His left hand was alreadly rotating his Wheeldex to the latter part of the alphabet. If he could reach Jackie O. in the next fifteen minutes she'd still be at work.

"Yes," Hallie Cooper was saying, "that would be fine," and they settled on a bar in Hell's Kitchen where Charlie could be reasonably certain that Jackie O. wouldn't turn up.

Half a minute later, on the phone with Jackie, he heard himself making the kind of schoolboy excuse that becomes only less believable as it becomes more elaborate. Why not tell her the truth: that this was cop stuff and could take a couple of hours and that he was already at the end of his day? He wouldn't have to include the rest of the truth: that he couldn't see Clint Eastwood refusing an offer like this, the chance to debrief an attractive and capable woman who was suddenly giving him who-knew-what, with this information, maybe even giving him an invitation for who-knew-what-else?

He was clear on one thing: Hallie Cooper was eager to lay this information on him. He would wonder, later, why he hadn't been more suspicious. For now, though, he had enough trouble handling Jackie O. The lady asked rhetorically, and not very charitably, why she hadn't stayed with the guy she was dating last year (an accountant) and Charlie said they both knew why. She asked him whether his police business was going to take all night and he said it was difficult to know. They did not part amicably but he called her "Babe" because he knew she liked it. Whatever they had together, they would patch it up.

And he was suddenly less tired as he left the station house to have a drink and some supper with Hallie Cooper, winner of a Pulitzer Prize and the only person in recent weeks to apologize to him. Charlie Zinck was a pushover for an apology.

• • •

Tony's Bar and Grill was like a hundred other places: local bar for the neighborhood regulars and local eatery for those who liked any kind of food as long as they didn't have to cook it themselves. Tony had long since departed for Buffalo with a passing love-interest, leaving his wife to manage a business that didn't even have her name on it. Her heart had never been in her cooking, but her food was several stars better than what her regulars were used to at home. Actually, it reminded them of their homes long ago: like their mothers long ago, Michelle made a good pea soup, a great meatloaf, a sensational rice pudding. The rest of the menu was usually inedible and, by a happy coincidence, usually unavailable. Charlie Zinck and Hallie Cooper were having a beer and a glass of wine while their meatloaf was being "specially prepared."

"You know what it is, Sergeant? It's guilt. Hanging in the air like fumes at a dry cleaner's. Everywhere I went."

"Who's acting so guilty, and what are they guilty of?"

"They aren't *acting* guilty, and I don't think they *are* guilty. It isn't guilt in the legal sense — in *your* sense, being able to go out and arrest someone." No doubt about it, she had extraordinary eyes, clear, concerned, intelligent. He was drawn by the grayness of them, the directness of them, as much as he was by the intelligence behind them. "What I mean," she continued, "is that all the people I talked to today seem to feel *responsible* for those two deaths in the subway. Whether they actually *were* responsible is another matter, of course."

Charlie Zinck nodded. "So who did you see?"

"I spent an hour with Anna Carr McElroy's husband. They've been separated for a while but they never got around to getting a divorce. You've probably heard of him. Chip McElroy. He was active in the late Sixties, early Seventies, against the war in Vietnam."

Charlie Zinck nodded again. "With his lovely wife beside him."

Hallie smiled at the sarcasm. "I didn't care for their style either."

"Not just their style. I didn't like their thinking. Anyone over the age of twenty-two, for Christ's sake, knew it was more complicated than what those college-kid hot-shots were saying. But they liked to keep it simple — better for the posters that way — even if it meant getting it wrong. I always thought it was more about Mommy and Daddy, some sort of grand communal tantrum against their parents, and why not their government too while they were at it, more than it was about the real world, or even about Good and Evil. So what's he like, old Chip, now that he's his father's age? And why does he feel responsible for his wife's death?"

"He was a basket case today. Utterly shaken. I think he feels personally responsible that he wasn't around yesterday to save her."

"And where *was* he at the time?" Charlie asked.

"He seems to have been handing out leaflets about nuclear power on the corner of Broadway and One-hundred-sixteenth Street. That's thirty, forty, minutes from the Village, at least."

"And I suppose he has someone who'll remember he was there?"asked Charlie.

"He has a *cop*, if you can believe it," said Hallie. "Seems the cop asked him something about what he was doing, and asked his name, and Chip McElroy asked the cop for *his* name, and they kept an eye on each other for the next two hours."

"That would seem to be a good alibi," Charlie smiled sourly.

"I thought so too," said Hallie, also smiling. "He's a very angry person, this Chip McElroy, but he's got a touch of sweetness too. He kept saying he was so sorry it had turned out like this. It didn't *have* to, he kept saying. She brought it on herself, he said at one point. What do you think *that* means?"

"I'd ask *him*."

"I did. No answer."

"In that case, we can jump in with both feet. Maybe he was sorry he'd had someone push her in front of a train. Or he was sorry he'd treated her so badly that months later she wanted to jump in front of a train. Who knows what people think they're responsible for? Why did they split, do you know?"

"I asked him. A bit crudely, but I just asked. He didn't much answer. Said they'd had 'irreconcilable differences' — 'ideological' more than personal. He did a lot of silent staring and a lot of wringing of hands, for minutes at a time. He wasn't altogether articulate the whole time."

"Ideological," repeated the detective. "Like whether they wanted to buy the same posters, or eat the same lettuce." Hallie smiled at him, the smile that members of a somewhat older generation give to each other when talking about members of a younger generation.

"You know," Hallie said softly, "I felt very sorry for Chip McElroy. He seemed very troubled."

"Well, it isn't every day that your wife, even your estranged wife, dies a messy death in a public subway. Do you think he *was* involved, by the way?" He liked the way Hallie looked at life, the way she observed things and came to decisions about them.

"I don't really. Not directly. He probably failed her in all sorts of ways. And she failed him too. But it doesn't sound like anything you could arrest him for."

"We usually have a lot more behind us before we go out and arrest someone," Charlie Zinck said wryly, hoping in the next instant that Hallie wouldn't take offense and clam up. "Don't take offense," he said; "I say that to everyone."

Hallie laughed. "I won't."

They ate their meatloaf. They talked about meatloaf, and Michelle, and Tony running off to Buffalo (Buffalo!), and cooking by oneself, and living by oneself. Nothing very intimate, except that it was all pretty personal. And then they talked *more* personally. Inevitably, in New York City, two people eating or drinking together soon exchanged the necessary information about marital status. It was one of the rules of decent urban intercourse, as open and casual as the sniffing that dogs do when they meet. If you were married, you said so. But briefly, please. And if you were not, you said so. But again, please, briefly. Nothing long and drawn out, about relationships gone wrong or going wrong. Hallie Cooper mentioned almost inconsequentially that her husband had died some years ago. She added that one of the things he'd said to her, in his last days, was that anyone who'd had a loving relationship would almost certainly use that experience to build another loving relationship. So far, though, it hadn't happened. She said this in a way that discouraged further conversation on the subject. (Mid-way through it, in fact, she had wondered why she was telling him all this.) Zinck told Hallie about his ex-wife, saying that the relationship had not been a terrific one, but that it had given him a profound determination to get things right the next time. No mention was made of Jackie O.

No mention was made of Bernie Novinsky either — by Hallie or by Zinck — leading Zinck to wonder anew about the geometric possibilities:Bernie sitting astride one angle of an isosceles triangle or a parallelogram, Hallie leaning provocatively against another. (Charlie Zinck had always liked math.) "You didn't know this woman, Anna McElroy, did you?" he asked Hallie. Hallie shook her head. Did Joan Novinsky, do you know?" Hallie didn't know. Zinck left that subject too, the mathematical possibilities having suddenly become too complicated for reasonable discourse.

"And you dug up other people today?" Charlie Zinck asked.

"I saw a friend of the fellow who was killed with Anna McElroy. A former roommate, actually: a lover. He was absolutely *drenched* in guilt. Sergeant, the fellow had *AIDS*."

"Which fellow?"

"The one who was killed in the subway. His name was Francis Minot. The roommate had thrown Minot out for the last few weeks of his life. Can you imagine the guilt of *that*? He was devastated today. And angry, about everything. He went into a long tirade about everyone being afraid of people with AIDS. He kept shouting at me about how people with AIDS can't keep their jobs if anyone finds out they have AIDS. Their lives are miserable. They lose their friends. They lose their apartments."

"They especially lose their roommates, I suppose," Charlie Zinck said dryly. "Did this man think Minot was capable of murder? Or was anyone after him? To kill him, I mean."

"Roberto Pereira is his name, the roommate. He said Francis wouldn't hurt a soul. There was a lot of anger in Francis, and a lot of 'why me?' stuff, but he was coping with it pretty well, Roberto said. There was a social worker helping him."

"Did Minot know the McElroy woman?"

"The roommate didn't think so. Minot didn't know many women."

"Did Minot know *of* her?"

"Probably not. I asked that. Minot didn't read much, and he didn't watch the think-stuff on television."

"What were his politics?"

"That was apparently not a big part of his life. When he was a kid, during the Vietnam War, he went on a few protest marches."

"So did a lot of people who didn't have any politics. It wasn't a bad way to spend a Saturday afternoon, if the weather was good. It wasn't *my* thing, but I can see the appeal of it."

Their rice pudding came and the detective asked the reporter whether Francis Minot, who wouldn't hurt a soul, might have been *self*-destructive.

"Well, I asked the social worker about that. He was busy with a client and couldn't see me but I had him on the phone for about fifteen minutes. He said Minot had been a very tormented person, abandoned by everyone, isolated, lost. More like someone heading into suicide, he said, not like someone out to commit a murder. He was pretty emphatic on that."

"And he took time out from his client to discuss Minot with you? Usually those people have answering machines for their incoming calls. Social workers, psychologists, they call you back later. They don't usually interrupt what's going on right there in the office."

"Not this one. Maybe he doesn't believe in answering machines. There could still be someone left in New York who doesn't."

"Improbable. But go on. Minot was 'tormented.'"

"I'll dig out my notes." Hallie leafed through a spiral-bound notebook. "Here it is. He said he'd had Francis Minot under his care for about six months, helping him to come to terms with his condition, for which the prognosis was not good. He said he'd been able to help Francis Minot in areas where the traditional medical personnel were still unable to deal with these realities on a direct basis with their patients. He said he felt reasonably certain that Francis Minot had not been of a murderous bent. But he could not be at all certain about suicide. Suicide, in a sense, would be consistent with Francis Minot's mental state, whereas murder would not. Francis Minot was exceedingly tormented, he said, but more likely to take it out on himself than on anyone else. More than that he couldn't say, since he was busy with a client."

"He mentioned Francis Minot so often by name, with another client sitting right there? Again, it's not orthodox behavior among the shrinking and helping professions. . . . Although maybe it's okay if the client is deceased."

"I gather he's not an orthodox social worker," said Hallie. "His specialty is thanatology, working with people who are dying."

"What did Minot do, by the way? What was his work?"

"He was a window dresser. Store windows. Unemployed."

They ate their rice pudding quietly, for a few moments, until Zinck asked Hallie to go back into her notes and her memory for a few details. Did Roberto Pereira know of anyone who might want Francis Minot dead? No. Did Chip know of anyone who might want Anna dead? No. Where was Roberto at the time of the accident? At the bank where he works as a teller. Not at lunch? It happened more or less during lunchtime. No. He takes an early lunch; he's back at the bank by noon.

"I also spoke to some of the people who were in the subway," said Hallie. "By telephone. Nobody saw anything. I've got pages of notes about nothing. The two people who actually remembered seeing Minot and the McElroy woman together said no one else was near them. Again, there was this vast guilt from everyone, as though they were somehow personally responsible for this terrible event. I find it odd. . . . Not suspicious, just odd."

"Why? How would you feel if *you'd* been there?" It was the first personal question he had asked her and she looked at him, startled and then bemused, before answering. "I would have thought it was one of the rare occasions on which I would have witnessed human violence — the ultimate human violence if it had been a murder, the ultimate human desperation if it had been a suicide. These things don't tend to happen in my presence. I've never seen a murder or a suicide. Outside of TV and the movies, that is. I would be struck by the finality of it, and I would probably brood about what had led up to it, but I would never think I had been a silent partner in it, helping it to happen." She paused, waiting for some response from him. The detective nodded his encouragement and let her talk. This was what any cop would do if he were trying to get to the bottom of a complicated situation — let the person talk. It was also, Zinck realized, what any man would do if he were interested in a woman, if he wanted to see whether his second impression of her was as good as his first.

Hallie gave the detective a quizzical look and went on. "The guilt of Anna's husband and Minot's roommate is something else, though. I think it's regret over the *life* of the dead person, not guilt over the *death* of the person. And maybe they have reason to feel guilty. . . . If *I'd* been in the subway station? I'd feel sorry, in some way, that I couldn't be more helpful in the investigation, but I wouldn't be oozing the kind of guilt that I heard pouring out of these witnesses who hadn't witnessed anything. It's not their fault they were daydreaming when violence was happening right in front of them. It's not their fault they can't prevent every misery and misfortune occurring in this city. One woman was so overwrought today she could hardly get her breath on the phone. No one cares about anyone else, she kept wailing, and now she's just like everyone else. I asked her whether she had any reason to think it was a murder rather than a double suicide, or a double suicide rather than a murder, and she could hardly get the words out. It was just one word, finally. No. She hadn't any reason to think it was one thing or another. She hadn't seen a thing, she said. . . . But *you* know, don't you," and Hallie looked at the detective with her wide gray eyes, "*you* know it isn't a double suicide."

"I don't know what it is," he answered warily, suddenly remembering that this was a reporter opposite him.

"Then you don't know it's a *double suicide*," she said, with triumph in her voice. "*I* certainly don't think it is. And therefore it's all wide open — maybe a murder and maybe not. And, if it's a murder, maybe linked to the murder of Bernie Novinsky and maybe not."

"I don't see that link, in what you've told me. Not yet."

"I don't see it yet either. But that doesn't mean it isn't there. I'm no detective. I just talked to some people. I could be overlooking something monumental."

Charlie's beeper suddenly intruded on them. "Be glad you're no detective," he said, "living with one of *these*, twenty-four hours a day. Worse than an unhappy wife. I gotta call in. Be back in a minute."

He was back in two, standing at their table just long enough to indicate to Hallie that he wouldn't be sitting down again. He got their coats from the extra chairs and signalled to the waitress for their check.

"Would it be anything relating to the Novinsky or McElroy cases?" Hallie asked him.

He looked straight into those goddam gorgeous gray eyes. "No," he lied.

chapter six

Charlie Zinck's car was easy to spot. It was an eight-year-old Plymouth Reliant, sand color, and it looked as though it couldn't give chase to anything faster than a mugger on a skate board. You couldn't see the powerful engine under the hood, and you couldn't easily see the assortment of police gadgets inside the car, including the red light that Zinck could clamp one-handed on the roof as he was careening after a bank robber in a BMW. A card saying N.Y.P.D. Official Business was out of sight under an old copy of the *Amsterdam News*.

Tonight, as usual, the car was the only eight-year-old Reliant in the block. It was also the only vehicle smack in front of a hydrant. Zinck and the gray-eyed lady had made their goodbyes in front of Tony's Bar and Grill. She was heading for the corner, for a cab. She didn't want a lift. He walked across the street to the Reliant.

He was aware of the glowering of a few pedestrians as he unlocked the car. Definitely unfriendly, he thought. Either they made me for a cop and they're sore on general principles, or they didn't and they're sore that nobody gave me a ticket. He smiled and tipped an imaginary hat to a woman of immense proportions who was scowling after the car.

He found another hydrant across the street from Hudson Hospital, and this time he stuck the Official Business card on top of the newspaper. Why not? Let people think the world was a little less unfair.

He ran into heavy pedestrian traffic as he entered the hospital. Visiting hours were just over, and people were streaming toward the clogged exits. People alone or in twos and threes, keeping their thoughts to themselves. If they exchanged worried looks, they were together; if they met no one's eyes, they were alone. It was not a talkative group.

"Where's your lab?" Charlie asked the elevator operator.

"It's closed, sir," was the quick reply. "You'll have to come back in the morning."

Charlie showed his shield.

"Oh, well, sir, the lab is down in the basement. But it's not open this time of night." The lad had a notable case of acne.

"I'm supposed to see someone named Sylvia Ascher," said Charlie, not one to give up easily. "I understand she's down there."

"It's not so simple, sir. I'll have to get permission for you," said the young man, not moving. "It would be much better if you came back in the morning."

"Not for me. And may I suggest that it would be better for *both* of us if I get to the lab *tonight*." He looked hard at the young man. Yes, that was impressive acne.

The young man stared at the floor for a moment, contemplating the terrazzo and his predicament. "OK, just a sec. I have to get clearance for you."

It wasn't that the fellow was uncooperative. It was more that he considered himself to be personally responsible for keeping the United States from becoming a police state. Zinck tried to humor these types, to a certain extent, but he didn't see any laughs in it tonight as he sat for twenty minutes in the lobby waiting for his clearance to arrive and then another fifteen minutes on an uncomfortable bench outside the lab waiting for Sylvia Ascher to return. The place had that special hospital smell, even in the basement: a combination of what they use on the floors and what they use on the patients. Zinck knew he'd be smelling it long after he left.

He jumped to his feet as the lab cart approached, pushed by a woman no longer young, no longer even middle-aged. She looked as lonely and weary as a charwoman.

"You're Sylvia Ascher?"

"All my life. And who are you?" She pushed a few strands of too-black hair from her face.

"I'm Sergeant Zinck. You phoned about the picture in the paper?"

"I thought they'd send someone older," she said bluntly. She shifted her weight. Her ankles were swollen.

"I'm getting older all the time," Charlie replied, but the woman didn't smile. "Tell me about the man in the newspaper," he said, taking out his notebook. "You've seen him?"

"I was in and out of his room like a revolving door. Every two, three, hours they wanted blood work. They should have moved him down here, put him in the corridor, save everyone a lot of wear and tear."

Zinck nodded understandingly. "Do you know his name?"

"It'll come to me." She frowned, trying to remember. "You know how it is, you can't wrap your little finger around it?" She smiled and shrugged. "It'll come." She busied herself with her cart, tidying some supplies.

Zinck lifted pen from paper and looked at the lined face of Sylvia Ascher, who didn't look altogether well herself. "Would you know the nature of his illness?"

"What's to know? Sick is sick. . . . You know, he came in only a few days before . . ." She shook her head.

Charlie had his pen poised above his notebook. The page was clean. He looked closely at this tired woman, and he tried to make his question sound kindly. "Does it strike you as odd that you're the only one in the whole hospital to call the police? The only person to see a resemblance between this man and the picture in the paper?"

She shrugged. "Well, the nurses are very busy. They have a lot to do, answer the bells, empty the bedpans, find doctors to marry." She did not mean it as a joke and Charlie Zinck fought a smile.

"*Everyone's* busy?" he asked. "All the doctors, and the X-ray people, and the EKG people, and the Gray Ladies, and the dieticians, and the . . . ?"

"Most people look at the chart and that's all. Or the bracelet. A patient could be wearing a Richard Nixon mask, and as long as it had good color nobody would bat a hair."

"But you look at the face, is that it?"

"I check the bracelet to make sure. I'm very careful. And I like to have a little contact with my people. Not just take their blood and run, if you know what I mean. . . . The new ones today, they call themselves *phlebotomists*. Fancy, schmancy. But they don't take time to know the person *behind* the veins."

"You've had some contact with this man?" Charlie asked.

"I ask him how he is, and he says, 'I did something good, didn't I?' So I say, 'Yes, I'm sure you did.' Some day I'll start charging $80 an hour for this kind of talk. . . . What did he do, he saw a murder? That's what the paper said. What's so good about that? Sounds to me more like he got caught with his pants in the cookie jar." Her hair growing in white at the roots gave her scalp an unusual prominence, seeming too white against her too-black hair from a bottle.

"We're not sure what he did, what he saw. I'd like to check with him, if you could tell me where to find him," said Charlie.

"Oh, he's gone now," said Sylvia Ascher. She picked up several of the glass tubes and swirled the blood in them.

"Gone? When did he leave?" Things never got easier without getting harder.

"He was gone when I came to work today." And then, seeing that Zinck seemed not to understand, "He died. Early Saturday he died. Two days ago. He was in a coma the whole night before. I couldn't even tell him, that night, he did something good. Well, I said so anyway, in case he could hear."

"Miss Ascher, could he have gotten up out of bed yesterday and gone to the subway?"

"He couldn't have gotten up to go to the toilet."

"You can be so sure?"

She became expansive. "Myself, I've never been to Lourdes — I'm not of that persuasion — but everything I've seen in this life tells me that someone in his condition does not get out of bed, hang up his tubes, waltz out of the hospital and go for a ride in the subway." She looked pleased with herself. "I'm no doctor but I know a thing or two about sick people."

"Did he know he was dying, do you think?" Charlie Zinck asked, making notes in his notepad.

"Oh, Officer, that man was looking at his last days on earth, sure as God made little green oranges." Zinck looked up at her, mildly startled, thought of saying something and then thought better of it. She looked back at him impassively.

"Anything else you can think of, about this man?"

"No. Just that he was here. Here today and gone tomorrow. And now it's yesterday already. . . . You don't happen to have a nice older policeman there at the police station, do you? A nice Jewish policeman?" She gave Charlie a grotesque wink, following it with an amiable smile.

"I'll keep my eyes open for you, Miss Ascher. I want to thank you for calling. It was very public-spirited. I wish everyone would take the time and make the effort, the way you did. It was very good of you." God, he was tired. Something about a hospital. It got to you.

"So how come nobody married me, I'm so terrific?"

"I don't know, Miss Ascher. I have a hard enough time trying to know the things I have to know." He smiled at her, as generously as he could.

"You can go to the records office and find out who he was. Past the elevator and down to the second corridor on the left. There wouldn't be too many dying that day, even here. I think his name was Kassof, maybe, or Karlov. I'm no spring chicken when it comes to names. . . . But I'm a good cook," she smiled.

The smile was off her face before she turned and pushed her cart into the lab. But she appeared a moment later and called to Zinck as he was heading down the dreary corridor toward the elevator. "Officer? One more thing." He returned to her door. "That man wasn't here all that many days, but he never had a living soul he knew poke their noses into his room. Not a friend, not a relative, not a business associate, not a rabbi, not a priest, not a living soul. The nurses noticed *that*. And there wasn't a greeting card in the room." Sylvia Ascher was torn between pity and outrage.

Then she added as an afterthought, "They brought him in when he passed out on the street. He was carrying garbage. Not garbage exactly. Dog stuff. You know, dog mess." She waited for Zinck's nod of understanding before going on. "In a shopping bag from that Republican What's-his-name, who wanted to be Governor a couple years ago. . . .You know, Officer," and she seemed both mystified in what she didn't know and wise in what she did, "this Kaslov, Arloff, What's-his-name, didn't look like a Republican to me. But it's hard to tell, with their clothes off. . . . Anyway, I thought you should make a note about nobody coming to see him. The world is a very lonely place, even with so many people breathing down your neck."

"Don't I know it," Zinck said, a bit too cheerfully. "Thanks again." She had just given him all he needed to close this case. A goddam shopping bag full of dogshit! Crazy goddam city!

But because Sylvia Ascher was watching him closely, and because she seemed to be a specialist in loneliness, he made a note about nobody coming to visit, and then he went off to the records office. He wanted to skip down the corridor, kicking his heels together like some Charlie Chaplin-type figure just before "The End" closes in on him. But he walked slowly, in deference to a place where good people — as well as murderers — came to die.

• • •

According to hospital records, the man with the dogshit in his shopping bag was Maurice Orlov. Nice when things worked out. Also according to hospital records, Orlov had died in the wee hours of Saturday morning, going to his just reward some eight or ten hours before Anna Carr McElroy and Francis Minot headed out on that same journey. This was good news to Charlie Zinck. There was no reason at all to think that the death of Anna McElroy was connected to the death of Bernie Novinsky. And every reason not to — beginning and ending with the general assholery of the transit cops, who were hell to work with and were stupid besides. Charlie Zinck was almost more relieved at not having to work with them on this case — almost, but not quite — than he was at having the Novinsky case solved. Let the transit cops worry about the McElroy/Minot case. As long as he didn't have to work with them on a Novinsky/McElroy/Minot case, he was happy.

From the hospital records, too, Charlie Zinck learned what had killed Orlov. Your basic Big C. Cancer. Orlov had passed out on the street and within seven minutes he was picked up and taken to Hudson Hospital. Within a day he was comatose. Within two days he was dead.

Could he have killed Bernie Novinsky earlier in the week, being so near death? A neurologist on duty at the hospital said yes, no question about it. The man had cancer and was greatly weakened from chemotherapy and all the rest of it. But he could get around. Nothing in his condition would rule out standing in a doorway for an hour and then, for a minute, firing a gun at someone.

With this information, Charlie Zinck should have had the sense to leave. But he didn't, so he soon got half of what the neurologist had learned at medical school. Orlov's disease had started out as lung cancer and then moved to several other places, one of them the brain. At the time of his death, the deceased had had a tumor the size of a golf ball in his brain. This would account for his limp, incidentally, said the neurologist. Charlie nodded. And in the normal progress of this abnormal growth, the tumor eroded a blood vessel in the brain and Orlov began to bleed into his brain. That's when he passed out in the street. The neurologist looked at Zinck closely — to see whether he was grasping the sequence of events, no doubt — but Zinck wondered momentarily whether he was showing symptoms of special interest to this man of science. . . . And then, when Orlov got to the hospital, they couldn't control the bleeding, or the pressure and swelling, and when it all hit the lower brain stem, which handles certain basic things like breathing, it was all over. . . . Charlie Zinck was tasting his rice pudding, which wasn't so good the second time around. He felt a stab of pain in his right temple — a pain about the size and shape of a golf ball. Hospitals did that to him. And neurologists. Still, he was glad to have the information and he thanked the doctor in his best professional manner. He was grateful to the doctor for taking the time, et cetera. Actually, he was grateful to Whomever for not giving him a golf ball in his own brain. But he didn't feel like spending much time in the hospital morgue — only enough to make sure that Maurice Orlov was there and dead and thin and gray.

A few minutes later, when he left Hudson Hospital and was breathing the sweet air of the city again, he was OK. Even the newly-scratched profanity on his fender didn't get to him. They had Orlov, and Orlov had killed Novinsky. That was that. Some satisfactions go deeper than a scratch on the fender. He moved the Plymouth out into traffic.

He worried briefly about why Hallie Cooper was laying all this McElroy stuff on him, but his reverie was interrupted by a taxi vooming past him on the right, almost clipping him before swerving in front of him and abruptly turning left. Dangerous place, this city. He'd think about Hallie Cooper some other time.

chapter seven

Steve Marino, a patrolman for the last two years of his twenty-four-year life, looked like an uncomfortable six-year-old.

"I just don't think it's a good idea, is all," he said. "What about Joanne doing it?"

Charlie Zinck sighed. "A lot of things don't seem like a good idea at the time. Just do it, OK? Joanne's busy."

"I'm busy too. . . . OK, OK, I never said I *wouldn't* do it. I'll *do* it. You said Hudson Hospital?"

"Yes, and I said Kimberley Dayline. I want her to see the body, and I want her to give a 'yes' or 'no' as to whether this was the man in the doorway of her building the night Bernie Novinsky was shot." He turned to some papers on his desk, signifying that he didn't expect a whole lot of discussion on the subject.

"What if she won't say?" Steve asked.

"Ask her nicely. She looks as if she knows how to say yes or no."

"What if she won't even go?"

"You're a cop, Steve. You're not asking her to perform unnatural acts. You're asking her to do her civic duty. Lots of people get asked to do this kind of thing. Especially if they live on a street where a murder took place. Just go and do it, OK?"

"She'll probably faint," Steve mumbled.

"Are you trying to say you're not up to the job?" Charlie asked. "If she faints, grab her. You know how to grab a girl." He permitted himself a smile, and then looked harshly at Steve Marino. "Get going, will you? There isn't too much time left, on Mr. Orlov."

"I thought he was on ice," said Steve.

"Of course he's on ice; they just need the space. They don't want him *permanently* on file, if you know what I mean. And as soon as they find some relatives there'll be all kinds of pressure to release him."

Steve Marino shrugged his way out of Zinck's tiny office.

"Christ," Charlie Zinck said to no one. The only thing more difficult than getting Steve Marino to do this job would have been doing it himself. He'd already seen enough of Maurice Orlov. And he didn't need to see more of Kimberley Dayline. That was greasy kid stuff. Let Steve get another eyeful. He, Charlie, would be spending the night with Jackie O., and she was woman enough for one day. Yes, he'd be with Jackie O. — unless something came up, of course.

• • •

Steve Marino waited. He had pushed the bell twice with no response, and he reached out to push it again. But the door buzzed open and he grabbed at the door instead.

"Ms. Dayline?" he called from inside the double door.

A voice called down from the top floor. "This better be important."

"I told you it was. It's, uh, Officer Marino. Should I come up?"

"You might as well."

"I could wait down here."

"No. Come on up. Just don't be surprised at the way things look."

"Are you alone?"

"I think so. But as I say, it's kind of confused up here."

Steve Marino had a few ideas of what he might find in the apartment,but he gasped even before he got there. As he walked up the final flight of stairs he caught sight of Kimberley Dayline on the top landing, backlit. Beng a policeman for two years, he thought he'd seen just about everything, but this vision of flesh made perfect, flesh revealed, life become art, almost stopped him in his tracks.

"So. Hello," said the wondrous woman.

"Hello. Like I said on the phone, this isn't going to be easy. But it's very important. Are you about ready?" Now *that* was a dumb question.

"Well, I'm not dressed yet. I can't go there in my bathrobe."

"It'd be OK by me," said Steve Marino, feeling a little heady. "I worked in a place once where everyone wore bathrobes."

"You're kidding. Where? In a hospital?"

"No, in a school. The principal wore a bathrobe because he used to be in the Peace Corps. In Africa. It was really a dress, an African dress — for a man, you know — and then everyone else did the same, not to stand out, you know." Steve was more than a little breathless. "It wasn't really a bathrobe. But I wore it over my pajama-tops, so maybe it was."

"Oh." She pondered this. "You sleep in pajamas?"

"Well, most of the time. Look, maybe we shouldn't stand around like this."

Kimberley shrugged disarmingly. "The neighbors don't mind. I do a lot of entertaining in the hall."

"I mean we should get to the hospital."

"Oh, sure. You can come in while I'm getting dressed."

Steve Marino ran up the last few steps, following the spectacular Kimberley Dayline into her apartment and into who-knew-what exotic sights and memorable moments. He held his breath, promising himself that he would always remember crossing this threshold into —

Good God! Her apartment! Sheets everywhere. Pillows. Dirty dishes. Half-empty glasses. The odd shoe here and there, one shoe resting against the congealed remains of a pizza. Piles of *things* everywhere.

"Sorry," said the lady, not altogether penitent. "I said it was a little confused up here. I only clean on Tuesdays."

"That's OK," said Steve, knowing that it wasn't. After all, she had destroyed something beautiful for him: the vision of mirrored ceilings and black-satin sheets and leopard-skin rugs. Are you going to get dressed?" he asked.

"Yes. In a minute. Do you want anything?"

"Nah." What kind of question was *that*?

She slipped into the bathroom carrying a bundle of garments. As she removed what she was wearing, she threw the discards out through the open bathroom door onto a small heap of things (clothing, newspapers, magazines, and quite possibly another pizza). Steve tried to concentrate on this heap rather than on the imagined body of Ms. Dayline, which he knew to be first clothed in her robe then to be nude, and then . . . (He was not very good at not thinking of the nude body of Ms. Dayline.)

She came out of the bathroom after a few minutes, wrapped in a skimpy towel which she held closed around her stupendous breasts. For the third or fourth time in this unusual morning, Steve Marino gasped. Jesus Christ, what the hell was going on?

"I didn't like what I was wearing, so I came out for something else."

"Well, I wish you could go this way," Steve managed to say, "but I'd probably have to arrest you."

"You don't arrest people for being indecent in their own home, do you?"

"No, certainly not." It sounded like a trick question.

"Good. I really hate clothes," Kimberley said, and she flung the towel onto a distant pile of things — yet another pile — and stood before him naked.

Steve stared at her. This was one fabulous female, no doubt about it.

"Do *you* like clothes?" Kimberley was saying.

"Not a whole lot," Steve replied, being very much aware of which ones he would like to be relieved of, at this moment.

"Well, get comfortable, then. We can take a few minutes to get comfortable, can't we?"

"Yes, sure," said Steve, and he sat down awkwardly on some things on a chair.

"No, really comfortable," said Kimberley, and she walked to him as if in slow motion, drew him up against her and pressed herself against him while she undid holster belt, trouser belt, button, zipper. She was murmuring about his body — particular attributes of it that she admired (a quick study, she) — as she released him to her attentive hands. His hands went where he and she both wanted them: to those astonishing breasts. He closed his eyes in pleasure and she, probably with her eyes open, went for it. Was there ever any question about it, he would wonder later. But at the moment he didn't think of much of anything, being preoccupied with the His and Hers of Now.

He remembered vaguely that he was on duty — but what the hell, even Charlie Zinck would probably go for it, he thought briefly, before he decided not to think about Charlie Zinck any more.

Kimberley led him exquisitely to her bed, one hand on that part of him that would have followed her anywhere at this point, her other hand reaching for a candy-dish of condoms of various sorts. Steve, who had never experienced such hospitality and was similarly new to some of the gaudier condoms in the dish, chose one he had never seen in a vending machine and never would have asked for in a drugstore.

It was all pretty wild. Juicy and noisy. Steve Marino didn't have words for it. "Wow," he said, finally. Afterward, he spent some thoughtful moments looking for various items of clothing he had shed in the heat of passion. Kimberley was helpful, and she had the grace to smile wordlessly when each of them turned up a pair of jockey shorts.

• • •

"No, I wasn't asking for your entire personal history," Steve protested. He and Kimberley were on their way to Hudson Hospital. It was almost lunchtime, and he felt empty and disoriented. A morning quickie — well, two — was not always all it was cracked up to be. Or maybe it was that other half-eaten pizza that turned up in Kimberley's bedroom, looking as inedible and unreal as those platters of fake food in restaurant windows. No doubt about it: this was not a good morning to look at a bunch of dead anchovies stretched out in a dubious sauce, all of it settled into a slab of dough that some fat guy had tossed around on his sweaty arms.

"All I asked," Steve repeated to Kimberley, "was if you do a lot of this."

"I don't see that it's any of your business," she answered. "Do I ask you for your whole life history?"

"But I'll tell you," he said. "Anything. What do you want to know?"

"Nothing. I don't want to know anything."

"Ask me anything. I'll tell you."

Kimberley sighed. "I just said I didn't want to know anything."

"Nothing?" Steve asked.

"OK. What are your hobbies? God, is this a drag."

Steve was still explaining the intricacies of beer-can collecting when they arrived at Hudson Hospital. Kimberley was silent and pouting.

"Did you ever see a dead body before?" asked Steve.

"Do I get to see the whole body?" asked Kimberley. "I thought I just had to recognize the face."

"Maybe you'd recognize the body," Steve smirked.

"That's gross," she answered. "Do you know how old that man was? He'd be old enough to be my grandfather."

"Are you saying you haven't done it with anyone that old?" Steve asked. He was trying to sound casual.

"Will you cut it out. I don't see why we have to discuss my personal sex life. I'm not constantly asking *you* about everything."

"But I'll tell you. I have never, and this is the truth, made it with anyone old enough to be my grandmother."

"This is really gross," Kimberley said.

"What's the oldest person you ever made it with?" Steve asked.

"How do I know? A hundred and five."

"I thought you said . . ."

"I didn't say *anything*. The only thing I said was that I would come down here to help the City of New York find a murderer. If I can. But if you keep this up I might just flip out when I see the guy, and lose my mind, and not be able to recognize him one way or the other."

"Well, it's got to be one way or the other. Either you know him or you don't."

"Not if I've gone crazy and just sit there twiddling my toes."

"You know, I'd really like to know, did a guy ever make it with you with his toes?"

"In about ten seconds I am going to lose my mind completely. You are about to hear the last words I will ever speak in this life, unless . . ." (and she lowered her voice because they were approaching the door to the morgue at Hudson Hospital) ". . . unless you shut the fuck up."

The balding man who welcomed them to the corpse collection enjoyed making up stories about the bodies he saw — the dead ones especially, but the live ones too. He looked at this young police officer with his blond good looks, his chunky strong body, and this young woman with her remarkable breasts (well, you couldn't miss 'em, with her coat flung open on them). These two, thought the man who saw more dead people than live people, these two are supposed to be a cop and a witness, coming to make a routine ID. But they have *really* just spent the past hour screwing. Passionately. Pantingly. Sweatily. "This way, won't you, sir? This way, ma'am."

• • •

"So what's the problem?" Charlie Zinck asked Steve Marino. "She identified the guy. She gave a positive ID. He was the guy on the steps of her building. What's the problem?" He raised his voice against the background noise that wasn't always in the background. Just outside the open door of Zinck's office, someone slammed down a phone and shouted an obscenity. A couple of heads looked up briefly.

"No problem," asked Marino.

"If you'll excuse my saying so, you look like you've got a problem. It's none of my business, unless it's about the ID in some way."

"It's not about the ID."

"Is it about the witness?"

"Not exactly."

"Christ, now we'll play 'Twenty Questions.' We have nothing else to do but play guessing games." He leaned back in his chair in a mockery of patience.

"It's not really about the witness. She identified the guy. Everything's fine."

"What else did she do? Give you a grope?"

"No. Jesus, I was on duty."

"You can't help who gives you a grope when you're on duty."

"Well, don't worry about anything like that," said Steve.

"I'm not worried about anything at all. We're almost home on this case. *You're* the one looks worried."

"Have you taken many witnesses to make an ID?" asked Steve. "On a stiff, I mean."

"Yeah. It gets to be sort of routine," Charlie said, remembering how he wouldn't have done it today unless his pension had depended on it.

"Do the witnesses ever act a little strange?" asked Steve.

"It's hard to know whether they're acting strange when you don't know what they'd be like normally. Did Ms. Dayline act strange?"

"I think so. I do most definitely think so." He paused.

"Well?"

"She kissed him."

"That's OK. A lot of people kiss a person who has just died."

"She *really* kissed him."

"That's OK. . . . Uh, where?"

"On the mouth. And I swear she had her tongue in there. The guy had to be ice cold. I think that's pretty weird."

"Don't worry about it, kid. There's a lot of kinky stuff out there. Maybe she hasn't had a live one for a while."

"Yeah. . . . You know, it was a long kiss. I just can't stop thinking about it. What do you think he tasted like?"

"Christ, don't ask me, ask her."

"I did, but she wasn't talking to me."

Zinck had a momentary concern. "She talked to you long enough to say she recognized the guy, didn't she?"

"Yeah."

"OK. Then what she does on her own time is not our worry. There's no law against it, and no one's complaining. Let it lie. It's all in a day's work." He began to shuffle through a pile of papers.

"Do I have to mention it in my report?"

"Nah, forget it. You got other things to think about."

"There was something else," Marino said.

"OK. Let's hear it." Zinck put aside the pile of papers.

"Well, she has this pair of knockers on her . . ."

"I am not unobservant," said Zinck.

"Well, she's kissing the guy, see, and her tongue is working, inside his mouth, and she's pressing her boobs hard against him and rotating her body around, sort of a circular motion . . ."

"Look, they weren't fucking, were they? Just forget it. . . . Uh, is there more?"

"Not really."

"OK, there's more." Zinck retrieved the Gaviscon bottle from his top drawer and opened it with resignation.

"We're leaving, see, and she leans against the little guy who's in charge there. I mean she really leans against him, puts her head on his shoulder and presses those giant boobs into him."

"And what does he do?" He popped a couple of Gaviscon tablets.

"He puts his arms around her and says, 'You go ahead and cry now, little lady, it'll do you good.'"

"Is that it?" Steve Marino nodded. "Steve, if you'll excuse my saying so, I think you're making a little too much of this with Ms. Dayline. If you see it from *her* point of view, it's all quite reasonable. She's overcome with normal emotion. It isn't kinky. She sees a guy who's dead, someone she talked to recently, someone who reminds her of her Uncle Harry . . ."

"Jesus H. Christ, I forgot all about Uncle Harry. Her *uncle*. Her own uncle. That *does* it." Steve lurched from Zinck's office as though reeling from a blow. Which, in fact, he was. He most definitely was.

• • •

By some understanding that went beyond words, Zinck knew he shouldn't ask Steve Marino to go back to Orlov with another ID. If you haven't seen that many stiffs, one a day was enough. And so, somewhat later that day, Joanne Liu reported back to Zinck that the black kid had positively identified Orlov as the man he'd seen kill Bernie Novinsky. Was he sure? *Yes*, ma'am. No doubts at all? No, *ma'am*. Joshua Tyrone Pemberton had then opined that a lot of white folks look alike, you gotta admit, "but this guy looked real different, and not just 'cause he's dead, you know what I'm saying'?"

Joanne Liu told Zinck that she liked the way young Joshua questioned the balding keeper of the corpses — intelligently, if a bit ghoulishly — and she reported confidently to Zinck that the lad was, in her view, a credible witness. She didn't mention the lad's excessive interest in whether a dead man goes to his grave with a permanent erection.

In spite of its being another all-you-can-eat Gaviscon day, Charlie Zinck was restrainedly ecstatic.

He OK'd the release of the facts to the media — Orlov had killed Novinsky in the course of a robbery, and Orlov himself had succumbed of unrelated causes a few days later. He omitted the curious fact that Novinsky's wallet was found near the scene of the crime with its money still inside, a fact that bothered Zinck only a little — and not at all when he didn't think about it.

"Hell," he said to no one in particular (this was getting to be a habit with him), "let someone else worry about that." And let someone else worry about the McElroy woman, he said to himself.

Someone else was.

chapter eight

Not exactly worrying. But for days now, Hallie Cooper had been thinking about Anna Carr McElroy, unable to clear her mind of Anna. It was as if Anna had moved into Hallie's apartment, out of some urgent need, and she, Hallie, lacked the power to turn the woman out.

Anna McElroy hadn't moved in alone. With her came all the Vietnamese women she had written about in the chapters Bernie had sent to Hallie. These women, too, had taken up tenacious residence in Hallie's mind. . . . The withered little woman, for instance, probably only forty-five years old, one of thousands of the new unemployed in Ho Chi Minh City. She didn't do too badly at scavenging. Widowed in the bloody year following North Vietnam's takeover of the South in 1975, she spent her days picking over pieces of used toilet paper at the garbage dump, selling it day after day for a few scraps of food. . . . And another: the sad daughter-in-law who watched helplessly as tax collectors took the rice saved for her mother-in-law's funeral; the dying woman's only son had left Vietnam three years ago, the first of their small family to bribe his way out. He was to have sent money back for all of them, but he was never heard from again. He had been a good son, they all said, and a good worker, trying to make the best of it when many had already fled. His disappearance could only mean that he had died at sea, a victim of the violent seas or the even more violent pirates from Thailand. . . . And another who would not leave Hallie's thoughts: the prostitute who had been manipulated through a long and mean re-education in a number of camps, the guards telling her how lucky she was to be alive since many in her family had died in re-education. On her release, she was told again how fortunate she was — she would now be privileged to serve the proletarian struggle by providing odd pleasures to Vietnam's Party officials and to their advisers from Cuba and East Germany. . . .

More women — and more violence to their spirit, their well-being, their freedom. The old crone, now an outcast, whose son had escaped from the army and disappeared; she had had to surrender her ration cards and was reduced to begging in the streets for food. . . . And the pitiful woman whose two fine sons had died in Siberia, part of the contingent of thousands of "export labor" workers sent to the Soviet bloc each year. She had lost her mind and fretted for hours each afternoon, thinking her sons had not yet returned from school. . . . And the young woman, a teacher, whose brother had been sentenced to thirty years in prison for trying to send his writing abroad. She had merely lost her *joie de vivre* and her health; her mind was still in service to the State.

The first time Hallie read these pages of Anna's — the final draft of the first part of Anna's book — she was stunned. She made a cup of tea for herself while she was reading, and when it was gone she sloshed a good brandy into the teacup. She sat for a long time sipping the brandy, thinking about Bernie who was dead and about the women of Vietnam who were alive in their hell-on-earth. These chapters seemed to carry a special message for her. They were, among other things, Bernie's last message to her.

Hallie read Anna's chapters again the next day and was struck almost physically by the power of the writing. Anna McElroy had cared about these women; her description of their suffering was poignant, memorable, intimate. The writer in Hallie saluted the writer in Anna. In her own reporting, Hallie often felt that she was speaking for people whose voices could not be heard, and Anna's work was fueled by this same passion. For with all the talk of a new "openness" in Vietnam, Anna had seen that Party control was still absolute, and in their own country the Vietnamese could not be heard. Their despair, fears, and sorrows — and their hopes if they still had any — could not be voiced. Anna had seen this. And through Anna, her readers would see it.

The third time in three days that Hallie Cooper picked up these extraordinary chapters she did not read them. She merely closed her arms around them and held them to her. Anna's death had been mentioned on the evening news between a pile-up on the FDR Drive, killing four people, and an explosion in a Con Ed line, killing two. Just another day in the life of the city. Hallie brooded for a long time, then, about Anna and Bernie whose lives were finished but whose work was unfinished. You ought to do a major story on her, Bernie had said. Too late, she apologized silently to him. Too late, too late. For the women of Vietnam, for Bernie, for Anna. It was very late at night when she fell into an exhausted sleep.

Driven by whatever melodramatic notion made her think of herself as a detective — no doubt furthered by meeting that detective, with whom she felt some indefinable kinship — she had spent a whole day looking into Anna's death. She'd gotten no real satisfaction from it. Or from the detective, who'd heard her out that evening. Still, she couldn't let it go. When this morning's paper carried the news that Bernie Novinsky's murderer had been found in a hospital, dead, she did the arithmetic before she finished the story: Maurice Orlov had died *half a day* before Anna was killed. So there *couldn't* be any connection between the deaths of Bernie and Anna. Let it go, she said to herself. Bernie was killed in a robbery, and his killer was now dead. Let it go.

But suddenly it wasn't Anna's death that filled her mind, it was Anna's life. And she knew she would write that lengthy piece about Anna. An obligation to Bernie, perhaps. She owed him this — at least this. An obligation to Anna, too, somehow. And beyond that, an obligation to the women who had trusted Anna.

Hallie Cooper had a reputation for being nobody's fool and in nobody's pocket. She also had a repuation for being one of the all-time romantics: a seeker after Truth, a fighter against Evil. Her readers loved every part of it, as did her editor. After the Pulitzer, he let her do whatever she wanted. She did her best when she went her own way, and she had a wall of awards to prove it.

When Hallie Cooper got hold of something, she didn't let go. And now, for better or worse, and wherever it might lead her, Hallie Cooper wasn't about to let go of Anna McElroy.

• • •

Ossy Blackwell's name, identified only as a member of the history faculty at Columbia University, was written in someone's handwriting (probably Anna's) on the first page of Anna's manuscript. Also on that page was the handwritten note (probably to Bernie) that Blackwell would be writing the introduction to her book.

Hallie Cooper reached Blackwell by phone at his office at Columbia. She had some questions for him about Anna, she said. He was pleasant, if wary, and suggested that they talk in person. He had some time this afternoon, if that would be OK. How about the West End Cafe? Fine, said Hallie.

She arrived early at the West End Cafe, near Columbia, and looked expectantly into the cheerful gloom: Not seeing anyone who looked expectantly at her, she asked for Ossy Blackwell. "He's gonna be late," said the bartender; "you just missed his call." Halllie settled into a table near the door. At a nearby table, three doughy students (probably female) were decked out in the layered guerrilla look and were eating huge portions of ribs and beans and rice and chips. Two middle-aged locals at the bar, in bleached-out sweatshirts, were laughing with the bartender. In a dark corner, two morose students were holding hands on top of the table. In a few other spots, solitary students were drinking beer and reading. Hallie waited.

She was startled by the large black man who entered the place and came directly to her table, smiling.

"Hallie Cooper? I'm Ossy Blackwell. Sorry I'm late." He smiled a quick greeting to a student he knew at another table and sat down.

"Oh, hello. It's quite all right." She returned his smile. Why had she never imagined he was black? "I've been soaking up the ambience. I haven't been here since my Barnard days."

"Anna McElroy spent some time at Barnard," Ossy said, sitting down and looking at Hallie closely.

"I didn't know that. I know very little about her. Is that how you met her?"

"No. I was off in 'Nam then, growing up and getting shot at, and she was spitting at the likes of me when I came back. We wouldn't have hit it off." He smiled and paused. Then, no longer smiling, "What's your interest in Anna Carr McElroy?" Hallie could feel him watching her; his eyes were like the fingers of the blind, leaving nothing unnoticed.

"I was shocked at her death. I was reading her manuscript the day she died. I'd like to do a story on her." That was hardly the whole of it, but Hallie was unsettled by the directness of this man, and — what was it? — his hostility. He was quick and blunt and wary and hostile. His smiles came as naturally as breathing; maybe his wariness did too.

"There was a lot to her," said Ossy Blackwell, suggesting somehow that Hallie wouldn't have known this.

"I'm sure there was," she said pleasantly. "I'd like to hear about her. From you." She was usually able to disarm the people she interviewed, either by flattery or by reasonableness, but Ossy was still circling around her, still sniffing her out.

"Why do you want to write about her? Because she's dead?" He smiled, without mirth. This was the kind of treatment a haughty professor might give a silly sophomore.

"No," Hallie answered. "Because her book is alive. Her book is extraordinary, the chapters I've seen. Had she finished it, when she died?"

"She had it about four-fifths done. I'll be pulling the rest of it together." He saw the question in Hallie's expression. "I knew her intentions, and I have her detailed outline and early draft. We had many conversations about the book. We taped 'em, as a matter of fact. She liked to listen back to our sessions, let 'em roll around in her mind again."

"Is her husband agreeable to this? Wouldn't he be the legal owner of the work, now that she's dead? Does he even *want* it published?"

Blackwell's soft dark eyes flashed. "It'll be published."

"It'll be a controversial book," Hallie observed, prodding him.

"It'll be an *important* book," he contradicted her, "for everyone who has the courage to say so. Everyone else will call it 'controversial' — implying equal validity to the other side. And some of those people will really do a job on it. They'll look first at Anna, how she lived and how she died, and they'll find a way to discredit her book by discrediting her." This wasn't just hostility, thought Hallie; he had thrown down the gauntlet.

"Give me a little credit, Dr. Blackwell. That's not what I do. That's not how I got to where I am."

His eyes pinned her. "I didn't get to where I got to the easy way, either. I'm a professor of *history*. Not *black* history. Everything I've done I've done the hard way — plenty of white folks, and a few black folks too, are still waiting for me to fall on my face. This book of Anna's means a lot to me. Not just 'cause she's right but 'cause she probably lost her life doing this book. I don't feature pouring out my guts about her, and about this book, and seeing it dished up in some piece of slick journalism."

Hallie leaned toward him and spoke without anger. "I don't do slick journalism. I'm here because I want to find out as much as I can about her. I'd like to hear as much as you'd like to say. Don't judge me before you talk with me. I haven't judged you." She raised her eyebrows as she finished these words. She inclined her head and smiled, ever so slightly, as if extending an invitation to him.

But he was the one to extend the invitation. "Let's have a beer," he said, smiling broadly.

And so they talked.

They talked about Vietnam during the war and Vietnam after the sorry end of the war. Finally, they talked about Anna Carr McElroy. As they both wanted it, Ossy Blackwell did most of the talking.

"There's a whole bunch of people who've had second thoughts about that war," Ossy was saying. "Not enough people, maybe. But they speak out pretty strongly." He was still wary, his eyes regularly scanning the scene, but he was comfortable now with Hallie. She was a good listener.

"What really forced these people to think about Vietnam" — and he grinned — "and maybe for the first time, not the second time, was learning what happened after North Vietnam took over South Vietnam. There was a bloodbath, pure and simple. At least 65,000 people were killed, by the most cautious estimate, and it was probably closer to twice that number. These weren't people who *died*, like in re-education camps; these were people who were *killed*. Slaughtered outright, in the bloodbath that all those people said wouldn't happen." His voice had gone up a notch, but there was no triumph in it.

"It has taken a while," he continued quietly, "but a few people in the anti-war movement have come to feel a certain responsibility for the way things turned out."

"Was Anna in that group?" Hallie asked.

"Well, not at first." He gave an apologetic smile. "For a while, she was like most of the anti-war people. They never looked back. I mean, there was 'peace,' right? And there was Latin America to turn to." He took a long drink of beer.

"Most of the anti-war people never understood what was happening in Vietnam after we left," he went on. "Hell, they never understood what was happening while we were *there*. They still think Ho Chi Minh was a gentle poet, a selfless nationalist. Believe me, Uncle Ho was a ruthless Leninist — he cared more about power than he did about anything else — and he sold out anyone he had to, in order to get and keep that power. Even some of the Vietnamese nationalists, to the French, in the early days. Uncle Ho was supposed to be primarily interested in getting the U.S. out of South Vietnam. The hell he was. He was primarily interested in getting himself *into* South Vietnam. Hell, the Ho Chi Minh Trail began *years* before the full-scale U.S. intervention, and the National Liberation Front was entirely the creation of Hanoi. Their own people have admitted it — now, when no one wants to talk about Vietnam any more."

Hallie saw that he had more to say, and she let him go on.

"It isn't easy for people to admit that what came after the war was more repressive than the French and Diem and Thieu combined. . . . You know, in four thousand years of history, the Vietnamese never left their land in any real numbers. Until the boat people started leaving in the Seventies. And they're still leaving in the Nineties. They have an expression there that if the gates were truly opened, even the lamp-posts would leave. . . . I don't know how much plainer it could be. But some people won't see it. Or maybe they see it and just don't want anyone else to see it."

"Anna finally saw it?" said Hallie.

"You damn betcha. And once she took off her rose-colored glasses, she saw clearer than anyone. One courageous lady. She knew she'd lose friends. Hell, we've all lost friends over this. But she probably never thought she'd lose her life over it."

Hallie raised her eyebrows. "You've said that twice. Do you have anything to base it on?"

"Nah. I'm not prowling around with a magnifying glass, gathering fingerprints. I can't know it here" — he tapped his head — "but I know it here," and he gravely touched his heart.

He was momentarily lost in his thoughts and didn't see the student approaching him. The tall young man loped in, close to the table, putting out his fist at the last moment to give Blackwell a mock greeting. The professor flinched and then turned angrily to his student. Embarrassed, the lad mumbled an apology and fled.

"That doesn't happen to me much any more," Ossy said to Hallie. "I guess all this talk about 'Nam had me thinking I was back there."

"You were there a long time?" Hallie asked.

"A full tour and damn proud of it."

"And you're glad you served," Hallie said.

"I'll never be *glad* I was there, but it was *right* to be there." Throughout their conversation, Hallie noticed how he kept correcting her, overriding her choice of words to make his answers his own. He was a man who considered subtleties important. He took no one else's formulations as his own. He was a self-defining man, a man who moved through his life with care. She liked him.

She had more questions about Anna. "So Anna eventually changed her mind about the war. But haven't things recently changed for the better there? They have a new person in the top position; they're making some changes."

For a moment, Ossy looked at her as though she were a not very bright student. "For fifteen years after the war was over, we heard nothing from 'Nam because the news was so terrible. It was a Vietnam only Stalin could have loved. Now, when even the Vietnamese admit how terrible it has been, our media make it sound like you gotta see the glories of Vietnam on your next vacation. But, follow me on this. It's still a country where the government *owns* the people: their thoughts, their labor, their 'votes.' People are still being sent to prison for their ideas. People are still fleeing — in huge numbers. There's still abysmal unemployment, and pervasive corruption, and stagnation, and mismanagement, and a rising crime rate, and a serious drug problem." He noticed Hallie's look of astonishment. "Oh, yes, six thousand opium addicts in Saigon alone. Their own people gave out this figure. . . . And there's a growing malaise affecting all age groups, particularly the young."

"Where do you get your information?" Hallie asked, curious more than challenging.

"Bad news like this comes straight from the Vietnamese government: from their official news agency and the official pronouncements of their various ministers. There are several reliable sources for this in the U.S. — we don't even have to read it in the original. The point is, the Vietnamese leaders don't say anything they don't want to say. And they're saying these things now, which makes every euphoric observation made by returning Americans just so much bullshit. Sure, there's an attempt to turn things around over there, but the reformers haven't won the day by any means. There's plenty of opposition to anything new, 'cause of all the people who'll lose a big chunk of power if there's any real change. And the changes in Eastern Europe have the Vietnamese top dogs very nervous. But even if everyone was behind the need for change — and they aren't — it's a long distance between *wanting* things to be different and *getting* 'em to be different." He chuckled ironically. "That's the basic reality of it. But our newspapers give space to just about any American who can show a ticket stub to and from Vietnam, no matter what kind of peculiar fantasies the person went in with or came out with."

"But surely the travelers see *something* that's worth reading about," Hallie argued. Her paper had carried one such report in the travel section, only a month ago: a woman had reported her delight in the lovely landscape of Vietnam, the interesting food, the unvindictive people.

"They see what they want to see. If they're Sixties-type kids who are mad at the U.S., they see that it's still All Our Fault. If they're academics who want to return to Vietnam to teach, they see what the government-approved academics over there tell 'em to see. If they're media people who want to be able to keep going back, they see hope in every admission of disaster. A lot of these people, don't forget, have a stake in a renewed interest in Vietnam. They'll want to be the ones to teach the courses, and write the newspaper pieces, and be the media authorities, when people start looking for Vietnam on a map again."

"Is a two-week trip under government control really worse than not going at all? I wonder," said Hallie.

Ossy laughed. "I wonder too. One assistant professor came back from his trip to Vietnam and began distributing Ho's Declaration of Independence. That's the document from 1945 that borrows from our own Declaration — people endowed by their Creator with certain unalienable rights, and so on, which is pretty bizarre considering North Vietnam under Uncle Ho's stewardship: not much life, *or* liberty, *or* pursuit of happiness. Anyway, this assistant professor doesn't understand that when Ho talks about how terrible the French were in Vietnam — they enforced inhuman laws, they fettered public opinion (these are Ho's words), they impoverished the people, they mercilessly exploited the workers — I think I have the words right — this poor sap doesn't understand that that's exactly what Ho and his henchmen did when *they* took over. He can't see it, this poor excuse for a scholar. He's so determined to *use* the Vietnamese — he'll go back, he'll teach there, he'll climb the academic ladder on this specialty of his — that he doesn't see how *they're* using *him*, using his gullibility, using his need to believe, using his hatred of his own country." He was trusting Hallie with his anger.

"What made Anna different?" Hallie asked.

"For a while she was like the rest of them. They talk big about things they don't know anything about. You see it in their approach to Latin America these days: Nicaragua under Daniel Ortega was just about the Promised Land. It isn't that they make up their minds after careful study. No, they take Daddy's money to go to school, but they don't want to contaminate their minds by listening to the propaganda of the other side. And only the *other* side is propaganda."

Hallie gave a knowing smile. She had her own experiences with people whose minds were closed. She trusted this man. "And Anna?"

"I'm making a lot of speeches," he apologized, knowing that no apology was needed. "Anna was just too tough-minded. Real grit to her. She was too honest, finally, to pretend she hadn't seen what she'd seen. Also, she stayed longer and saw more. And spoke the language. Which isn't easy, believe me."

Hallie waited, but he had finished. He took a swig of beer. "Damn fine woman," he said to his beer mug.

"Were you drawn to her?" Hallie asked. "I mean, in a personal way."

"No," he answered, genuinely surprised. "Not my type." He was a handsome man, handsomely turned out (in tweed jacket, button-down shirt, chinos, shined loafers), and Hallie thought he was probably saying, without saying it, that Anna was unattractive. "You don't know Maureen, I guess," Ossy continued. "Maureen and I met at Oberlin, and we are gonna be goin' strong until we are in our eighties at least. I get her to stop by at school every so often, to show the students what they're up against." He grinned. He had a disarming grin.

"Anna was not beautiful, I gather, but she was tough. No home-coming queen, but no fool."

"No fool at all," said Ossy. "Except maybe in marrying the guy she did. *He's* a fool."

"In what way?"

"Do you know what he tried to do to Anna, in Vietnam? He tried to turn her in to the authorities. Maybe that's stating it too strongly, but he wanted to tell 'em her faith was wavering. And you know where *that* would have gotten her — *out*, in a hurry. She knew Chip was uncomfortable there, but she didn't think he'd turn against her like that."

"What did she do about it?"

"She sat *him* down and she said she had a few things she could tell the authorities about *him*, if he wanted a real Show-and-Tell session. So the way the two of 'em settled it was for Chip McElroy to leave the Socialist Republic of Vietnam immediately, on the pre-text that his father needed to see him." Ossy chuckled. "I'm glad I was never on the wrong side of Anna Carr McElroy."

"Do you know what she had on Chip?"

"Haven't got a clue. But the guy was probably into several kinds of endeavors that the Socialist Republic of Vietnam believes im-proper for Socialist Man."

"Like what?"

"Like anything the 'Me Generation' would have experimented with in the States and would have been 're-educated' for in the new Vietnam. Anything sexual. Anything pharmaceutical. Anything intellectual. Something entrepreneurial. Something criminal, for all I know. It'd be hard for anyone brought up in the States to stay out of trouble in the Socialist Republic of Vietnam. And he's got problems of his own: he's not one of your 'together' types."

"In what way?"

"I don't know details, but I know he hangs out at Columbia a lot. He was never a student here but he hangs out with some of the loonier types. The ones who want peace — the lion and the lamb all chummy together — and then blow themselves up in someone's basement, trying out their bombs."

"Do you think Chip could have had something to do with Anna's death?"

"I don't know. I hope the police are discussing the matter with him."

"They are. But he has a good alibi. He was up here handing out leaflets."

"Just 'cause he wasn't at the scene of the crime don't mean he had nuthin' to do with it," Ossy said, smiling at his down-home language. "Hell, one of his nonviolent *compañeros* from the basement could have done it for him."

"Well, the person who seems to have done it is a bit outside Chip McElroy's circle. A homosexual, well out of the closet. A store-window decorator. With AIDS."

"Doesn't exactly sound like a match." Ossy looked suddenly at his watch. "You've heard enough from me for one sitting. . . . Say, I've got an open lecture on all this, on Tuesday evening next week. You're welcome to come."

"Are you the lecturer?" she asked, surprising them both with the little-girl shyness in her voice.

"No." He did have a beautiful grin. "The lecturer is Vietnamese," he continued, serious again. "Someone high in the ranks of the National Liberation Front. He had no idea the NLF was going to be abolished as soon as the North Vietnamese swept in. He was re-educated, and re-educated some more, and finally managed to get out. It's a hair-raising story. Ballsy little guy. And now he goes around saying a lot of things that a lot of people would rather keep quiet. It's a wonder no one has thrown *him* in front of a subway train."

"Bad joke," said Hallie, no criticism in her voice.

"Yeah. Sorry. I've always had a weird sense of humor. It keeps me from crying sometimes. This might be one of those times."

"I know what you mean. . . . I'd like very much to come to the lecture. I wish I could bring someone."

"Sure. No charge." The smile again.

"I can't. He was killed. Eight days ago. Bernie Novinsky. I asked you whether you knew him. I'm surprised you didn't. You'd have liked each other. You'd have been able to finish each other's sentences."

"I knew *of* him. Anna said she'd get us together."

They talked a while longer and then went their separate ways, each of them grieving for someone who wouldn't be able to attend the lecture this coming Tuesday.

On an impulse, Hallie looked back at him after she had crossed the street. He had turned and was looking in her direction. She waved tentatively, but he either didn't see her or chose not to wave. She felt oddly connected to this new acquaintance, this handsome black scholar. She had a sudden stab of anxiety for him: the link from Bernie to Anna — if there was a link — could well extend to Ossy Blackwell. The air was cool and she shivered. She passed a pair of students handing out leaflets and gave them an anxious look before hurrying into the subway.

chapter nine

Charlie Zinck didn't see his name in the paper until the next morning.

He'd been up half the night with the latest of the newly deceased — a man clothed only in a raincoat, found at about 11 p.m. inside one of the larger movie theaters. The call came from a woman who had sat through two hours of movies near the man and had begun wondering, upon getting home, whether it was quite proper for someone to go to a PG-rated movie wearing only a raincoat. The whole thing was brought to Zinck's attention when Zinck was wearing even less than a raincoat, as was the athletic Jackie O. (She was understandably miffed to see the back end of Zinck's raincoat going out the door, and she had been trying unsuccessfully all morning to reach him with the news that she was seriously thinking of going back to her accountant.)

As he flipped through his messages — three from Jackie O. alone — he came across the newspaper folded open to Hallie Cooper's column. One of his colleagues had scrawled a possibly good-humored note: "What did you have to do to get this kind of publicity?" Zinck smiled, closed his hand over the bottle of Gaviscon (just in case), and began reading.

He saw his name in the first paragraph and needed to read it twice to get the full sense of it. Your own name in print does that to you, he said to himself, as though he had daily experience with the phenomenon. When he was sure he wasn't looking at early retirement or worse, he read it for a third time, more slowly. The piece started off about Bernie Novinsky, who had been killed, and about his murderer, who had been caught. Then in a new paragraph, Hallie Cooper did the kind of thing for which her many readers admired her — she gave them something to think about.

> *Solving a murder in under two weeks is rare, and Det. Sgt. Charles J. Zinck deserves full credit for the painstaking police work that brought this case to its conclusion. But was this culprit brought to justice? No. The culprit had already gone to his death. In effect, then, the murderer cheated us twice: the first time by killing an excellent human being, the second time by escaping from any justice meted out by the community.*

Zinck's face registered his surprised approval. He hadn't much read this columnist, although he knew who she was (*everyone* did). She had really entered his life only this past week, partly as a pair of beautiful gray eyes, partly as a limp, partly as a help in his work, partly as a nag. He read on:

> *The murderer died from a disease whose name is difficult for many of us to speak. Undoubtedly he suffered. But we, the living, continually suffer when we are denied the catharsis of depriving a criminal of his pleasures, his freedom, even his life, for the violence he has done. We, the living, need to respond to the actions of violent criminals, and the name of this response is similarly difficult for many of us to speak. That name is vengeance.*

Zinck shook his head in disbelief. "Hey, she's OK," he said aloud to no one. He scanned the rest of the column quickly, to make sure his name didn't appear again. The media were usually up to no good, Zinck believed, and no sensible man wanted to see his name in print too often. Finding no further mention of "Det. Sgt. Zinck," he leaned back in his chair, smiled broadly, and released his grip on the Gaviscon bottle, leaving it on top of his pile of telephone messages.

He read a long paragraph on the rationale readily given for locking people up — to protect society, or to deter crime, or even to rehabilitate the criminal. Hallie Cooper seemed surprised that this last reason was given any more, but she mentioned it anyway. Then:

> *But vengeance? We do not so easily say that a violent criminal should be punished simply because he has violated society's rules and because society needs something to restore its reliance on those rules.*
>
> *When people do not control their anti-social impulses, our own response quite properly is a righteous anger, an anger crying out for something that will restore balance and civility to our world. In this sense, vengeance provides not only a necessary catharsis for society, but also an affirmation of society's moral code.*
>
> *Let us speak the word "vengeance," then, without shame or apology. Let us at least speak it. Our vengeance need not be spiteful. It can simply be the payment exacted for a serious wrong that has been done. The alternative is that our criminals will "get away with murder" in every sense of* those *words.*

The look on Zinck's face was one that Jackie O. had wanted to see last night: something between happiness and whatever is directly above it — bliss? He put down the paper and laughed aloud. "*Vengeance*," he said triumphantly. Several heads looked up. Zinck smiled impishly and returned to his work. The several heads returned to theirs. Zinck didn't realize, until later, that there were several more paragraphs to Hallie's column. He knew it dimly at the time, catching Anna McElroy's name further on, but this was not his problem. Seeing your name in print did something to you, Zinck knew, but he didn't care. For a short while today he was very happily full of himself. He wasn't about to worry about someone else's Anna McElroy.

• • •

The call from Hallie Cooper came in to Zinck a short while later, when he had started taking calls but wasn't yet answering previous ones.

"That was a terrific column yesterday," he said. "Thanks for the good word."

"You're very welcome. Thank *you*. But that's not why I'm calling. I've just had a telephone call from one of the people I talked to the other day. This woman was in the subway when Anna McElroy died."

Zinck grimaced silently.

"She told the police she hadn't seen a thing," Hallie continued. "But after she read my column, she decided to tell the truth. She had seen it *all*. She saw the young man *push* Anna McElroy, and this woman is outraged that he'll never be brought to justice. It's not enough if he just dies, she told me. It's too easy. That's exactly what I was saying in my column."

"Some people would say it's *easier* if he just dies. Easier on the whole judicial system, yes?"

"But harder on the whole moral system, yes?" said Hallie.

"Yup. I agree." Zinck said no more.

"There's more," said Hallie. "This woman is sure he *jumped*, after he pushed Anna."

"Well, *that*'ll make a few detectives happy."

"Why?" asked Hallie, surprised.

"They can stop looking for a *third* party who maybe pushed *both* of 'em. They can wrap it all up. Neat and sweet."

"Like the Novinsky case."

"Yeah." He was uneasy about the direction this converation was taking.

"OK, let's look at the Bernie Novinsky case," said Hallie, a schoolmarm's forced patience in her voice.

"What about it?"

"What I said in my column, basically. That another *possible* murder — now confirmed as a *definite* murder by this woman who just called me — may *possibly* be linked to the Novinsky murder." Zinck winced. This was the part of the column he hadn't read.

Hallie continued: "The two victims knew each other, don't forget. And I find it curious — don't you? — that Bernie's murderer and Anna's murderer are both dead."

"Curious, yes. Suggestive, no. Sure it's odd that two people who knew each other should die violently within a week of each other. But unless you've got a connection between the two men who were the last ones to see Novinsky and McElroy alive, you don't have much you could bring into a courtroom. That's if you even went into a courtroom, which you wouldn't, in this case, since both Perps — if they *were* both Perps — are deceased. You follow me?" Why was he giving the time of day to this media person and her crazy ideas? Why wasn't she writing *movies* instead of talking to him? Ah, maybe she *was*. His train of thought was interrupted by the lady, who was speaking with the same impatience he was feeling.

"Of course I follow you," said Hallie. "And do you follow me? This has to be more than coincidence, Bernie Novinsky and Anna McElroy being killed in one week."

Zinck was growing tired of the whole discussion. "OK, what about the ones who did it? One of 'em dies in a hospital, presumably fighting for his life, and the other — if we can believe the woman who just phoned you — does himself in at the scene of the crime. If you want a connection, you should try to get a similar M.O." Then he laughed, not kindly. "Hey, maybe this woman who phoned you could rethink her story *again*. Maybe the young man who *maybe* pushed Anna was *maybe pushed*. What makes her so sure he jumped?"

"She *saw* him jump."

"Yeah, but she wasn't inside his head. Maybe he tripped. Maybe Anna grabbed him. Maybe their clothes got tangled up together."

"Sergeant, we can't get inside *anyone*'s head, not the man who shot Bernie, and not the man who threw Anna onto the tracks. But we've got our hunches. The police go on hunches, don't they?"

"You better believe it. But I don't see that you've —"

"Sergeant, you seem to be doing everything possible to avoid making any connection beween the Novinsky and McElroy cases. I'm not sure why. But I'll tell you my hunch. It's that maybe Bernie Novinsky was killed for his ideas, not his money, and maybe he's one of a series of people getting killed for their ideas — killed in apparently unconnected assaults."

"Maybe, maybe," said Zinck without conviction, "and maybe you're just selling newspapers." He winced, knowing that this was the wrong thing to say.

There was a moment's silence from Hallie Cooper's end of the line. Then she said, rather pleasantly, "I can see you're a man of firm views." (Zinck didn't think she meant it as a compliment.) "I shouldn't be taking so much of your time. I'd like to congratulate you again on finding Bernie Novinsky's killer so quickly."

"Thank you," he said bleakly. "I don't usually read your column" — oh, Jesus, what made him put the *other* foot in his mouth? — "but I'll be reading it from now on."

"Fine," said Hallie Cooper, laughing. "A lot of my readers are people who've been mentioned once and are afraid they'll be mentioned again."

"Thanks for the warning," said Zinck, with a chuckle, "and thanks for calling."

"Thanks for listening," said Hallie Cooper, with a chuckle of her own.

Zinck put the phone down and smiled. Here was a woman you could argue with, and she doesn't end up having a tantrum. There weren't many of them, these days.

Hallie Cooper put the phone down and smiled. Here was a man you could argue with, and he doesn't end up calling you stupid. There weren't many of them, these days.

• • •

Uptown, the man known as Keith clipped Hallie Cooper's column from yesterday's paper. He would think about it more carefully later. In the meantime, he had people to see.

chapter ten

Stubborn man, thought Hallie Cooper. But clear-thinking. So . . . Anna's murderer could have jumped onto the tracks or could have been pulled. Maybe his clothes got entangled with Anna's. Hallie nodded her approval at so practical a theory, so intimate a detail.

It was rotten luck, no longer being able to get inside the head of Francis Minot. Then she stopped short, her hand still on the telephone from her conversation with the stubborn detective. What about the next best thing, get inside the head of the man who had been inside the head of Francis Minot — the man who had been Minot's confidant during the last six months of that tormented young man's life. She ran for her notes, found the social worker's number, and dialed it.

"Yes, I remember your call," he said pleasantly. "Have you been successful in your search for information?"

"Not really," she said. "I'd like to talk with you again, if I may. Could you spare me some tme?"

"Yes. I don't have a client for another ten minutes."

"I have quite a few things to ask you about," said Hallie. "Could I come to your office?" The social worker made no reply. "Or we could meet at some other place," Hallie suggested.

Again there was a pause. "No, we can meet at my office. If you can be here at two o'clock, I've had a cancellation for that time." He gave Hallie an address.

• • •

Miles K. Aldrich, M.S.W., buzzed Hallie into his building. It was a residential building — only a few apartments to a floor — and by the look of the professional identifications on the doorbells, many of the people who lived here also worked here. The place had an air of consulting rather than homemaking.

Miles Aldrich was in the hall to greet Hallie as she got off the elevator.

This was no proper professional in a three-piece suit; Miles Aldrich was wearing a turtleneck tucked into his corduroy pants, a woolen shirt opened to his hand-tooled belt. The belt buckle was a dazzling silver, with a large turquoise at the center of a tasteful swirl of curlicues. He was striving for the casual look, he had paid good money for it, and he had achieved it. An image straight out of a magazine ad.

"Ms. Cooper? Come this way. Are you writing an exposé?" He wasn't handsome so much as assured and accomplished. Maybe thirty-five, at the most.

"At this point, I'm looking for some explanation as to what happened the other day in the subway."

"Of course." He led the way down a longish corridor to his study and motioned Hallie to a seat opposite him. The room was rich and soft: a brown leather couch, beige velvet chairs, a handsome rug in muted colors. Very tasteful. The work of a decorator, probably, but not meant to look it.

Hallie commented briefly on his building — how comfortable and reassuring these old apartment houses were — but he made no reply. He merely nodded, as if telling her to get on with what she'd come for.

"You'd known Francis Minot for about six months, you said on the phone the other day," Hallie said.

"Yes. I'd been seeing him for that length of time." He waited for the next question.

"Did you have any idea he was about to kill that woman?"

"I had no such idea whatsoever. In fact," he added, "I don't believe the police have come to the conclusion that he killed her. Unless you have some new information." He said no more.

"Wouldn't he have been angry enough to kill someone? He was dying, you told me. Of AIDS."

"Ms. Cooper, the dying are often angry. But that doesn't mean they want to kill someone. They want to stay alive. They are often utterly incapable of seeing beyond themselves. . . . Then, too, the anger that a dying person may feel is only part of a sequence of emotions. You've read Kübler-Ross?" Hallie nodded. "Good. Then you know the full sequence. First, there is denial of the death sentence. The X-rays must be wrong, the doctor must be incompetent, a cure will be found, a miracle will happen. Then, when the truth sinks in, and when the second and third and fourth opinions verify it and the condition only worsens, there is anger. Why me? the person asks. Why now? Why this way? Often this anger fastens onto others: the doctor, the family, anyone who will go on living. But dying people do not go out and kill their doctors or their families. . . . Then there is the bargaining stage, when the dying person seeks a postponement of his or her fate, with all kinds of promises to his or her God — and often to a God not acknowledged until now. This stage is soon followed by depression: a deep sadness over the loss of health, the loss of vitality, the loss of meaningful relationships and work, and a deep grief, too, over the impending loss of life itself. . . . Finally, after all this furious and deeply felt emotion, there is acceptance, almost devoid of feeling: a quiet acceptance of death as the inevitable and proper and universal end to life." He had been looking earnestly at Hallie as he spoke. Now his look was expectant, and perhaps a bit arrogant. He would answer any questions, his look said, but he would be annoyed if his presentation left any need for questions.

Hallie looked at her notes for a moment. "Would you say that Francis Minot had come through his anger and arrived at an acceptance of his death?"

"I would say so." He brushed a speck of dust from the arm of his chair.

"Do you think he had any connection with the woman who was killed in the subway?"

"He never spoke of her to me."

"Not at all?"

"That is what I meant when I said 'never,'" answered Aldrich without affect.

"Yes, of course," replied Hallie. "You saw him frequently during the past six months?"

"Yes. Once a week at least."

"And you knew him well?"

"Yes." Something gurgled in the radiator, the only sound in the well-insulated room.

"I had the oddest thought today," said Hallie. Aldrich looked at her impassively. "That perhaps Minot was doing his murder for someone else," Hallie continued.

"I think it would be best not to refer to this as Minot's murder," Aldrich chided. "Unless there is solid reason to think of it as such." He arched his eyebrows. His statement became a question.

"I have only my own hunch to go on," said Hallie. Instinctively, she decided against full disclosure with this man. He didn't need to know about the woman who called to confess what she'd really seen in the subway. "I thought," she went on, "that he could have been under *contract* to perform this killing."

"That he was *paid* to do it?" asked Aldrich, his eyes widening.

"Paid in kind, possibly — his partner would be killing the person Minot wanted killed."

"Sounds like something on television, more than anything Francis Minot would have been involved in. He was a simple person, really. Something of an artist. Very frightened. Very much alone."

"He had no family?"

"None he could turn to. He left them in Nebraska when he came to New York. They had abandoned him long before — abandoned him emotionally, that is."

"Were you and he . . . close?"

"We were not intimate, if that is what you are asking. I am a professional person, giving professional help to clients who seek that help. We were as close as that professional relationship will permit."

"Did you know any of his friends?"

"I did not."

"Could you give me the names of any of his friends? I'd like to talk with them."

"I don't recall their names."

"Could you refresh your memory with your notes?" asked Hallie.

"I take no notes. Notes can easily disrupt a fragile mood, damaging one's concentration and threatening the client's trust."

Hallie smiled patiently. "Could you tell me a little more about him, then, from your memory: where you think we might look for any help in unraveling what happened in that subway station."

"I ought to make clear, Ms. Cooper," and Aldrich smiled charmingly,regretfully, at Hallie, "that Francis Minot was a client of mine and as such is entitled to full professional discretion on my part. I cannot discuss him with you in the detail you might wish. I can only say that it seems hasty for us to conclude that he committed murder. We were not there. Neither of us." He turned his head, smiling in the direction of an original oil painting, a landscape of some distinction.

"I considered the possibility of his having committed suicide," Hallie ventured, without real commitment, "but it would seem that —"

"A very real possibility, I would say."

"Yes, I recall your saying so, the other day."

"I am still of that opinion. Francis Minot's personality and frame of mind would be consistent with violence directed at himself, more so than with violence directed at others. I believe it is very likely that he jumped, and inadvertently dragged this woman onto the subway track with him. It is even more likely that someone else pushed both of them, someone still at large. But I am not a homicide investigator."

He smiled, boyishly, ingratiatingly, making clear that the discussion was nearing its end.

"You're the first thanatologist I've met," said Hallie. "Tell me about the field."

"The word is from Thanatos, the ancient Greek personification of death," explained Aldrich, looking at a point six inches above her head. "The field is specifically focused on death and dying. We are trying to provide a full theoretical framework covering death and the human response to death. We are also trying to offer full practical care and guidance to the dying and to their families." Hallie nodded her understanding.

"Thanatologists come from a variety of specialties, both professional and academic," he continued. "From medicine, of course — every conceivable branch. Also from nursing, pharmacology, law, theology, philosophy, psychology, sociology, social work, gerontology, and undoubtedly a few disciplines I've forgotten."

"Which of these was your own route into the field?" asked Hallie.

"I came from social work. I'd been doing fairly straightforward case work, in private and public settings, until I saw that the problems I found most interesting were precisely the problems being explored by this new specialty called thanatology. I had suffered a major loss myself," Aldrich added, "and realized I was in a position to help others to the same easing of suffering that I myself desired."

Something in his detachment stirred Hallie, reminding her of a psychologist she had dated briefly: a Lord Bountiful who dispensed sympathy and understanding to everyone else but never needed any himself.

Aldrich was sitting back in his chair, surveying a pair of handsomely framed prints on the far wall. "It was the time of the Vietnam War," he continued, "and we were all thinking a great deal about death."

"Were you in the war?" asked Hallie.

"I was in the movement *against* the war," he said pointedly. "My father had been in the war, early on." Again, when Hallie expected a longer answer, he said no more.

"Did you, by chance, know Anna Carr McElroy in the anti-war movement?" asked Hallie. "She was quite prominent in it."

"We never met. I heard her speak many times, years ago, and I saw her recently on television."

"That must have been on Bernie Novinsky's program."

"I believe so."

"Did you watch his program much?"

"No. I have a lot of reading to do. I don't watch much television."

"You know that he also died this past week?"

"Yes. I recall seeing that on television."

"Did Francis Minot ever mention the name of Bernie Novinsky to you?"

"Ms. Cooper, I think we should leave Francis Minot to his rest. I can assure you that he was *not* connected with the death of Bernie Novinsky."

"You seem more positive of that than of his connection with the death of Anna McElroy," said Hallie.

"Ms. Cooper, I did not intend to suggest anything of the sort. I know nothing of any connection Francis Minot may have had with the unfortunate Ms. McElroy and I know nothing of any connection he may have had with the unfortunate Mr. Novinsky. I can hardly be more positive of one theory than of the other. They are equal in my mind, and each seems equally unpromising as an avenue for the amateur detective." He smiled indulgently at Hallie, as though he had caught her stealing a fistful of mints upon leaving a restaurant: a grown-up amused at the child-like behavior of another grown-up.

"And speaking of detectives," he continued, "I must tell you that I saw your column yesterday on these two murders. I compliment you on your writing skills."

"Thank you," said Hallie, momentarily disarmed.

"With you on this case of Anna Carr McElroy," added Aldrich, "things should go very quickly. . . . I don't imagine the police have much to go on, yet." He paused, apparently ready to continue, then stopped.

"Well," he said briskly, giving a too-obvious look at his watch and rising suddenly to conclude the interview. "I hope I've been helpful, Ms. Cooper, but you see that I'm not in a position to know what happened on that subway platform. I do hope you'll come to me again, though, with further questions. I can't guarantee to be of real assistance but, like you, I'd be happy to see this mystery solved. And I'd be grateful to you if you could keep me informed, since Francis Minot — poor fellow — was a client of mine. I hope the police are looking for the felon responsible for his death and for the death of Ms. McElroy."

Hallie rose, too, folding her notepad and putting her pen and notepad into her purse. "I'm very grateful to you for your time," she said. She would have said more, but Aldrich had already turned from her and was waiting for her to leave his study. He followed her out of the room and down the hallway to the door of his apartment. At the door, he shook her hand as if he were greeting her on a receiving line, exerting just the slightest pressure to move her on.

He smiled at her as he closed the door.

• • •

Charlie Zinck was wondering about that wallet of Bernie Novinsky's. An expensive calfskin, but worn. Full of snapshots and membership cards and credit cards and money. OK, so a robber didn't want the trouble of fencing the credit cards — or the risk of using them. But *money*? Two hundred and forty-five dollars in good American greenbacks. Where was this robber coming from that he didn't look for real money? Or didn't recognize it? Or didn't want it?

Zinck looked back over the case, and the positive IDs from the aging blood lady and the black kid and the provocative Ms. Dayline. Orlov had done it, that was clear. Ms. Dayline had seen him waiting to do it. The black kid had seen him do it. The blood lady had comforted him in his hospital-bed confession of *something*. But here was this newspaper broad who was sure that money had nothing to do with it. So? She was entitled to her opinion. They still had their Perp, still dead. They still had their case solved. And solved in a little over a week, he was proud to think. If only things would go so well with the lady who had no hands or feet. Or the La-Z-Boy stiff. Or the Raincoat. . . . Or Jackie O., who was not returning his calls.

• • •

The man known as Keith was alone in his apartment. The column from yesterday's newspaper was on the table beside the easy chair in his living room. He had trimmed the clipping carefully and noted the date in the white space at the top of the column.

He looked closely at the picture of the columnist: a tiny portrait the size of a postage stamp. Handsome woman. Clever, too, mentioning the deaths of Bernie Novinsky and Anna Carr McElroy in the same column. Dangerously clever, he mused.

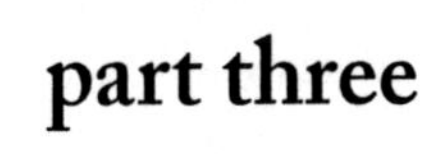
part three

chapter eleven

The elevator door opened and a woman of uncertain age looked out, momentarily startled to see Miles K. Aldrich waiting for her in the dim hallway.

"Professor Rupert," he said. "I'm very glad you're here. Please come in. I live here, as you can see, but I also have a room that serves as my consulting room. Right this way."

The woman had the gait of an elderly person, thought Aldrich; she took small steps, and there was little movement of her upper body. But with her unlined skin stretched taut over her cheekbones, she had the face of a thirty-year-old who did aerobics three times a week. In fact, as Aldrich knew from her doctor, the woman was forty-seven. Her major exercise for the past year had probably been hailing the taxis that took her to and from her doctors.

Associate Professor Marjorie Rupert was uncomfortable with her latest specialist.

"I don't know why I'm here," she began, bewildered but docile.

Aldrich could see that this would take time. "Dr. Motzkin thought —" .

"I think he's sicker than I am," Marjorie Rupert complained.

"— he thought you might want to see someone who advises

people in your condition," Aldrich continued patiently.

"Well, he said it wasn't essential, but he thought it might be helpful, yes," Marjorie conceded. "I've been very ill, for a year now."

"Yes. I have your history from Dr. Motzkin. But I gather you've seen him for only a few months."

"Yes. I seem to want new opinions, from time to time." She smiled, as if to apologize for her bad manners in changing doctors so frequently.

"Dr. Motzkin thought you might benefit from my opinion," said Aldrich. "Or rather, he thought you might benefit from talking with me on a fairly regular basis. Not about your physical condition — I am not a physician — but about your state of mind. It can be very helpful to talk with a trained person about these things: about life and death, sickness and wellness. I can assure you that nothing you say in this room will be repeated. I do not discuss my clients with their other specialists. In other words, I am not here as a member of the team, but simply as someone who can help you sort out your feelings and come to terms with your life." His mind was still on the woman who had just left his office, the reporter Hallie Cooper. Why did she seem not to understand that what a client discussed with him was privileged information? *Everyone* understood this.

Marjorie Rupert brought him back to the present. "I don't know what there is to discuss, really," she said. "I don't feel any *worse* than usual." She fiddled with the folds of her dress.

"Yet you aren't getting *better*."

"That's true. But I'm managing to keep on with my teaching. I'm not *disabled*. I'm not *terribly* ill." Typical denial, thought Aldrich. All of Motzkin's patients were stuck at denial. Francis Minot had been one of the stubbornest. And with *AIDS*, of all things.

"I understand," said Aldrich. "Tell me what it means to you, that you're not getting better."

"Well, I suppose it means I'm either staying the same or I'm getting worse." She gave him the nervous smile of a child hoping she was making a good recitation. Aldrich nodded a nonspecific approval.

"Did it ever occur to you that you might be getting worse?" he asked.

"No, not really. I don't believe in taking the gloomy side of things. Have you been talking with Dr. Motzkin? Oh, yes, of course you have." She laughed quickly. Then: "He seems to think I'm not doing very well."

"He has said that to you?"

"Not exactly, but he has pretty much said they've done all they could do for me, with the current state-of-the-art on diseases of the blood . . . on my particular disease of the blood." She looked at Aldrich without expression.

"Has he said you might be dying?"

"Well he . . . not in so many words. Are *you* telling me that?"

"I'm not a physician. But I see your records, and I know a little about these things, and I have Dr. Motzkin's —"

"What *are* you telling me?"

Aldrich took a deep breath: one more time he'd have to do the job every doctor wanted to avoid. He knew a brain surgeon who got himself booted up into administration because he hated giving bad news to patients. "I'm suggesting that you might be more ill than you've let yourself believe."

"Am I . . . dying?"

"It is possible. One never likes to say for sure."

"Why didn't he tell me this himself?"

"I imagine he —"

"He's a bastard, that's why." Marjorie's cheeks had reddened and her face had become a mask of hate. "I ask him what's happening, and he tells me they're doing all they can. What a dishonest little bastard. You know, I bet he's dying himself. He looks sicker than I do. I think he *is* sick. And I'm *glad*. God, you give these doctors your whole history, again and again and again, and what do they give you back? Not an ounce of sympathy. He doesn't even look me in the eye. I hope he *is* dying." She paused after this outburst, then looked around uneasily as if wondering who had been speaking.

The face of Miles Aldrich showed an expression that might conceivably be compassion. And Marjorie's tears flowed. Tears of self-pity. Of need. Of bitterness. Of rage.

Aldrich never knew what to make of these things. Maybe this Herb Motzkin was an inarticulate wretch who couldn't give his patients a clear message of bad news. Many doctors could never do it without judging themselves a complete failure. It was like bringing a bad report card home. . . . Or maybe Marjorie had been given the news and not heard it — had listened to it with her ears but not heard it in her mind. The brain is a magnificent machine, working instantaneously except when refusing to work at all. And the brain often balks at comprehending the worst.

Marjorie cried for several minutes, without restraint, without self-consciousness. Aldrich offered her a box of anonymous tissues in an embroidery-covered box. They sat for several minutes with neither one speaking, the doomed woman looking for the first time into the abyss, and the thanatologist looking for at least the three-hundredth time at someone else taking the measure of that landscape.

"It is good to cry," he said finally. He was on automatic pilot.

"I don't think . . . there's anything . . . good about this," she sobbed. "I can't bear it that my life could be . . . ending . . . just *ending* . . . just like *that.*"

"Your life has been better than most, I'm sure," said Aldrich. "Tell me about your life. Tell me about the important things in your life."

"My teaching," she began. With prodding, she told Aldrich about her special concern in teaching chemistry: that people should understand — really understand — the basic stuff of which man and the world were made. It's a magical science, she confessed shyly, showing the creation and composition of substances not even remotely like the substances that went into making them. . . . She had been successful in her field, and had recently been granted tenure at Columbia's chemistry department following an unusually high output of scholarly papers.

"And what else is important to you?" asked Aldrich. He was still thinking of Hallie Cooper's visit. He briefly flashed on the subway station, and the crucial contact that Francis Minot had had with the McElroy woman.

"Well, I never married," Marjorie said in a tone of apology. "Never even had any close calls," she added, making an attempt at a laugh. "There's no one now."

"Friends?"

"Just a few. People to go to the movies with, mostly. I spend a lot of time on my work."

"Family?"

"I have no family."

"Your father and mother are both dead?" He was fully attentive now.

"Yes." Her answer was barely audible through her tightened lips. Only the "s" was sharp and clear, before it too was absorbed into the quiet of Aldrich's well-furnished consulting room.

"No brothers or sisters?"

"Well no."

Aldrich looked at the Navajo rug on the wall behind Marjorie's head and made a mental note. "You have some siblings then?"

"Only a sister. We don't have much to do with each other."

"Are you in touch with each other at all?"

"No," she said. Aldrich highlighted his mental note.

"You don't plan to tell her of your . . . condition?"

"No." She brushed a strand of graying hair from her eyes.

"How long since you've seen her, or talked to her?"

"She sent me a letter when our mother died. That was twelve years ago."

"Did you reply?"

"No."

"Was she your mother's favorite?"

"Our mother had no favorites. She was in an institution for the last two decades of her life."

"I'm sorry. And before that?"

"That was a long time ago. Let's just say she wasn't a very good mother. . . . And her daughters aren't very good sisters."

"And your father?" He saw a glistening of sweat on Marjorie's pallid forehead.

"What about him?"

"Was he a good father?"

She laughed a short brittle laugh. "Hardly."

"Has he been dead a long time?"

"He died when I was eight." She paused. "For most of my childhood, they told me he died before I was born, but then he got ill and had nowhere to go, so he came home to die. . . . He took a long time to die."

She was tiring, Aldrich could see, but he needed to get something more from her — and leave her with something more. "Do you do much that gets you out among people? Volunteer work, or political activity? Church, maybe? Or some other group?"

"No, my work takes all my time. And I'm not really a belonger. Well, years ago, I was involved in the anti-war effort — you know, Vietnam." She gave him a questioning look, and he nodded. "And recently there's a group that wants me to get involved in getting the U.S. out of Latin America. But I haven't had the energy for it."

Aldrich nodded his understanding. "You need to *get* help, not *give* it, these days." She smiled weakly in gratitude. "And you need a friend." Her eyes again filled with tears as she searched his face for answers. He held her glance with his own.

Miles Aldrich had seen all this before, too many times to count. This woman was like so many others who'd been told of their impending death. She was stunned, bruised, holding tight to civil discourse as to a lifeline. But underneath the quiet agony, he knew, was a rage against the gods, a rage against her fellow man. He knew how to manage this. He would be her support, her friend, her confidant, her counselor. And she, now weak and alone, would come to the end of her life as a tower of strength — and, in doing so, would give him strength. It was a fair exchange, he felt. . . . And who could fault this work of his? It was admirable work: help to the dying. It was also progressive: a new specialty in the helping professions. If he got an extra reward from it, who could complain? Didn't everyone need something extra? Saints were in short supply.

Their time was almost up. He prided himself on knowing, almost to the minute, when the forty-five minutes were up. He practiced, of course, but it was something like perfect pitch — either you had it or you didn't. He had it.

He also had Marjorie Rupert, had her in a good place for a first session."This has been a good beginning, today, wouldn't you say?" He reached for her hand and held it in his own. "We'll talk again soon. Do you have time tomorrow? I see people on Saturday."

Marjorie nodded dumbly.

"Good," said Aldrich. "Same time?"

Again Marjorie nodded.

"Good. Between now and then I want you to let your feelings

go wherever they take you. If you are sad — sadder than you've ever been — let yourself feel it. And if you are angrier than you've ever been, let yourself feel it. We'll talk it through, tomorrow." He gave her hand a squeeze as he helped her up. He smiled at her. "I'm very glad you've come, Professor Rupert. I can help you."

"Thank you," said Marjorie.

She said no more, but she clung to his hand as he guided her down his hallway and out of his apartment.

"Until tomorrow, then," he said, as the elevator came for her and closed on her and took her away. She went unwillingly, he knew.

• • •

Marjorie Rupert was tied to Miles Aldrich by invisible cords. She knew no one else who might want to help her. She was speeding away from him, in the elevator, but in a sense she was still with him, clinging to him hard. And she was already looking forward to tomorrow, when she could return to him more fully.

The elevator arrived at the ground floor and the automatic door opened but Marjorie made no move to leave. Facing her, ready to enter the elevator, was a younger woman, dark circles under her eyes. Was this woman also dying, Marjorie wondered, and also seeking solace from Miles Aldrich? No, most people *weren't* dying at any given moment. Was she now going to wonder how long everyone had left to live? "Get hold of yourself," she said aloud in a low voice.

Still, she felt an immediate flash of rage, a surge of hot jealousy. The young woman started to enter the elevator, a lively spring in her step, and Marjorie shouted at her, "Wait! Can't you see there's someone *in* here?" Marjorie swept past the surprised young woman and blundered tearfully toward the front door.

On an impulse, however, Marjorie turned back to the elevator and watched its progress in the brass pointer above the elevator door. She watched the arrow move slowly to Aldrich's floor and past it. She found no consolation in knowing that the young woman was not precisely her rival, for a deeper knowledge told her that the young woman was her enemy as surely as if she had lunged at Marjorie with a knife. Marjorie understood, suddenly and grimly, that the sages have it all wrong; when a person's life is being squeezed out, the object of that person's full and complicated hatred is not Death, but Life.

With tears streaming down her face and sobs choking her breath, she lurched to the outer door and exited the building with her terrible new knowledge. It was the middle of the afternoon on a bright autumn day, but it was late in her life and she was full of hatred for the lucky living.

• • •

Upstairs, Miles K. Aldrich, M.S.W., American Society of Thanatologists, stared without comprehension at a delicate watercolor on the wall of his study. His mind was on the two women who had been in this room this afternoon: Hallie Cooper, so full of life, and Marjorie Rupert, so shatteringly aware that the life-force was draining out of her. Such were their destinies, it would seem. But what about the unpredictable random events, and their unpredictable consequences? . . . He wondered again whether Francis Minot had jumped, in the end. Or been pulled.

He made out a card for Marjorie Rupert, noting the date of her first visit and making a few other marks on the card.

chapter twelve

Sometimes a guy could be too thorough. That was Steve Marino's view. It wasn't a view he had held for long. In fact, he hadn't held it until this very day. Right after lunch, Charlie Zinck had handed him an address book — the cheapo kind the telephone company used to give out for free — and told Steve to find out anything he could about everyone in the book, especially anything that might concern a relationship between the deceased Maurice Orlov, owner of the book, and the deceased Bernie Novinsky.

Steve Marino put the phone down again. And sighed again. Was she *never* going to answer? He ran a hand through his wavy blond hair and looked up to see Charlie Zinck standing over his desk.

"How's it going?" asked Charlie.

"OK. It takes a while," Steve answered.

"Any problems?"

"Nope."

"Anything turning up?"

"Nope."

"OK. Let's meet in another twenty minutes." Zinck left Marino with the distinct impression that he thought Marino was goofing off, which seemed — to Marino — unfair. It didn't matter, in Marino's mind, that he *was* goofing off. Christ, this was no picnic, doing goddam telephone work. He dialed the next number. Dial-A-Joke. What, again? No, he'd forgotten to cross it off earlier. (*This* wasn't goofing off — the Dial-A-Joke number was right there in the book. Under J, though; not under D.) Dial-A-Joke was never busy. Ah, but if Dial-A-Joke didn't answer — now *that* would be funny. . . . Yeah, this was the same number as before. Same joke. He listened to it again, and decided again that it wasn't funny. Must have been made up by the owner's wife. Marino knew a thing or two.

The next number in the book was busy, so he tried Kimberley Dayline again.

Again he found no one at home, or no one answering. He imagined why no one was answering. Yes, he definitely knew a thing or two about this world.

Back to the busy number. It was now ringing and a man answered.

"Hello?"

"Hello, I'm Officer Marino of the Twentieth Precinct, New York City Police Department, and I'd like to ask you some questions about Maurice Orlov, if you can spare me a couple of minutes. Is your name Howard? And are you an acquaintance of the — of Mr. Orlov's?"

"Yeah, I'm Howard. And you might say I'm an acquaintance. Why are the police interested in him?"

"I'd be glad to tell you, sir, but first let me get your full name and how long you've known him."

"I've known him all my life."

"How long would that be, sir?" Was this guy being evasive or did he have nothing else he wanted to do this afternoon?

"I'm thirty-one. Do you also need my height and weight and the color of my eyes? What's this about, please?"

"We're trying to find out anything that can help us in a murder."

"Was *he* murdered?"

"No, he wasn't. But does the name Bernie Novinsky mean anything to you?"

"No, but I wouldn't know any of his friends. We haven't seen each other in — oh — fourteen years. Jesus, I hadn't realized it was so long. All those birthdays without a single phone call between long-lost father and long-lost son." He laughed without amusement.

"He was your *father*?" Steve Marino hadn't expected this. Orlov wasn't supposed to have any relatives. The hospital said he didn't.

"The only father I ever had. . . . What do you mean, *was* my father? Did he actually have the good taste to die?"

Steve was embarrassed. He didn't like a son to speak ill of a father, especially a father who was dead. And now he, Steve Marino, had to deliver the final news. Why didn't the hospital get it straight? "Uh, I'm afraid I have some bad news for you, Mr. — uh — Orlov."

"It couldn't be any worse than what I've had from him for thirty-one years. This man was bad news for me from the minute I was born."

"He's dead, sir, I'm afraid I have to tell you."

"Ha! If you'd known him, you wouldn't be afraid to tell me that. It's really comical, you know?"

"What is, sir?

"The whole fucking world is comical. Remember, you heard it first from Howard Orlov." Steve Marino checked his watch. Not even four in the afternoon. Was this guy drunk already? Probably not — his next utterance was quite sober: "Is there something in particular you wanted, Officer?"

"Well, I hadn't expected to reach any of Mr. Orlov's family. Could I ask you about any others in the family?"

"There are no others. . . . Now, if you'd like to know the color of my eyes, they are brown, like my father's. And, like him, I have one hell of a disposition. I don't enjoy talking to people I don't know. And you're not someone I know."

"Uh, sir, could I ask you if you had any contact with your father in the past few years?"

"I don't think you get the picture, Officer. I haven't seen him for fourteen years."

"No, I guess I didn't get the picture. Did you two write to each other? Or call? In the past few years, I mean?"

"Without airing the family linen in public, let me say there wouldn't have been much point in that."

"Yes, sir. Well, I'm sorry to take up your time. We might want to call you again. Are you reachable at this number?"

"It would seem so, wouldn't it?" And then his tone changed. "Officer, I'd like to know how he died."

"He had a brain tumor."

"Was it painful?"

"I don't know, sir."

"OK. Let's just hope it was."

"Yes, sir. Thank you very much. Have a nice day, sir." Steve Marino hung up the phone and mopped his brow with the back of his hand. Jesus Christ, what a mess people made of their lives. He went over to the cooler and got a drink of water. Kimberley might be home now — or answering now. She wasn't, so he dialed the next number. He promised himself another try at Dial-A-Joke soon, to see when they changed the joke.

A woman with a deep and unattractive voice answered his call.

"Excuse me, ma'am, I'd like to speak with Rita Stavin."

"Slovin? I'm Rita Slovin."

"I'm sorry, ma'am, can't read the writing too good here. I'm Officer Marino from the Twentieth Precinct, N.Y.P.D, and I'd like to ask you whether the name Maurice Orlov means anything to you. . . . If I'm not bothering you."

"No bother, honey. His name doesn't mean much to me one way or the other. Did he give you my name?"

"We got it from his address book, ma'am. He just died and we're looking for information about him."

"If you ask me, he died *years* ago."

Steve leaned forward in his seat. "You mean, he's been dead a long time? We're not looking at the real Maurice Orlov here?"

"No, honey, nothing like that. You have a lot of imagination for a cop. All I meant was the guy was none too lively even when he had sweet fresh air going in and out of his lungs."

"Oh. Funny you should mention his lungs. That's what went on him. His lungs. He had lung cancer, and then a brain tumor."

"Well whaddya know? Still, something has to go first."

"Yeah. . . . Uh, have you seen him in a while?"

"Not since maybe four years ago, maybe five."

"Did you know any of his friends? Or his family?"

"Honey, I didn't even really know *him*. We just went out a couple of times. A boring movie, once. And a boring lecture, another time. He was nothing to write home about, if you know what I mean."

"Yes, ma'am. Would you think he might kill someone?"

"Well, you never know. I mean, *anyone* could kill someone. It all depends on whether you mean putting rat poison in someone's dinner, very quietly over the months, or whether you mean stabbing him with a kitchen knife while he's bending over the dishwasher."

Steve rolled his eyes. He could undertand why Maurice Orlov hadn't pursued the lady. "Yes, ma'am," he said. "One more thing. Would the name Bernie Novinsky mean anything to you.?"

"No, not really. My first husband's name was Bernie, but his last name wasn't Novinsky." Steve moved the receiver to his other ear, not expecting to miss anything. He looked up to see Charlie Zinck looking at him, and he moved his hand over his notepad — "4-5 yrs," he wrote.

Rita had nothing else to impart, it turned out, and Steve Marino began to get out. "Uh, if we need to talk with you again, ma'am, would it be OK calling you at this number?"

"Honey, it's no trouble at all."

"Thank you. Have a good day."

"You too, now. . . . Oh, tell me something. Were there a lot of numbers in his address book?"

"No, not too many. Not many at all."

"OK, just curious."

"Yes, ma'am."

"'Bye now, honey."

"'Bye, ma'am."

• • •

And so it had gone, through the small pages of the worn address book. A few numbers were no longer current. *Keith*? No, said the man who answered Keith's number. *Gloria R.*? No, she was the previous tenant. We only kept her number because she said there wouldn't be many calls. She'd still be out in Kansas. She went out there a couple of years ago to take care of her mother. *Dr. Meagher*?

Yes, this is the office of Dr. Meagher, but Mr. Orlov hasn't been in for a dental checkup in eighteen months. Perhaps you could tell Mr. Orlov that good dental health depends on regular dental checkups. Steve said he would; he was easily intimidated by dentists. . . . Other numbers too. A local talk-back show, which gave a recorded announcement of the week's forthcoming shows. And a neigborhood Chinese place offering take-out and delivery, with a flat-voiced man rattling off the day's specials in one breath. (No, he didn't know Misser Orroff, and he'd like to get off telephone, please, unless gentleman was ordering, because this was most busy time, please.) And a nearby movie house, with four different movies on four different schedules. If you liked the sound of a female voice — and this one wasn't bad — you sure got a lot for your message-units on this call. . . . And then there was Dial-A-Joke.

Steve Marino was depressed. In the entire list, there was no one Orlov might have eaten Chinese food with, no one he might have gone to the movies with, no one he might have shared a laugh with over the joke of the day. There was literally no one Orlov might have *connected* with, in a moment of sadness, or worry, or need, or fun, or celebration. Maybe he was one of those people who call the Weather number the last thing at night — not to listen but to talk.

Steve tried Kimberley Dayline again, and she caught him off balance by answering.

"Oh, hello," said Steve.

"Who's this?" said the wondrous woman. She had no clothes on, Steve was sure.

"A friend," said Steve, admiring her body.

"A friend who'll be talking to himself in a minute," she snapped.

"Kimberley, this is Steve. Steve Marino. You know, a coupla days ago."

"Oh. Sure. Is this police business?" she asked. She was admiring her body too, Steve guessed.

"Sort of. I was wondering, did you happen to see my handcuffs lying around?"

"What?"

"My *handcuffs*," said Steve, raising his voice and simultaneously regretting it. (Was it his imagination, or did several heads turn around? You couldn't say *anything* in this place.) "My handcuffs," he hissed. "I think I left my handcuffs there. You know, when I was there."

"Well, I cleaned on Tuesday and I didn't see them. But I'll keep an eye out. You never know. . . . Is that all?"

"I guess that's all," Steve said, disappointed. "I'd really appreciate your looking for them. We're not supposed to let them get away from us."

"OK. Anything to help the men in blue."

"We certainly appreciate it, we men in blue." He felt like a jerk. He looked up to see Charlie Zinck standing there again, and he put his hand over the mouthpiece. "Just calling my sister to see if she found a pair of handcuffs I think I left there."

Charlie laughed. "You're not supposed to do that to your sister."

Steve turned his attention again to the phone, which was giving him the steady buzz of no one at the other end. "OK, Sis, that's terrific. Probably in that big easy chair where I was watching TV. Thanks a lot. 'Bye." He hung up and gathered his notes to discuss two hours of real phone calls with Charlie Zinck.

• • •

Hallie didn't see the man approach. Obviously. He would have approached from behind and stalked his quarry for a while as he sized up the situation. And she didn't anticipate the blows: a hard punch to her left shoulder and a slam to her mid-section, both from the rear. She felt her handbag leave her, sail off into the man's arms as smoothly as if the two of them had been part of a relay team. Spent, she was now sprawled on her hands and knees. One knee was grated raw on the pavement. One stocking was in shreds. One wrist was already hurting. Her "team-mate" was speeding on down the street toward Broadway, where he would soon lose himself in the heavy sidewalk traffic.

She choked back a brief nausea. But even as she got groggily to her feet, helped by a man walking a very large dog, she knew exactly what had happened.

She had been mugged. In a city where someone gets mugged every six minutes — or is it every six seconds — this someone had never before been Hallie Cooper.

Checking over her bruises, and feeling the nausea subside, she was surprised not so much that she had finally been mugged but that she hadn't yelled, hadn't even called out. Manners were a liability these days, she suddenly knew. And then she also knew, without any surprise whatsoever, that no one would have seen any of it anyway, on this quiet side-street. Someone might have noticed the guy as he bolted for Broadway if she had yelled. But she hadn't raised her voice, hadn't even found her voice.

Worse than that, she hadn't even seen his face, hadn't even registered his skin color. He was thin and tall and young and quick — and he was wrapped in brightly colored scarf and hat and gloves — but she knew this wasn't much of a description to give to 911.

They soon told her so, when the man and his dog walked with her to a street phone and stood there protectively (apparently waiting in line) while she made the call.

"Go home, dearie," said the gravel-voiced woman who took the call. "Get your super to let you in. There isn't much we can do. The hat and the gloves and the scarf he'll get rid of before he goes a block. Put some iodine on your cuts, and call the people you have to call about your cards being stolen. And if your keys were in your purse, change your locks. Get a locksmith in. That's about all you can do. I've been mugged myself, dearie. Be glad you can *walk* home."

Hallie did it all. And she thought furiously about the event during all the time it took her to get herself and her apartment and her credit life back together. The balding locksmith was wryly amusing, as he described his good fortune with New York's increasing crime rate. "I come from Ukraine. Hard to get out of Ukraine, I tell you honestly. Only clothes on my back. Nothing else. But where else could I go, to make such a good living with locks and keys? . . . I looooooove New York." He sang the advertisement off-key. Hallie gave him a cup of tea as he worked on her locks; his good humor was good medicine for her.

Finally, left to herself in her newly secure stronghold, she called Charlie Zinck to ask the question that had been nagging at her since the attack.

"I'm sorry to call you with such a trifling situation. Muggings must be a dime a dozen for you. But I can't help wondering whether this could all be *connected*, somehow. I did write that column about Bernie Novinsky and Anna McElroy. Am I being *warned*, somehow? . . . Or even *targeted*?"

"I don't think so," said Charlie Zinck, but he had bounced forward in his chair and was giving the call his full attention. "You live in New York City, you gotta expect this kinda inconvenience," he laughed easily.

"I've been expecting it for *years*." Hallie laughed too. "But I just wonder why it came *now*."

"I dunno. What's your sign?" asked Zinck.

"Surely you don't —"

"No, of course I don't. But I don't really think you should worry about this incident being aimed at you personally. What were you doing, walking where there weren't any people? Not paying attention? That's enough, these days, to get one of these characters attached to you. He wouldn't have to know anything else about you. . . . By the way, this kinda thing, they're all independent operators. No contract work. If it was a contract, it'd be more than a mugging. You follow me?"

"That's very reassuring," said Hallie, not at all sure it was.

They talked a few minutes more, Hallie again apologizing for bothering him. "But you're the only cop I know," she said, laughing at her excuse and then apologizing for not knowing any other cops.

"That's OK. Now that you've been mugged, take it from me, your whole life'll change. Some of the more extreme types, the ones used to spit at the 'pigs,' they even *talk* to cops today — 'Hello, Officer,' that sorta thing. Amazing what only one mugging'll do. If I didn't know better, I'd think it was the public relations office of the N.Y.P.D. behind half the muggings in this city." They laughed together.

"Detective, I think I need some personal police protection on something. There's a lecture up at Columbia this coming Tuesday. A professor named Blackwell is sponsoring it. He knew Anna Carr McElroy very well. I talked with him the other day. At some length. I'll tell you about it. It's rather interesting."

"Lectures aren't really my thing," said Zinck.

"Blackwell said there might be trouble."

"I was just thinking I could make an exception in this case.

What kind of trouble?"

"Protest of some sort. Who would think Vietnam could still get people all riled up? The lecturer is Vietnamese, did I mention?"

"No you didn't. Sure I'll come. Vietnamese are getting killed all across the country these days. Big flap in the Vietnamese refugee community about whether the U.S. should recognize the Hanoi government, after all these years. Most of the Vietnamese-Americans have always been dead set against recognition. And now it's getting some of them killed."

"I'll be glad to have your company," said Hallie, a bit distractedly. Why did every bit of comfort serve only to add to her discomfort? She had thought the protest at Columbia would be only verbal, but maybe you had to be a homicide detective to see broader possibilities. Then why didn't Charlie Zinck see broader possibilities in her being mugged today?

They hung up soon, Hallie allowing herself to be convinced that the attack on her was of little consequence — especially since she now had three new locks on her door and a direct line to her own private policeman. She didn't know that the incident was considerably more troubling to Charlie Zinck, who scribbled a few notes while they were talking and who made several urgent calls the minute he said goodbye to her.

• • •

The phone call that came to Hallie Cooper, exactly eight minutes later, was a jaw-dropping surprise to her.

"I've been thinking," said Charlie Zinck, "you could use some police protection sooner than next Tuesday." He tried to make it sound light. "I'm driving up to Vermont this weekend. Want a ride? I have to look at the bed-and-breakfast my cousin just bought. He has plenty of room, he says, with the leaves all down and the tourists all gone. Want to come? I'd even listen to more of your television plots." He laughed warmly. "Really, I'd like your company."

"You think I should get out of town, is that it?"

"I didn't say that." But that was exactly what he thought. "I think anyone who gets mugged should take a few days away from the city, look at some scenery, get calmed down. Look, if I thought you were in any real danger, I'd get round-the-clock on you." (He had, in fact, tried to do exactly that, but nobody was available for a job he couldn't really make a good case for. Somebody even accused him of spinning out television plots.)

"I have work to do," Hallie argued.

"That's OK, bring it with you. You can look out at the mountains while you're doing it. I'll be busy with my cousin, figuring out some security stuff he needs. He just retired from the Sheriff's Department up there, but he's not into the latest security stuff. They don't much need it in Vermont. . . . And really, you'll have a room to yourself on Saturday night."

"So you're inviting me to meet your family, but we're staying in separate rooms, is that it?" She was chuckling.

"That's it," he laughed. "Still, bring your best nightgown. You never know what hour of the night some crazy fire alarm might go off."

Hallie smiled. This man knew a lot about women.

"So. You'll go to Vermont with me?" Zinck asked. He didn't know what he'd do if she said no. Cancel his Vermont trip and follow her himself? What was it, about her? He wanted her safe, was all he could think of.

"Well, yes," the lady replied. "I'd love to."

They decided what time Zinck would pick her up the next morning."And don't go walking by yourself on any quiet side-streets tonight, OK?"

"OK." She liked his protectiveness. Something very nice about a man watching out for her, she thought. Even if she didn't need it.

chapter thirteen

Marjorie Rupert looked hard at her image in the bathroom mirror. She could no longer hide from herself the knowledge that she was dying. In her mind's eye she could already see the sockets of her eyes deepening, the prominences of her cheekbones growing more exaggerated. For a second she had a hideous vision of her skull without its flesh, and she turned from the mirror repulsed.

She ran cold water over her hands and held her dripping hands to her eyelids and forehead. She'd had a full day yesterday — an endless class, an interminable faculty meeting, a string of unwelcome conversations in hallways, and then the meeting with Miles Aldrich. It took a terrifying effort to do what she'd taken for granted even a few months ago. How much longer would she be able to go on? And did anyone appreciate her? All they did was take, and all she did was give. She was tired of giving. She was just plain tired. The cold water felt good.

But she wasn't too tired to keep the appointment with Miles Aldrich this afernoon. She dried her hands and dabbed at her eyes — with Miles Aldrich, *she* would take and *he* would give. Not that these specialists were doing any good, any of them. She was still ill, wasn't she? But they had come to seem like family, somehow — the family she'd never had. Each new specialist was like a distant cousin turning up from out of town. Marjorie would be cordial to the cousin, and the cousin would give her special attention. That's the way it should be in families, Marjorie thought, although she had no first-hand knowledge of any of it. Her own family had been a disaster: the sort that ends up in textbooks. Maybe some cousins would have helped, she used to think. Together they could have defied everyone. Together they could have run away.

She would see Miles Aldrich again today and he would soothe her. He would make her feel calm and generous and saintly. And whenever people spoke the name of Marjorie Rupert in the future they would never suspect that, at the end, she had hated everyone — everyone except perhaps for Miles Aldrich.

She was tired and full of bitterness, but she had strength for Miles Aldrich. That, and need of him.

• • •

Aldrich felt the energy in her the instant the elevator door opened. She began talking as soon as she saw him. When he offered his arm for the few steps to his apartment door, he felt the urgency, the intimacy, of her grasp. He was intrigued by this change in her. Attracted by it.

"I'm so full of anger today. . . . I wanted so much, and now there's no time. There's no time for anything but rage. . . . I was so furious at *everyone* today, I've been burning up with rage." Marjorie was breathless as she sat down on the beige velvet chair. "Please help me," she said softly, her voice apologizing for having skipped the niceties of greeting.

"Of course I'll help you," said Aldrich. "That's what you're here for." He looked at her in what he knew to be a compassionate way. "Tell me," he said, leaning toward her, "tell me about your anger. Tell me about all the people you've been angry at since we saw each other yesterday."

And so she told him. It wasn't a long list. Her department head, who didn't see why Marjorie couldn't offer remedial work to the students who were doing unsatisfactory work. "Is it *my* fault they're failing?" Marjorie had shrieked at him. He hadn't answered. . . . And the student who thought she could get a better grade just by asking for it. "Spoiled brat, she can't con *me*," Marjorie raged to Aldrich. . . . And another student, who swore he'd handed in the assignment but couldn't remember how he'd done it. . . . And still another. "He was talking up a storm in class — in *class*, can you believe it? — about some Vietnamese refugee who's coming here to tell us how terrible everything is in Vietnam today." Her voice indicated her scorn for both the messenger and his message. "It's all the doing of that trouble-maker, Blackwell. Does he think he knows everything about Vietnam just because he fought there? And does he think he can do anything he pleases just because he's black? When have *I* been able to do anything I please?"

Aldrich leaned forward in his chair and extended his hand to Marjorie. He knew of Blackwell and hated what he knew. "And these are the people you've been so angry at," he summed up.

"There are even more," she said. Aldrich nodded. There were always more. His nod was meant to urge her onward to her own summary, and she went willingly.

"I don't know if you undertand this," she said. "I'm not just angry. I'm full of *hate*. I hate them *all*. . . . I'd like to see them all wiped off the face of the earth. That's a terrible cliché but it's exactly what I want. Why are people like Ossy Blackwell or this refugee or these students allowed to stay alive and do their mischief and twist everything to their own advantage when I — just — *die*?" It had cost her something to say this, Aldrich could see. Her lower lip was trembling. Sweat stood out on her forehead. She had asked him her unanswerable question and she wanted a response from him.

"There are many things we're not able to know in this life," said Aldrich. "We can only try to do our best with each situation as it presents itself to us."

Marjorie looked at him skeptically and her eyes filled with tears. "I thought you were here to help me."

"I am," said Aldrich. He handed her the box of tissues and was startled at the way she took the box from him: this was only their second session and already she seemed fully dependent on him, fully open to him. He experienced a thrill of anticipation for the relationship he so often sought and so rarely found, a relationship in which he would give all and his client would take all. Marjorie *would* take all, he suspected — the hints, the suggestions, the commands, the instructions, all. He fixed her with a steady glance that shut out everything else. "I *am* here to help you," he repeated.

"Then tell me how to get rid of this anger," Marjorie ordered. Again, Aldrich was startled. Marjorie Rupert was dependent yet strong: a complicated woman. And was she really forty-seven years old? She seemed more like *twenty*-seven, at the moment.

"We will talk about it," he said.

"I'd rather just go out and *do* something about it," said Marjorie. "I don't *feel* like talking. I don't have *time* for talking." Aldrich was aware of his breathing. Extraordinary, what was happening.

"You *must* talk," he said firmly, and he saw Marjorie relax very slightly into the velvet chair. Soon he would be doing the talking and she would be doing the listening. It remained to be seen only what they would be discussing. "Your day today —" Aldrich began.

"I told you already. I hated everyone. And I can't bear to think that I'm about to — leave. I won't be able to fight them any more. . . . I'd like to — damage some of them before I go. . . . Now *that* would get rid of my anger." She looked at Aldrich triumphantly, even defiantly, at this last utterance.

He looked back at her, evenly and without rebuke. He sensed the remarkable nature of the moment — everything that followed would either be redeemed or tainted by what happened during the next blinking of an eye. He waited for that fraction of a second and Marjorie moved in. "Help me," she said quietly, "help me — to *do*."

Miles Aldrich looked at her steadily but said nothing. In all his days of death counseling, a client had never been in the position of leading *him* and he was unprepared for it. He needed time to think.

"You need time with your thoughts," he said. "I want you to sit quietly here, with me. We will meditate together for fifteen minutes." He put his hand out to touch her hand, and placed her hand quietly in her lap. "I will be here. Let us close our eyes and be silent now." He removed his hand.

"But isn't our time almost up?" asked Marjorie.

"When I ask you to lean on me, I do not think about time," said Miles Aldrich. But in the moments that followed, he thought a great deal about time. It was too soon. She was too strong. Perhaps she was a provocateur? No. She was truly dying. And he would help her to a fulfillment, an ecstasy, that she could not achieve without him. This was firm ground for him. He knew this. Except that she was in step with him already, even ahead of him. It frightened him. It also excited him.

Fourteen and a half minutes passed before Miles Aldrich looked at his watch again and decided to re-establish contact with Marjorie Rupert.

"Tell me," he said calmly, "tell me what you are thinking at this very moment."

"At this very moment," and she took a deep breath, "I am thinking of what Ossy Blackwell would look like dead." She looked unflinchingly at Aldrich. Neither looked away. Unspoken questions were exchanged, and unspoken answers.

"You are a strong woman," said Aldrich. "And you are lucky, knowing ahead of time that you are — departing. It is a gift not given to most people. No one who isn't at the end of life would be able to think as decisively as you are thinking now. *Your* last days can be more important than the *years* in someone else's life. What you do now can make your whole life meaningful."

His voice took on the ministerial tone of One Who Knows, and Marjorie looked at him with the glazed eyes of one who is in the presence of One Who Knows.

"I knew you could help me," she said, her voice a whisper.

"Yes, I can help you. I am very glad you came to me." Marjorie looked suddenly tired, to him, and he feared going further at this session. "I'd like you to come again. On Monday. We will work together, Marjorie." It was the first time he had used her name. He repeated it: "Marjorie, Marjorie." His voice was soft, intimate.

"Thank you, Dr. Aldrich."

"Your beautiful name is Marjorie. And you may call me Keith." He extended his hand to her, to help her rise.

She took his hand and fell against him as she struggled to her feet. "Oh, Keith, Keith, no one has ever known me the way you do. I've been looking for you for a very long time. Thank you, thank you. Keith, I am yours." She pressed herself to him.

• • •

The man who called himself Keith went back to his consulting room and lay on the leather couch for a long while after Marjorie Rupert left. He was spent, emotionally and physically. Where did she get the energy, this woman who was almost at the end of her life? Where did she find the strength for what the old jokes used to call "fancy fucking"? She had not only been the initiator of this sexual episode, she had also been the instigator of every heated escalation — from the first minute when she had steered him to this couch until the last moment when her own prolonged convulsion had triggered his. Even her voice had signaled his: a series of high-pitched cries from her, at the end, had brought forth his own wordless cry. She had been the first to rise too, lifting herself off him and untangling their bodies and clothes with a detachment that reminded him of something long, long ago. Nothing he could place, but something hurtful. Not a major trauma — just a small wound that had never fully healed. She had touched him deeply, in ways he didn't fully understand.

Aldrich had long known that he despised most of the people who sought him out. They were needing and suggestible and he loathed them for it. But these poor weaklings (or so he thought of them) were sustenance to him. Their need to follow suggestions pointed only to his own ability to give suggestions. Their despair pointed only to his own level-headedness. Their dependency pointed only to his own solid stature. An impartial observer might have said that Aldrich could well avoid the despair and dependency his patients were suffering: he had health, and he had life ahead of him; his patients had neither of these. But impartial observers did not have access to Keith's thanatology practice. His consultations were carried out in the privacy of his well-turned-out study. His patients didn't last long enough to complain, and he worked hard (played hard too: tennis and golf primarily) to maintain good connections with his referring physicians, who felt relieved to be able to provide *something* for these people of unfortunate prognosis. The referring doctors, moreover, didn't want difficult emotional scenes with such patients in *their* offices. Although no one knew precisely what went on in Aldrich's office, any referring physician picked at random would probably have said that Aldrich was an excellent practitioner of this very promising new specialty.

It all worked — for Miles K. Aldrich and for everyone else. If an impartial observer were to say that Aldrich might be taking unfair advantage of the situation, or might be manipulating his patients (dreaded accusation), the observer would surely be accused of lacking impartiality and would probably be called a foe of the entire mental health field.

It worked. Or did it? Keith was unsettled. Here was Marjorie Rupert leading him, running way ahead of him, finally handing him Ossy Blackwell — and who knows how many other people — on a platter. She was not at all like the others, Keith could see. He felt elated. And uneasy.

She wasn't the first client he'd had sex with, of course. That wasn't what was bothering him. He did whatever needed to be done, and sex was sometimes part of what needed to be done. People expected him to take charge, didn't they? That's why they came to him, and spilled their guts to him, and allowed themselves to be directed by him.

But, and he stared at an expensive piece of primitive sculpture without seeing it, Marjorie Rupert hadn't "allowed" this sexual encounter to happen, she had positively insisted upon the encounter. This was a new experience for Keith, and he found it perturbing. And appealing. . . .

Marjorie hadn't wanted to leave, but Keith said he needed to be in possession of his wits for Monday, when they could continue their work together. He gave the word "together" a meaningful emphasis. He said he would call her on Sunday, but couldn't see her; he would be in a meeting all day. She left, then, without a kiss or an embrace. Her emotions came not from affection but from far deeper currents.

And Keith, dreading Monday but looking forward to it, knew that this woman had stirred something in him that was profoundly disturbing. He remembered how Marjorie had settled her urgent body onto his, how she had forced his responding body into hers. It was she who had done all the thrusting. He hadn't resisted, or fought, or seemed unwilling, but he had the odd feeling now that somehow he had been violated. Used. Raped.

• • •

Ossy Blackwell, alone in his quiet office on this Saturday afternoon, was unsettled. Never before had he received a call like this. Should he cancel the lecture? Urge people not to come? Postpone it? Hold it somewhere else?

"Hell, no," he bellowed.

And then he called the police.

• • •

Hallie Cooper and Charlie Zinck were well out of the city on this beautiful Saturday before they fully relaxed. And then — something about talking in a car, not seeing the other person's face and not having your own reaction immediately visible — their conversation turned personal. Before they hit the Taconic Parkway, they discovered they'd had similar parents, principled and hard-working, and similar fourth-grade teachers, encouraging and exemplary.

Things moved on from there. His boyhood days camping on Lake George; her girlhood days earning merit badges. They liked the children they had been, and the children they saw in the other person. They'd been the same kind of children — earnest, sweet, hopeful.

They slipped easily into grown-up talk. When the conversation turned (inevitably) to the impending trial of the mayor of New York, they found themselves in complete agreement on the case. They laughed heartily over this. The chances of any two random New Yorkers agreeing completely on this perplexing case were almost non-existent. About one in twenty, she thought. He talked in terms of odds, which she didn't precisely understand. When he explained it as best he could, she listened carefully before deciding she still didn't like odds. He liked her femaleness, her amused self-awareness, stamping her foot about something utterly inconsequential. She liked his maleness, his pride at knowing how the world worked, or at least how odds worked.

She thought briefly about the nightgown she had brought. As did he. But neither made mention of it. The closest was her observation that the air was getting pretty crisp out here — it would be a chilly evening — and his reply that the nights get pretty cold in Vermont, this time of year.

As it turned out, Hallie never took the nightgown out of her overnight bag. The call to Zinck came almost as soon as they arrived at his cousin's place. They'd just been shown around — the seven guest bedrooms of this early Vermont house, the carriage house beyond, the cozy tavern area off the living room. They were in the living room, the four of them, looking out at the majestic but gentle Green Mountains — Marybelle bustling about with the sofa pillows — when the call came. Charlie took a deep breath, rolled his eyes extravagantly and excused himself to take the call out at the desk.

He returned to the living room with a scowl on his face. "I don't know how to tell you," he said, "but I've gotta get back right away. Christ, some day I'm gonna get a job as a toll-taker on a bridge somewhere." He turned to Hallie. "Whaddya think? You wanna stay? Or you wanna drive back with me?"

"I'll drive back with you. And I could do some of the driving, if you'd like. Leave you with a bit more energy to handle whatever's waiting for you." Zinck's cousin's wife later opined to her husband that Hallie and Charlie must be very involved with each other. What other woman would offer to help with the driving?

So the four of them had a quick snack together — Marybelle's pea soup, with thick slices of sourdough bread, followed by tart Vermont apples with chunks of good Vermont cheddar cheese. Then the two men had a quick consultation over the security problems that had ostensibly brought Charlie to Vermont. Their business was over in ten minutes. Expressing farewells that were too fond by half, but regrets that were altogether honest, Hallie and Charlie got back into Zinck's eight-year-old Plymouth Reliant and headed south.

They had a relaxed drive back to New York, talking now about their early adulthood and how each of them had fallen into a profession they hadn't fully understood at the time. From various things that each of them said, they understood that they were roughly the same age — beyond forty but short of fifty. Things didn't get more personal. They had each volunteered the information, some days ago, that they were each (more or less) unattached. But any history or details of those circumstances remained unspoken. And as they came down the East River Drive, into headlights coming strong at them, their seven hours in the car that day began to tell on them. They wanted to be done with this journey. There were long moments without talk.

Zinck hadn't mentioned what was calling him back to the city, and Hallie hadn't asked. Well, she *had* asked, in a way: "Anything to do with Bernie or Anna?" And he had given a one-word answer. "Nope." For her part, Hallie didn't know whether to believe him or not.

For his part, Zinck didn't know *what* to believe. A pair of ears had arrived at the precinct house in today's mail. Bloody, hairy ears. Personally addressed to Zinck. No hospital had yet produced anyone, dead or alive, with head to match. They were large ears, with wax in them and hairs coming out of them and dried blood all over. And hand-addressed to *him*. Christ. He was not relishing this case.

His mind was too full of those ears to let him make a proper goodbye to Hallie Cooper. He was sorry it hadn't worked out, he said. Yes, she answered. And then he was pulling away from the curb in front of her building, thinking about ears — his, hers, everyone's — and she was upstairs unpacking her nightgown and thinking about the work she'd be doing for the rest of the weekend.

• • •

Indeed, it was a quiet weekend for both of them. Zinck was up to his ears — so to speak — in this new case, hanging interminably on the phone and wading interminably through records. "This is about as exciting as taking the goddam *tolls* on a goddam *bridge*," he growled to the wall.

He called Hallie a couple of times, wanting to remind her to be careful out there, maybe not even *go* out there — how had he forgotten to say this, last night, when they parted? — but he got only her answering machine. Was she already out there, maybe already in trouble? He felt like a dope. Like the kind of dope who gets a prom date with the girl he has been afraid to ask out all year, then discovers he has forgotten to get her a corsage. . . . Well, back to the ears. He was so bored he'd almost be glad to hear from Jackie O., he thought. Or even from her accountant — they could swap accountant jokes. . . .

Hallie, too, was having a quiet Sunday. She was doing a long-postponed column on the continuing development of Lower Manhattan — her "beat" being Manhattan in all its facets — and she suddenly wanted to refresh her memory about the buildings surrounding the giant towers of the World Trade Center. But wouldn't it be almost deserted, today, in that part of town? Should she go, today? She was thinking of Charlie Zinck wanting her to stay off the quiet side-streets, as he put it, or even leave town altogether, as he ultimately arranged it yesterday. Well, she wasn't about to succumb to needless panic. She'd already been mugged. It couldn't get any worse, could it?

She tried calling him, to thank him for the scenic drive to Vermont, but she got only a busy signal. OK, she'd call him later.

It never crossed her mind that there might not be a "later."

chapter fourteen

Marjorie came again to Miles Aldrich — to her Keith — in the middle of Monday afternoon, and it was a new Marjorie Rupert who exited from the elevator. She had a more determined step, Keith noticed, and as she walked ahead of him to his door she seemed not to notice or care whether he was following.

He felt an immediate apprehensiveness. Which of them was coming for help, and which of them was dispensing it? He was annoyed with this woman for not staying "in her place," as he viewed it. But he was annoyed with himself, too, for wanting inexplicably to *be* in her place. He didn't usually meet this kind of person here. And he didn't usually have this kind of desire. It was beyond anything sexual. Or was it? He no longer knew.

"And did you have a good —?" he began.

"I think you are a brilliant man," Marjorie interrupted, "and I have been thinking of nothing but what you said to me on Saturday."

"And what have —?"

"I want to see Ossy Blackwell dead before I die," she said, looking hard at Aldrich. "And that isn't all. That is only the beginning," she said slowly, emphatically. He looked back at her, aware that he was blinking rapidly.

"I'm so *indebted* to you," Marjorie rushed on. "I see a *use* for my terrible rage. I see a *reason* for my life. . . . I wish I could thank Dr. Motzkin for bringing you to me. I wish I could thank him properly."

"No, you wouldn't want to tell Dr. Motzkin . . . all of this," said Aldrich.

"It'll be just between us," said Marjorie. "You can trust me, Keith."

"Yes, just between us," he echoed. He saw that Marjorie had closed her eyes and was rocking gently back and forth. "I am glad you have put your trust in me," he said in a soothing tone. He was trying to right the balance, get things back to where they should be. "I will help you," he said.

"You will tell me . . . how," she said, looking hard at him again. It wasn't even vaguely a question. It was a command, and again Keith felt the ground slip out from under him.

But didn't he want what she wanted? *Didn't* he? "I will tell you . . . how," he responded slowly. He closed his eyes and felt her reach out her hand to him.

"Now," she said.

• • •

In the back of his mind, Charlie Zinck had been brooding about Maurice Orlov. There has to be more to a man than a Chinese restaurant and a son who loathes him. Yeah, I know, not one of us will end up more than a handful of dust, in the end, but still . . .

He called Steve Marino into his office and nodded for Steve to close the door. "You been thinking at all about that Orlov guy since you made those calls?" he asked Steve.

"Not especially," said Steve. "Just that I can't get over how he had no women in his life. Jesus, the only woman I talked to, she couldn't remember how long it was since she saw him. I mean, it was *years*."

"There was one other woman, you said."

"Yeah. She wasn't there any more. Left town. . . . You figure he was some aging queer? Without any women, I mean." Women meant a lot to Steve Marino. Not individual women, but the *idea* of women.

"It wasn't just women," said Zinck impatiently. "Orlov didn't have any *anybody*." (Had he heard that from Hallie? No, she had said that about Minot.)

"He did have someone. Named Keith. But he wasn't there any more, either. Well, don't they say everyone ends up alone? We're born alone and we die alone," said Steve. Steve liked old Westerns.

"Yeah, but there's alone and there's *alone*. Hell, I don't even know why we're bothering with it. It's a closed case."

"Yeah," said Steve.

"Yeah," Charlie echoed. "OK, thanks. I just can't get over how alone the guy was. And I think about his apartment. You wouldn't know anyone *lived* there." He excused Marino, and leafed absent-mindedly again through Orlov's little book. If there *was* some connection between the Novinsky murder and the McElroy murder — some connection between Orlov who killed Novinsky and Minot who killed McElroy — did he expect to see Minot's name in this little book? Under M? Come on, he said to himself. If everything was gonna be that easy, what would they need detectives for?

Then, on a hunch he wouldn't have been able to verbalize, he dialed the number for Gloria R. No answer. He dialed the number for Keith and got a recording: Dr. Miles Aldrich would be happy to call the caller back, if the caller would give the necessary information at the sound of the beep. Zinck, on another hunch, gave his home number and said it was important. He said he would like Dr. Aldrich to call him back tonight any time after 8 p.m., and as late as necessary. On still another hunch, he left no name.

• • •

The call came in at 11:50 that night. Zinck had been out like a light for half an hour. It took him a few seconds to get his bearings — and a few more to climb over the body of Jackie O., who lay stretched out and snoring between him and the phone.

"Hello," he growled into the phone. Jackie O. mumbled a reply and he scrambled away from her, tangling his feet in the blanket as he moved down to the foot of the bed and onto the floor. The phone cord was looped around one of the not-so-comely arms of Jackie O. and he tugged at it.

The lady was now fully awake and up on one elbow, no blanket on her, and looking at him with what could only be — even allowing for the dim green glow from his digital clock — an expression of a distinctly unfriendly sort.

"Christ," he breathed, not precisely at Jackie O., but in her general direction.

"Hello," said the caller. "This is Dr. Miles Aldrich. You left a message on my machine."

"Yes, I did. I called you this afternoon." Fully awake now, he tugged the phone free of Jackie O.

"You said it was important," Aldrich was saying. Zinck sensed that the doctor was experienced in talking to people who didn't talk easily.

"Well, yes," said Zinck.

"You're calling about yourself?" Aldrich prodded.

"Mmmmm." This was a game the cops worked at, finding out as much as they could while giving out as little as they could. Zinck was damn good at it. Even on the telephone, even in the middle of the night, even simultaneously wrassling with someone over a tangled blanket. Jackie O. had tried to retrieve the blanket. Without thinking, Charlie Z. had tugged it back around him.

"Perhaps you could tell me what the situation is," said Aldrich.

"Well, it's a long story." There was a long pause, not filled by Aldrich, and Zinck went on. "I'm not sure if you're the right person." He noticed that Jackie O. was getting interested in the conversation.

"We could settle that fairly quickly if you'd tell me more about the situation," said Aldrich.

Why is this guy so cagey, thought Zinck. "I wanted to hear more from you, sorta know if you're the right person," he replied.

"Who has referred you to me?" asked Aldrich. No doubt about it, thought Zinck, this guy is uneasy: a coyote sensing a baited trap and sniffing around it.

"I got your name from a friend," said Zinck.

"And which friend would that be?" asked Aldrich. Zinck didn't answer. He winked at Jackie O., who was looking at him suspiciously in the green light.

"Look," continued Aldrich, "I don't mean to be difficult, but I don't know that I'm going to be able to help you. The fact is, I'm going away for a while. If your situation is — uh — urgent, you'd do better working with someone else."

"I could wait until you're back," said Zinck.

"I wouldn't think that a good idea."

"I got your name from a friend who died," Zinck said suddenly, giving a little and hoping to get more.

"That does not altogether surprise me," said Aldrich.

There was another long pause.

"I don't know if he'd want me to mention his name," said Zinck.

"That is your privilege, of course. If you don't mind, I don't think we can work together. That is *my* privilege, you understand."

There was still another long pause, and Zinck was puzzled. Why isn't the guy hanging up, he wondered. The words just spoken seemed final enough. This game was always easier in person, when you could see what the eyes were doing, see whether sweat was coming. But this, now, was like a sword-fight in a pitch black room. If the guy was still there, Zinck needed to make some contact.

"The friend," said Zinck in a rush, "told me that *Keith* was someone I should see." He emphasized the name Keith and again he waited. And now he could sense the sweat breaking out on the face of the man he could not see. He heard the man breathing and he heard the words, "I'm afraid I can't help you." And then Charlie Zinck was holding a dead telephone in his hand.

"Who in blazes was *that*?" said Jackie O., as Zinck hung up the phone.

"No one you know," said Charlie Zinck. "No one I know either," he laughed, "but he sure was scared I *might* know him."

"You're sure it was a *he*."

"I'm pretty good at telling the difference," he chuckled, reaching for her.

"No one calls an *accountant* in the middle of the night," she mumbled.

"And look at the fun they miss," Charlie said, putting his hands on the lady's breasts.

The call nagged briefly at him for another moment. Why had

the name Keith alarmed Dr. Miles Aldrich? And what would Orlov have been doing with this Dr. Aldrich? The cops had already queried the few specialists Orlov had been seeing, and to the best of Zinck's recollection there was no Dr. Aldrich.

But all of this nagged only briefly at Zinck's consciousness. He'd think about it tomorrow. Right now, Jackie O. was ready and willing, and he was able.

• • •

Seven blocks away, Miles Aldrich padded nervously through his apartment. He didn't like people asking for Keith. Didn't like it at all. What kind of joke were they playing? Was it *even* a joke? The only trouble with his line of work was the people he had to work with. (Now that *was* a joke.)

He wanted urgently to get away. Let Marjorie Rupert do her thing, if she was up to it. And if she wasn't, well, he didn't want to be around to hear from her. And he didn't want to hear from anyone else asking for Keith.

He wanted only the sun, the sand, the ocean. And perfect strangers. . . . If they were dying, let them have the decency to keep it to themselves.

chapter fifteen

The next day it was suddenly winter, crisp and clear and cold. Charlie Zinck hadn't left his office all morning. He was itching to get away from the place — get away anywhere, especially from these grotesque ears (which weren't any longer on the premises but were still very much with him).

He was especially eager to have another go at Dr. Miles Aldrich — find out what he was hiding. Of course he was hiding *something*. *Everyone* was. More so when they talked to cops. Could the good doctor have pegged Zinck for a cop? Zinck wouldn't have pegged Aldrich for a doctor. Well, he sighed, there was a lot he didn't understand. Like Jackie O. talking constantly about her accountant. Zinck was finally fed up. Let her go back to the guy — if he even existed. (That had come up in the wee hours of last night. It wasn't a happy discussion.) . . . Zinck needed to find his Gaviscon.

He also needed to have his head examined. Wasn't the Novinsky case all wrapped up? So *what*, if there was something about Orlov, or Dr. Aldrich, or Mrs. Novinsky (quite the lady about town) that didn't smell so hot. He was *crazy* to keep poking around. Even if it *was* what they paid him for.

And tonight he was going to a goddam lecture with Hallie Cooper. With maybe some trouble at the lecture. And maybe some trouble from her — she'd probably have some hot new theories about the Novinsky murder being tied to the Orlov murder being tied to the La-Z-Boy murder being tied to the raincoat murder being tied to these ears. Funny, he and she had a really good time on the trip up to Vermont and back. If only they could manage not to talk about murder all the time. Well, they could. He tried her phone again, to ask her where he'd be meeting her.

Was she *ever* going to pick up her phone? He resisted the thought that maybe she wasn't able to.

• • •

By the middle of the morning, a sleety snow was coming down, and Charlie Zinck was not too sorry to be still in his office.

One of the few people out when he didn't have to be was Chip McElroy, who was standing at the corner of Broadway and One-hundred-sixteenth Street, shifting his weight from one foot to the other and passing out flyers about the lecture tonight. The speaker would be some Vietnamese guy, a defector, a big shot in the National Liberation Front of years ago, now bad-mouthing the Hanoi government everywhere he went. Chip stamped his feet in the cold. In the old days, a guy like this wouldn't be able to *speak* on a campus like this; now he not only speaks, he's sponsored by a fucking professor in the fucking history department. Christ, it was cold.

"Boycott this lecture," he shouted into the sleet, thrusting a flyer into any hand that met his. "Hell no, we won't go," he said to a dark-haired woman who raised a fist (at him? with him?), as she laughed in the direction of the man striding along beside her. . . . Another young woman reminded Chip fleetingly of Anna, and he was sorry Anna couldn't see him now. She would admire him, he thought, bucking the tide of this complacent group. Or would she? Best not to think of Anna.

When the flyers were gone, he was chilled through and through. He ducked into the subway, vaulted the turnstile and walked up the platform to wait for the downtown express. For the next stretch of hours, he'd be scraping the leavings off the dishes in one of Midtown's better restaurants. The leavings infuriated him — as did the people he worked for (talk about complacent!) — and he didn't think he was long for this job. Today might be the time to leave for good.

Recently he had taken to imagining the final hour of his final day at the restaurant. He would scrape his last dish — no, he'd heave it against the cracked-tile wall — and he'd march from the steamy kitchen into the cool elegance of the dining area. He'd have a bunch of flyers with him (about *something*) and he'd stop at every table and forcibly press a flyer onto every elegant plate. He would manage to splatter food onto every elegant patron and they would react exactly the way his parents did whenever anything got dirty or broken or spilled. Everyone would soon be shouting at him. And he wouldn't give a shit.

• • •

But the day didn't go the way he wanted it to. Back in his furnished room now, Chip McElroy was agitated and angry. He'd been ready to launch into his final farewell at the restaurant when the sweaty black chef had said "Move over, boy," and the moment was gone. He'd been ready again when "Hot stuff behind you" had distracted him. Finally he just left, and not through the dining room after all but certainly for the last time, two hours before the end of his shift. Outside, he felt as though he'd forgotten something — of some importance, he thought — and he squinted hard into the middle distance on the trip uptown, trying to figure things out.

Now on the phone in the hallway outside his room, he was shouting, "You don't understand, this is gonna be a big event tonight." He punched abruptly at the air with his free fist. Then, just as abruptly, he leaned calmly against the wall. Keep cool, he chided himself. These media types don't like to think they're dealing with some kind of psycho. He took a deep breath and let it out slowly. "It's not really true, you know," he said evenly, "what people say, that nobody wants to read about Vietnam any more." He listened to the voice on the other end.

"OK," he interrupted, "but what you don't seem to understand is there's probably gonna be a whole lot of violence at this thing tonight. Real violence. Like we haven't seen since the Sixties or Seventies maybe. . . . OK, that's all I'm asking, just think about it."

He hung up with deliberateness, looked down the hallway with a half-closed eye, then spun around to kick the wall. These people had taken him seriously during the anti-war days. They would take him seriously again. They would write stories about him, do interviews with him, run photos of him. They had done it before. They would do it again.

He wanted suddenly to get out and get some air — hand out more flyers, drink a couple of beers, have a burger, get there early.

Inside his furnished room, he turned to the cardboard chest of drawers in the corner and moved it away from the bare brick wall. Just above the floor was a loosened brick, pried out by Chip himself soon after he rented the place. He pulled the brick out now and reached down into the wall until his hand met a plastic-wrapped Smith & Wesson .38 caliber Bodyguard. He withdrew the gun and placed it on the blanket of his unmade bed. His hand went back in and came up with a second plastic-wrapped package, this one of Super Vel ammunition. This too he placed on the bed. "OK," he said with emphasis and approval. He remembered buying the gun — from another guy who worked at the restaurant — and being told, "this piece has a history, you know what I'm saying?" Indeed, he knew. This gun had killed someone. And as Chip told himself now, it might again. It just might.

Very carefully, he unwrapped both packages and loaded a cartridge into each of the five chambers of the revolver. A handful of ammo went into his pocket and the remaining ammo went back inside the wall. He then placed the brick back in the wall, pushed the chest of drawers against it, and picked up the loaded revolver. As he grasped the weapon in a proper hold, he glanced into the mirror. But only his head and torso were visible in the dime-store mirror.

"OK," he said anyway, with emphasis.

On his way out, he looked back into the room, checked the brick wall and remembered at the last minute to take the stack of flyers. As he left, he gave the door jamb a good hard kick and slammed the door.

• • •

An hour later, he was on his third beer in a stale-smelling little place on Upper Broadway. He liked to think that beer calmed his nerves. Not that his nerves needed calming, of course.

"How're ya doin'?" the bartender asked him.

"Just fine," said Chip. "Just fine." Beer always helped, whatever his mood. Not that he spent much time checking out his mood, for Christ's sake.

"Just fine, just fine," echoed the man sitting on Chip's left at the bar. Quiet and self-contained until now, he suddenly turned toward Chip and exhaled a long puff of smoke.

"Whaddya think *you're* doin'?" said Chip.

"I'm having a drink here, having a smoke, having a fine time. Just fine." He took another puff and admired the smoke rings heading in Chip's direction.

"You've got a lotta nerve," said Chip, leaning quickly against the man and pushing him sideways.

"Who're you shoving? You don't like smoke, all you gotta do is say so." The man reached for his drink with the hand that was holding his cigarette. Smoke curled toward Chip.

As quick as a snake going after its prey, Chip grabbed the cigarette from the smoker's right hand and snuffed it out in the man's fancy drink. The butt sizzled briefly before it settled among the skewered fruits.

Phil the bartender had seen it all. "Sonny," he yelled to his nephew, "run and get Ruiz, will ya? He was just in here. Probably up to the taco place at the corner." Then, under his breath, he put his questions to no one: "Who needs *this* shit?" and "Why are the cops *never* here when you need 'em?" To the two drinkers he managed an authoritative order: "Break it up, you guys, break it up."

The smoker was not to be appeased. "You saw what he did. He took the cigarette right outa my hand, put it out right in my drink."

"You better believe it," said Chip.

"Guys, look, it's only a drink, it's only a cigarette, the night is young, let's wind it down."

"I suppose you're on *his* side," Chip challenged. "You don't think there's anything wrong with some prick breathing smoke at everyone."

The bartender sighed. "I try to stay out of these little disagreements," he said to Chip.

"How can you stay *out* of it? You saw what he did," said the smoker. "He's gotta get me a new drink."

"Look, *I'll* get you a new drink. It's on the house. Maybe you could move down one seat and not get any more smoke on our friend here?" He gave the smoker a phony smile.

"Why should *I* move? He doesn't like smoke, let *him* move."

"Go fuck yourself," Chip said pleasantly.

Sonny was suddenly back with Ruiz, both a little breathless.

"What'sa trouble here?" said Patrolman Ruiz, running his tongue around his teeth looking for bits of his supper.

"This prick was smoking at me," began Chip.

"You mean this gentleman here," said Ruiz.

"He's a prick," said Chip defiantly.

"And this fucker is a juvenile delinquent," said the smoker.

"OK, now we've all been introduced," said Ruiz, "let's try to find out what happened."

"I told you. He was smoking at me."

"Were you smoking at him?"

"Well, smoke may have been going in his direction . . ."

"Fuckin' liar."

"Fuckin' delinquent."

"Gentlemen, gentlemen."

"He shoved me," said the smoker. "He nearly shoved me offa the stool here."

"You shoved him?" Ruiz asked Chip.

"I had to get his smoke outa my face," said Chip. "I just nudged him over a little. Fuckin' prick."

"Fuckin' juvenile delinquent. Fuckin' asshole."

"Sir," Ruiz said to the smoker, "let's calm down here. It doesn't help to call anyone names."

"Whaddya think he's callin' *me*?" the smoker complained.

"I'm about to address the situation, sir. Just hang on there," said Ruiz. He turned back to Chip. "Sir," he said, using the word with some difficulty, "I'd like to suggest that in the event of future situations like this, you try to handle it at a lower level of response, you know what I mean? Like not shoving the guy, OK?" He looked steadily at Chip, and Chip (who suddenly remembered the Smith

& Wesson in his pocket) nodded.

"OK," said Ruiz. "And you," turning to the smoker, "you might just want to think about which end you're blowing your smoke out of, in the future, OK?"

"I want a new drink. He ruined this one."

Phil the bartender spoke up. "I *told* you, you'll *get* a new drink. But I want you guys separated. I don't want you two sitting near each other."

"You won't have me sitting here at all," said Chip. "Don't get yourself worked up. What do I owe you?"

"Three beers, $4.50."

Chip counted out his money, bypassing the bartender's outstretched hand to slam the money down on the bar — exactly $4.50, nothing more — and with a surly look at the smoker he walked out of the bar. He did, after all, have other things to do this evening.

Ruiz stayed a few minutes more, getting Phil's observations on the decline of civility since he had come to this bar fourteen years ago. "The only people acted that way, back then," said Phil, "were your real psychos. Now it's every third guy who's some kinda weirdo. I see you don't even take anybody's name any more, you've probably got filing cabinets full of 'em already."

"Yeah," said Ruiz, who was in elementary school fourteen years ago. "If we can settle outa court, so to speak, that's what we do. No need to read 'em their rights and all that. . . . This one was a weirdo, no doubt about it," motioning toward the stool recently occupied by Chip McElroy, "but not basically one of your dangerous types."

• • •

Charlie Zinck put through another call to Dr. Miles Aldrich — his fourth of the day. Like the other calls, it was not answered. Not even intercepted by machine. Why would the guy not want to know who was calling him? Could he be so rattled he forgot to turn the machine on? Or was he sitting there in the dark just listening to the phone ring?

Charlie had a few choice questions for Aldrich. But they could wait, he figured. In another few moments he'd be off to meet Hallie Cooper — he had finally reached her — and he was looking forward to an evening with a woman who wasn't constantly talking about her accountant. So what if there was trouble up there at the lecture. Trouble, he could handle. It was accountants he was sick of.

chapter sixteen

Miles K. Aldrich (who liked referring physicians to call him "Dr. Aldrich," and who allowed certain patients to call him "Keith"), was selecting a wardrobe and an image for his immediate departure for the Caribbean.

His destination was the island of Nevis — a tiny volcanic protuberance midway down the island chain — and he had a seat on tomorrow's early flight to San Juan, with a connection to Antigua and a final hop to Nevis. The return flight was open; his stay would depend on what he found there, and what he left here. He'd see the morning papers before he left. It might even hit page one of the *New York Times*, which didn't usually play up violent crime unless it was very gaudy or very big or very intriguing — and God knows, this thing tonight could be all three.

He didn't want to be any closer to it than tomorrow's newspapers, though. And if Marjorie came out of it, he didn't want to be around to hear about it from her. That reminded him to change the message on his answering machine. He'd be "called away" on an emergency, unable to specify his return. A complete fabrication, of course, but there was no reason to be unkind. Or truthful. For the truth wouldn't fit onto the tape of any answering machine. It went back to his earliest years, to a time when, if he didn't like what was happening around him, he just . . . left. No one, in those years, was ever successful in explaining to him that he couldn't leave *himself* behind.

And the truth went back twenty years and more, to a time when the young Miles was grieving for a father he had never known, a father who had never cared for him. Your Dad died in Vietnam very early in the war, his mother said to him, in a voice that might have been proud or angry or grief-stricken but was none of these. Miles's father, in fact, had not been anywhere near Vietnam at the time of his death, or at any other time. But Vietnam was in the air then, and it was as good a place as any for a fictional father to die a fictional death. The boy began to hang out with the older kids who went on the protest marches. They weren't old enough to go to war themselves, and weren't young enough to have fathers in the war, but they went on all the marches anyway, running, chanting, yelling, thumbing their noses at everyone — and then, afterward, comparing notes about the dumbest people they'd seen along the way. Maybe, Miles said once, if the soldiers don't go to Vietnam but go to Washington instead, we could be *done* with this stupid war. Whaddya mean? the other boys asked him. Well, he answered, if they murdered everyone in our government, the war would just be *over* — there wouldn't be anyone left to send the soldiers off to war. The other boys had a good laugh over this, although a couple of lads waxed precociously philosophical, wondering whether killing some people to keep them from killing others should even be called murder. Maybe, said Miles, the soldiers who should go to Washington and kill everyone (and probably get killed) should be the ones who were gonna die anyway in Vietnam. Everyone had a good laugh over that too, although Miles didn't see what precisely was so funny.

That was long ago, and he had other things to think about today. What should he *be*, for these weeks or months in the Caribbean. An archaeologist on sabbatical, perhaps, or a novelist plotting a new book, or a film producer reading up for his next project. He wouldn't be *doing* anything, of course, but he wanted to look as though he *had* done things, and would again. He would take with him a collection of notebooks, which he would fill with unreadable snippets and unintelligible outlines. He would take an armload of books, none of which anyone else would have heard of, some of which he might even read. And he would take an impeccable wardrobe. You never knew who you might meet: a wealthy young widow, a retired executive, all sorts of lonely people with heaps of money and lots of time.

His things were scattered throughout the apartment, grouped to fit his luggage, which was also scattered about. On the doors and doorknobs, hangers with jackets and slacks. In the hallway, near a small satchel, shoes already wrapped in their gray woolen socklets. On the bed, piles of sportswear and underwear. In the living room, on various chairs, assorted paraphernalia: books, notepads, stationery, pens, cameras (maybe he would be a world-traveling photo-journalist), a radio, his scuba gear, a sailing hat —

The doorbell rang. Jessie, his travel agent, no doubt. She had promised to deliver his ticket on her way home, since his flight was leaving early tomorrow morning. She'd be delivering the ticket herself. She didn't like to spend money on messenger service.

The bell rang again — with some urgency, Aldrich thought. Who *else* could it be at his hour? Almost six o'clock. Not a patient, certainly. It *had* to be Jessie: energetic and effusive, tickets in hand, hair flying.

Before he got to his buzzer, the bell rang a third time: an insistent ring.

"Jessie?" he called into the intercom.

"No! . . . Keith, it's *Marjorie!"* came the reply.

Jesus Christ! "Marjorie you shouldn't be here."

"I have to *see* you! I'm not at all sure . . . I don't know if I —"

"Marjorie, it's not wise to talk about this now. Not here."

"Please buzz me in. I'm so worried about how —"

"Marjorie! Please don't talk any more." Keith looked frantically around the apartment. Unmistakable signs of his departure were everywhere. He couldn't let her in. "Marjorie, I want you to stay right where you are. I'll be right down. Do you understand me?"

"Yes. Why can't I come up?"

"I'll be right down. You must wait for me right there."

"Keith, you have someone up there. You have some woman up there."

"Marjorie, don't get excited. I don't have anyone up here."

"Who is Jessie?"

"Jessie is the kid from the cleaner's. Marjorie, you wait right there for me. I'll be right down."

Jesus Christ!

• • •

She was waiting by the doorbells, leaning against the wall, when Keith rushed down to the lobby a minute later. Christ, she looked terrible.

"Oh, Keith, I've had such a —"

"Not here, Marjorie, We'll have some supper together. You'll like that, I know." He took her arm, fighting the revulsion that ran through him.

"I don't know if I can eat. I just want to talk with you. I want to be with you. I've been so —"

"We'll be together. We'll have a good talk. I know just the place." He opened the outer door for her and guided her through it. Her ailing body and disoriented mind were dead weights against him. But he was the strong one again and that was as it should be.

"Keith, you've no idea what I've —"

"Marjorie, I say this to you for the last time. You must not talk here. If you talk here I shall simply walk away from you. Is that quite clear?"

"Yes," she said, mouthing the word more than speaking it. She allowed him to guide her along — a block and a half to busy Broadway, then a block down Broadway to a small restaurant, one of the many Cuban-Chinese places that did a steady no-star business in Manhattan.

He steered her to a booth in the rear, and she sank onto the seat. She said again that she didn't want to eat, but he put his index finger to his lips to silence her protestations (and postpone her outpourings). "Two bowls of your soup," he said to the pouting waitress, pointing to the worn menu. "Every cuisine in the world has its chicken soup," he said to Marjorie, aware that he was stalling for time and had no interest whatsoever in talking with her about cuisines of the world.

"Yes," she said dully.

She sat silently, waiting for the chance to speak. They listened together to the people around them talking volubly in Latin tongues; Keith soon felt secure in their Anglo anonymity. "What seems to be the matter?" he asked. "But talk quietly now. We don't need to share this with everyone." He forced himself to smile.

"I couldn't remember what to do . . . what to do . . . *afterward,*" she stammered. "I mean, should I put the gun away? Or just drop it? Will it be smoking? It could burn a hole in my knitting bag, couldn't it? . . . Oh, Keith, why can't I remember what to do afterward? We had it so carefully planned."

Keith took a deep breath. She was finished, for the moment. Yes, it had been carefully planned, even how she should hold and aim the weapon. He just hadn't planned on her going to pieces, that's all.

"It doesn't really matter, Marjorie dear, whether you drop the gun afterward or take it with you. We went over that, you remember. It doesn't matter at all." He gave her a long look. She stared back at him.

"As to the rest," he began, and then stopped. Their soup was arriving. He was silent while the waitress set down the two heavy bowls and the two paper napkins (one, a little soup-sodden) and the two tarnished spoons and the two packets of cellophane-wrapped crackers. Keith's look menaced Marjorie into silence. "As to the rest," he said again after the waitress had gone, "I don't think it's necessary to worry. I showed you exactly what to do. Nothing could be simpler. You said so yourself. You will be sitting in the first row, you must be sure to do that, and then you simply have to concentrate, that's all there is to it."

"But what if —"

"Now Marjorie, the great figures of history didn't spend their time saying 'what if' — they simply did what they had to do. What destiny demanded of them. What destiny *offered* to them."

"Yes, but —"

"Marjorie dear, you're worrying needlessly. I wouldn't have let you even consider this if I hadn't thought you were up to it. And worthy of it. And fully able to carry it out. You are an important person. Your life will be important in a way that few lives are important."

She put her spoon down and looked at him. "I want you with me," she said.

Jesus Christ! This was not going well. "I can't, Marjorie, you know I can't."

"I promise I won't tell anyone that you gave me the gun. I won't even tell anyone that we talked about this together. You know you can count on me."

"I know I can." He knew it less and less with each moment. "I am absolutely counting on you about that, Marjorie. Absolutely. And Marjorie, I must repeat to you that I can only take care of you afterward" (and he gave the word a meaningful emphasis) "if I am strictly out of this whole thing. You must tell no one. *No one.*" If she brings me into this in any way, he thought, if she tells *anyone* that I aided and abetted or even knew about it, I'll tell them that in my professional judgment she was *crazy.* Stark, raving mad. Sure, she came to consult me, I'll say, but the rest was stark, raving *lunacy.* The lunacy of a woman who was out of her mind because she was dying and alone. He looked long and hard at her, and allowed his eyes to narrow. "You understand, don't you, Marjorie, that if you involve me *in any way* I will have to say that you are not in control of your mind. You do understand that?"

Marjorie's eyes opened wide and she spoke slowly and firmly. "You *must* come with me. The only way I can promise not to do anything foolish is if you come with me."

Jesus Christ! Dangerous business, blackmailing someone who was ready to blackmail you back.

"Finish your soup, Marjorie. We'll want to get there early. We'll want to be sure to be in the front row." He was thinking furiously as he spoke. He'd have to find a way to get himself out of this. Or to stop her. . . . He couldn't concentrate. Relax, he said to himself. It'll come. "Relax, now, Marjorie. Sit quietly. We'll go soon." And with luck we won't meet Jessie who is probably messengering a batch of tickets all through these streets.

• • •

Hallie Cooper asked for a sugar-cured ham on rye and Charlie Zinck did the same. He liked her choice of dessert too — one of the

European tartlets for which this off-campus deli was justly famous. He took the same.

"And coffee?" he asked.

"Yes, please," she said. He poured two cups from the machine further down the counter, near the cash register, and she moved on ahead of him to pay for her tray.

"I thought you two were together," the heavily made-up woman at the register said dully. She spoke without cordiality — almost without civility.

"Neither one of us is together," laughed Zinck as he paid for his own tray. Hallie turned to laugh quickly with him. The woman at the register frowned at a broken fingernail and made no response.

"You know what scares me a little," said Hallie, when they were settled at a table. "Chip McElroy called me this afternoon — at my office. He seemed to want *me*, in *particular*, to come to this lecture. He'd seen my piece in the paper the other day. Didn't say anything about it. Just that he'd seen it. And of course, a week ago, right after his wife was killed, he and I talked for an hour or so. He may feel there's something unfinished between us. I'm uneasy about him."

Zinck was thoughtful. "He's pretty near the edge with all of this, I'd say. He was never too stable, from what I gather. But I wouldn't worry about it." (Zinck worried about it, quietly, for a moment.)

"Do you know him?" Hallie asked.

"Let's put it this way — I have access to people who know him."

"Can you tell me about him? I'd be interested."

"Sorry."

"OK," Hallie said, with a shrug and a smile.

"Good."

"What do you mean, good?" Hallie asked.

"I mean, don't go 'way mad."

"I'm not planning to go 'way at all." Hallie laughed. "I'm planning to go to a possibly dangerous lecture with you." There was just a hint of coquettishness in her voice.

"Other people from the paper gonna be there?" he asked.

"Mmmmm, I think so," she answered noncommittally. "Other people from your outfit?"

"Mmmmm," he answered. "In fact, with your people and my

people all over the place, there may not be much room left for civilians. Let's get there before all the good seats are gone."

They ate silently for a minute or two. "I had a thought," said Hallie. "On how the two murders might be connected. Maybe Orlov was doing Minot's murder, and Minot was doing Orlov's. Or maybe the circle is larger. Six people. Ten. Twenty."

"Large enough and they could support an 800 number."

"I'm serious."

"I know."

"Did you ever come across anything like that?"

"Sounds more like TV," said Zinck, finishing his coffee. "No suspicion of any conspiracy until exactly seven minutes before the end of the show, at which time the detective uncovers the mastermind behind it all."

"Why *seven* minutes?" asked Hallie, amused.

"Because he has to explain it to his girlfriend for five minutes and then they tumble around together for the last two minutes. Heavy breathing. Raunchy jokes."

She laughed with him. "Why does he need so long to explain it to her? Maybe she's very smart."

"I'm sure she is. My error. Ok, he explains it in *two* minutes and they have *five* minutes for the sexy stuff. Much better."

"You don't think much of my idea," said Hallie.

"For TV, I like it fine," he said. He wondered how long she'd be pushing ideas at him. Would they still be having supper together in a couple of months? His place or hers? He smiled at her, and she smiled back: a dazzling, open, surprised sort of smile. That's when Charlie Zinck remembered he was here to protect her.

• • •

Maureen always knew when he was worried, thought Ossy Blackwell. Uncanny woman. Sometimes she knew it before he knew it himself. Like tonight, when he arrived home for dinner, and she picked up on it as soon as she put her hands on his cheeks and stretched herself up to kiss him.

"Nguyen Nhu Thanh is going to be just fine," she said. "I spoke to him half an hour ago. He refuses to let you worry."

"I know, honey. I just called him too."

She stirred something in a pot on the stove and said, "Then why are you worried?"

"My dark brooding nature," he said, forcing a laugh and knowing he wasn't fooling her.

Nguyen Nhu Thanh hadn't wanted to eat with them. He was suffering from a recurring intestinal difficulty, the result of his years in the jungle with the Viet Cong. Early today he canceled an invitation to have dinner before the lecture with a small group at the Faculty Club. By midday he canceled a later invitation to have a quiet dinner with Ossy and his family at home. A few minutes ago, when Maureen called him at the Faculty Club to ask whether she could do anything for him, he said gently but firmly that she could not. He would be at the lecture hall at eight o'clock; she and her husband and her husband's university had no need to worry about his being on time. . . . But her husband wasn't worried about that, and Maureen knew it.

"Something's happened." She studied his face with concern.

Ossy didn't reply directly. "I think I'll swing by the Faculty Club and pick him up. He says he knows the way but I'd like to pick him up anyway."

"Of course. Should Robbie and I go with you? Or should we meet you there?"

"I was thinking you don't have to come at all." Ossy busied himself pouring a cup of coffee. Maureen frowned slightly.

"I *always* come to your open lectures. And Robbie's very much interested in all of this."

"And you're not even apple-polishing the teacher," he laughed.

"You think not?" she said, chuckling with self-confidence. Then, because he hadn't really answered her, she asked again, in the soft but serious voice he loved, "What *has* happened?"

"You are some persistent woman."

"You tell me when you're tired of that," she said, still smiling, still waiting for an answer.

"OK, OK," he said in mock surrender. And, then, looking at her with full seriousness, "It might get a little ugly tonight. A protest of some kind. Before, during, or after — it's hard to know when. Or what. Or even who. A bunch of students, probably, and some others who wish they were students. They either want people to boycott this lecture entirely — there's some indication of that — or they want people to show up and harass the guy. They don't think we've 'learned the lessons of Vietnam' yet. Or they don't want people to hear what *this* guy thinks are the lessons of Vietnam."

"The campus police will be there, won't they?" asked Maureen.

"God help us, yes. They think they're doing a good job when they remember to take their walkie-talkies. And when they get to the place while the demonstration is still going on."

"That bad?"

"They call it a low profile. I'd call it a few other things."

She laughed. "You always did have a way with words. . . . Should there be *other* police there? I mean *real* police?"

"The place'll be crawling with 'em. All trying to look like students. So anyone who looks *too* much like a student probably isn't."

Maureen smiled. "You don't think the lecture should be canceled, I suppose."

"I do not. Do *you* think it should be canceled?"

"I do not." She tossed her blond curls for emphasis, and he hugged her fiercely.

"How'd my Momma's flat-footed child get such a beautiful female?" he whispered. He hadn't told her of the call that came in to him on Saturday afternoon. Didn't want her to worry. Didn't want her to talk him into canceling the lecture. Ha! *He* would have backed down long before *she* would have. This Maureen was a sweetheart, all right, but she was plenty tough. I'm glad you're on *my* side, he was always telling her. And she always was.

The caller on Saturday was almost certainly Vietnamese. Something about the intonation. And the imperfect English — imperfect in the manner of the Vietnamese. If this lecture isn't canceled, the caller said, you must bear responsibility for the fate of the traitor Nguyen Nhu Thanh. . . . The opportunist Nguyen Nhu Thanh. . . . The liar Nguyen Nhu Thanh. Ossy listened to the whole stream of it, and when the voice wound down and the two of them were listening to the other one's silence, he just hung up. Maybe it wasn't the smartest thing to do. But the police (whom he called as soon as he got a dial tone) thought he'd done exactly the right thing. "Don't worry," they said to him.

"Don't worry," he said now to Maureen. Don't worry, he said to himself. He left the kitchen abruptly, to talk to his son before dinner.

• • •

Nguyen Nhu Thanh knew he ought to eat. But he hadn't enjoyed food for years now. He ate to stay alive, much as he did any other necessary thing for his body, like keeping warm, or staying dry. Perhaps because his body had been so badly abused — first in Diem's jails, then in the malarial jungle with his comrades, then for years in the Communists' jails, finally for seventeen days on the open seas in the tiny hold of a fishing boat — he preferred not to care what happened to it, preferred not to think about it. Only when his body was achingly wet or cold or unfed did he pay attention to it, and then only grudgingly.

Tonight would be difficult; he should eat if he wanted to keep his strength up. After a long telephone discussion with the head of dining services at the Faculty Club he decided upon a bowl of soup (chicken and rice) with some extra rice on the side and a banana and a pot of tea.

"Is that all, sir?" We have some very nice veal tonight — a light veal stew in a delicate white wine sauce."

Nguyen Nhu Thanh mumbled his thanks. "I am not well. I do not want to eat heavily."

"Do you need a doctor?"

"No. I have been ill a long time. We are well acquainted, my illnesses and I."

"I'm sorry to hear that. I'll have this sent right up, sir. Have a pleasant evening."

"Thank you, thank you." So kind, the Americans. So well-meaning. So naïve.

He wondered why he kept speaking, kept standing politely before one audience after the next to recite facts that seemed sometimes to wrench his very heart from his body. But who *would*, if he didn't? Few people in this part of the world knew what he knew, and fewer still wanted to talk about it. Sometimes, when he found his spirits flagging, he was glad to take himself home — to the place in Texas he called home — and rest until his next speaking engagement. He could never really go home, of course, back to Vietnam. He could only go on, explaining what had happened there and confessing his own part in the tragedy. The "tragedy of Vietnam" and the "agony of Vietnam." How often he had heard those expressions from Americans. But how little they knew, the Americans. How naïve they were, in spite of their elaborate news media.

He mopped his brow. A heavy sweat was oozing from him in this heated hotel room. He was not a well man. But he was a patient man. He would keep on speaking. It was necessary. For himself, as much as for those who came to hear him.

Surely, though, it was for them. In every audience there must be *some* who could understand the truth. That the Cold War, in the Far East, was far from over. That Vietnam wasn't on the path to real reform. That Vietnam could only look good because Pol Pot's Cambodia had been getting all the bad press. There must be *some* in every audience who could see that memory and truth must survive. And that proper payment must be exacted.

He felt secure here. Only a rudimentary lock on the door, but he felt protected. He lay down on the single bed and thought of nothing until he heard the knock on the door.

part four

chapter seventeen

Charlie Zinck took Hallie Cooper's arm as they walked into Columbia's Miller Theatre, formerly the MacMillan Theatre and still the site of major events at the university. She leaned into him a little, and he liked it a lot. He knew women who got annoyed at this traditional gesture, moving away as though you had just proposed some unspeakable act. He was sick and tired of women who worried about unspeakable acts.

For no special reason, he smiled at Hallie, and she beamed him back one of those fabulous open smiles of hers. The two of them could be on the verge of something, those smiles said to Charlie Zinck. And he didn't mean going to lectures.

"Hall is really filling up," he said to Hallie. "Not very comforting to the folks who told everyone to stay away."

"That's *if* they wanted everyone to stay away," said Hallie.

Charlie nodded his quick approval. "And you've never been a detective?"

"Only in my fantasies," she laughed. "I've been everything, in my fantasies."

"That's probably more fun. In my job, I *see* everything," Charlie said. They chuckled together briefly, comfortably.

Charlie spotted someone he knew. "I'll just be a sec. Gotta say hello to someone." He moved off in the direction of a lean young man wearing faded jeans and a worn woolen shirt. "You working?" Charlie asked him.

"Yeah," said Henry Barrkman. "You too?"

"Nah, date. Culture." He nodded toward Hallie, who was studying the crowd. "You got a lotta friends here?" Charlie asked.

"Enough."

"I like your get-up."

"Whatever works," said Barrkman with a touch of a smile, his eyes already moving past Charlie.

"Yeah. Well, I better get us some seats, while we can. Down front. See ya around."

"See ya," said Barrkman.

• • •

Upstairs, at the front of the balcony, Chip McElroy was also looking over the crowd. Where were the city patrolmen? Where were the guys from the Tactical Patrol force? Why weren't they taking this thing seriously? . . . On the other hand, the crowd was great. Ha! Tell people to stay away and they came in droves. . . . But he wanted more cops. Why weren't there more cops?

He made the sign of a fist at someone he thought he knew downstairs. Actually, he should be down there himself, be seen and heard better. He felt a rush of exhilaration. Before the evening was over, they'd know who they were dealing with. He checked for the gun in his pocket. Then, keeping his right arm tight against the pocket with the gun in it, he shoved his way downstairs against the incoming crowd. This was gonna be some evening!

• • •

Marjorie Rupert's knitting bag lay in her lap. She clutched it to her in an uneasy grasp. She looked up at the two empty chairs on the dais, not eight feet from her. Despite her coat and two sweaters, she shivered in the overheated hall.

Keith, next to her, looked straight ahead. At his insistence, they would not be talking to each other. Indeed, they walked in as though they had never met, as though the force of the crowd had funneled them into these front row seats together. She glanced at him now. He was still looking straight ahead. He blinked rapidly but did not shift his gaze.

She searched carefully in her knitting bag, slowly bringing forth a long piece of knitting. She smoothed out the work and stabbed into a stitch. Keith sighed deeply. His face was a mask, as was Marjorie's.

An observer might well take them for strangers — for two of those odd birds who come to public events and speak not a word to anyone.

• • •

Maureen smiled expectantly as Ossy Blackwell strode onto the stage, but her smile faded when she saw the frail man with him. Nguyen Nhu Thanh was pitifully slight, even by Vietnamese standards. The sweat of illness stood out on his skin. Maureen made an effort to smile again at her husband, and Ossy returned her greeting with the merest wave of his index finger — one of their public signals with each other.

Ossy advanced confidently to the microphone. Nguyen Nhu Thanh waited attentively in one of the over-sized chairs flanking the lectern. With his feet barely reaching the floor, he looked like a child playing at being grown up.

When the audience settled down, Ossy began to speak.

"Welcome to you all. I am Professor Blackwell of the history department. . . . Perhaps you saw the news item, some months ago, that 30 per cent of American schoolchildren don't know which side we were on in the Vietnam War. Well, some of us who followed that war fairly closely might also wonder which side we were on." He paused to sense the reception of that remark. Some liked it and some didn't. He went on.

"There was a significant war on our home-front, as you know, with one side saying we were against the march of history because we were opposing a revolution of purely nationalist dimensions. You don't hear much of this argument today because the very march of history has discredited it. We know now, and we know it unequivocally — from the horse's mouth, as they say — that the true backers of that revolution were the Communists of North Vietnam. What was behind that so-called revolution was *not* nationalism and a love for the Vietnamese people; it was Communism and a hunger for power. This was *not* an indigenous revolution; it was a continual aggression from outside. And barely two years after America pulled out of South Vietnam, the North Vietnamese moved in openly to crush the South Vietnamese — crush both the Government forces and the National Liberation Front, and all other citizens, high and low, who now live under one of the world's most oppressive regimes. . . . We will hear tonight from a man who was a key member of the National Liberation Front of South Vietnam from its start. The NLF, as you know, was the political arm of the Viet Cong. Whatever we may have thought about the NLF during the Vietnam War, I am sure we're in for some surprises tonight."

Ossy Blackwell looked down at a small notecard in his hand. "Nguyen Nhu Thanh, who is with us tonight, is a product of traditional Vietnamese society. He was born sixty-eight years ago into a well-to-do family in Saigon. He was sent to France by his family for professional studies, as were many of his peers, and when he returned to Saigon in his late twenties, he was both a physician and an ardent nationalist. In France, he had met people who had met the fabled Ho Chi Minh, and it was a fateful time for this young idealist, changing the course of his life and in due time urging him and others to change the course of their country's history. Nguyen Nhu Thanh will tell us tonight how Ho Chi Minh and his comrades and successors betrayed the NLF. Yes, betrayed. There is no other word for it. And our speaker will tell us tonight why he decided that he must escape — must leave the beloved homeland he had helped to betray and leave the treacherous government he had tried to serve. Our guest tonight became one of his country's thousands of 'boat people' — one million people, it has been estimated — whole families who left in whatever boats they could get, who left even when they couldn't be sure they would ever arrive at a refugee camp or would ever be allowed to leave the camp for a permanent home somewhere on this earth, indeed who can't be sure today they won't be returned to the Vietnam they have fled."

Ossy took a deep breath and looked out into the filled hall. "The physical and intellectual courage of Nguyen Nhu Thanh is beyond my powers to describe. Let me say only this, to you and to him. We honor his bravery. We weep for his country. We welcome him to *our* country, where he now lives. We were not on his side during the war, but he is now on *our* side. We welcome him here tonight. Nguyen Nhu Thanh."

Ossy Blackwell, smiling, extended his arm, and under the pretext of shaking hands with his guest helped him from his chair and escorted him to the lectern.

There was a commotion along the side wall of the auditorium as two students unrolled a cloth scroll. "NGUYEN NHU THANH. TRAITOR TO HIS PEOPLE." Ossy Blackwell covered the microphone with his hand and spoke a few words to the frail Vietnamese, smiling to him as he left him alone in front of the audience.

"Thank you for coming. I am no longer your enemy. You are no longer my enemy. We have a common enemy." Nguyen Nhu Thanh gripped the side of the lectern for a moment until the pain in his gut subsided.

• • •

His voice was higher than Marjorie Rupert had expected. She was disappointed in him altogether. Where was the jungle guerrilla with his fervent rhetoric about struggle, his virile stance against oppression? Had this delicate and aging man ever been such a figure? She found it difficult to concentrate and caught only a few words from the earnest presentation that followed.

"Our goals were glorious in the National Liberation Front. They shine still, in my heart. We desired the most broadly democratic coalition . . . a foreign policy of peace and neutrality . . . the North and South to be unified by peaceful means. Our manifesto and program of action pronounced all this. But our allies in the North had other plans, even though they helped us to write these very documents. . . .

"I did not know that our early leadership was filled with secret members of the Lao Dong, the Workers' Party — now the Communist Party. Much later I comprehended how we had been used.

But in 1960 we were so hopeful. I remember well the organizing Congress of the Front. . . ."

Marjorie Rupert noticed the young boy next to her busily writing in his notebook. He was perhaps eleven or twelve, the child of an interracial coupling. Why did he seem familiar? He looked like nobody she knew, yet he reminded her of someone.

The lecturer was leaning forward against the lectern. "We in the Front soon established many other groups, all of them careful never to have visible ties to the Front, never to express sympathy with the Front. The Movement for Self-Determination, for instance, with the slogan 'South Vietnam for the South Vietnamese.' Your media liked this. And the Committee to Defend the Peace, which brought some of the best families of Saigon to our struggle. And the Young People's Association of South Vietnam, which organized the energies of our nonaligned youth. And the Alliance of National, Democratic, and Peace Forces, which permitted the Front to use the reputations of people who would never have joined the Front itself. . . .

"Always, we were conscious of your media and your anti-war movement. Deliberately, we sought a moderate political image when we formed our Provisional Revolutionary Government. I was thought to be merely a doctor — all my activities with the Front had been secret — and so I was chosen Vice Minister of Health, Social Action and Disabled Soldiers."

The boy next to Marjorie Rupert was no longer writing. Marjorie remembered, long ago, keeping a little notebook of questions to ask her father, before she understood he would have no answers for her.

• • •

Next to Marjorie on the other side, Keith Aldrich shifted uneasily and looked at the speaker through narrowed eyes. Why was this wasted old man telling them all his secrets? Ossy Blackwell, self-righteous bastard, was behind all this. Why couldn't the bastard leave well enough alone? Was it wrong for Keith to have wanted to end the war — a war that had taken his own father from him, made an orphan of him and many like him? That wasn't a wholly accurate account of his history, Keith knew, but he usually forgave himself this little embroidery on the truth (even though he knew that the truth was long gone and the embroidery was all).

"You may say, perhaps," the frail Vietnamese was saying, "that we were dishonest toward our brothers in South Vietnam. But we thought our goals were worth it. We were honorable in our way. The Communist North was not. They proclaimed to the world their commitment to our goals. How often did their Pham Van Dong say to his Western visitors, 'No one has this stupid and criminal idea of annexing the South.' Always, your media believed him. . . . The North *used* us."

He stood there a moment, a pathetic little figure, confessing his treachery and his gullibility, asking for — what? Keith saw Ossy Blackwell take a pen from his pocket, write something on a notecard, and look in Keith's direction with a slow smile. Keith looked back; and behind a mask that gave away nothing, Keith alone knew the extent of the turmoil inside himself.

• • •

He's smiling at me, thought Marjorie, looking at Ossy Blackwell. No, he's smiling at the boy. It must be *his* boy. She felt queasy. "I have to go to the bathroom," she said to Keith. "Shall I take this? Or leave it?"

"Leave it," growled Keith under his breath, glowering at her for speaking to him. He snatched the knitting bag from her as she got up. For an instant her hand maintained contact with the knitting bag as she wished that Keith could be — well, *nicer* to her. She felt a slight dizziness and sat down again. Keith didn't look at her. A moment later, she got up slowly and walked to the rear of the hall to find the ladies' room. She turned once to look back to Keith. He was still looking straight ahead.

• • •

The chance to leave, Keith thought. The chance to be rid of this irksome woman. He could walk out now, he realized, go home and pack, spend the night in a hotel, and fly off tomorrow to the Caribbean. She'd never find him. He glanced toward the back of the auditorium. Marjorie was nowhere in sight. Now, he thought. Go now.

But he couldn't go out carrying a *knitting bag*, for Christ's sake. He'd have to leave it. Which meant she'd probably go through with the whole plan. And fall apart afterward. And spill his name to anyone who was kind to her. . . . OK, he could handle it. He'd wait a while and then contact the N.Y.P.D. himself, from the island of Nevis, offering his help in connection with the dreadful deed done by his recent client — perhaps by then his *late* client. He'd tell them he had just learned of the event from an old newspaper.

Now, he decided. Go *now*!

He walked quickly to the back of the hall. He didn't see the plainclothesman approach their two empty seats, ask their nearest neighbors whether they were the owners of the knitting bag, and then walk rapidly (knitting bag in hand) to catch up with Keith.

"Did you forget this, sir?"

"No, I . . . oh, yes. Thank you. You're certainly on your toes. I appreciate your coming after me." He had his hands on the knitting bag now. "We wouldn't want to lose this. My, uh, wife, is, uh, making a . . ." He stopped, understanding suddenly that no such explanation was needed."Thank you."

"Quite all right, sir. Didn't want you to leave anything behind. In case it was on purpose, you know." He forced a laugh. "We worry about things like that."

"Uh, yes, of course."

God, here was Marjorie again! "Keith," she said in surprise.

"Had to stretch my legs," he said. "Getting a little cramped in there." He smiled idiotically at the policeman.

"You have my . . . knitting," she said.

"Of course, Marjorie dear. I wouldn't leave it."

The policeman stood there awkwardly, seeming not to know how to extricate himself. "You two going back in again?" he asked.

"Yes," said Marjorie. The policeman opened the door to the auditorium.

Keith took Marjorie's arm and whispered to her savagely as he escorted her back down the aisle. "We have to change our plans, Marjorie. You will not be doing anything we talked about. Do you hear me? You will do *nothing*. Do you understand?"

She looked at him dully.

Whether she understands or not, Keith thought, I have the knitting bag. And tomorrow I will be gone. They sat down again in the front row, each of them staring straight ahead..

• • •

Four rows back, Hallie Cooper nudged Charlie Zinck. "That's the social worker who was counseling Francis Minot," she said. There was surprise in her whispered voice. "The *thanatologist!*"

"Hmmmm," said Zinck. It's a small world, he thought. He said nothing more. He was thinking about how observant she was.

Hallie, too, said nothing more. She was interested in what Nguyen Nhu Thanh was saying.

• • •

At the front of the auditorium, the plainclothesman took up his former position along the side wall (with others in the overflow crowd) and looked out across the crowd. Christ, was he glad he wasn't married! Carrying someone's *knitting* around with you all the time.

He noted that the couple had sat down again. And the guy was still clutching that knitting. . . .

• • •

Zinck's mind was wandering. He was studying the back of the head of the thanatologist. Gotta be an Emotionally Disturbed Person, thought Zinck. The guy never moves his head.

Zinck was suddenly distracted from his distraction by a growing restlessness in the hall. A gray-haired woman in the middle of the auditorium had just cried out angrily, "Why tell us now? Why didn't you tell us then?" A buzz spread through the hall. And still the social worker didn't turn his head. Save us from social workers, thought Zinck.

Nguyen Nhu Thanh kept on. "You must understand," he said, his thin voice barely heard above the background noise, "that we nationalists in the National Liberation Front were hoping merely for assistance in our liberation effort. We didn't know that the North had created the Front and had always controlled it. And that as soon as military victory was in sight the North would treat the Front like . . ." — he was searching for the proper word — "like poor relatives, as you Americans say. We people from the South were accused of not having the proper politics. We were bypassed for all important positions in favor of cadres from the North. We saw our Provisional Revolutionary Government dissolved by the North as soon as they accomplished their military victory. We became prisoners in our own country. We became mourners at our own funeral."

He had taken a deep breath, ready to proceed, when a middle-aged man near the back of the hall shouted, "Why tell us *any* of this? We're sick and tired of being the world's referee." A rumble spread through the hall.

"This could get ugly," Hallie said.

"Yes," Zinck answered, thinking she was reading his mind. Not that he had any real objections. . . .

The two students with the "TRAITOR TO HIS PEOPLE" scroll thumped their wooden poles on the floor. The scroll bobbed up and down. Ossy Blackwell moved to the lectern. "Nguyen Nhu Thanh has agreed very generously to answer all questions after his lecture. Please hold all questions until then." He smiled in the direction of the students with the scroll. "And you two, you can stay if you can manage to keep that thing quiet. Get it calmed down, OK?" He patted Nguyen Nhu Thanh's arm as he stood beside him. Then, smiling as if to say "Carry on," Ossy took his seat again.

Charlie Zinck, in the fourth row, was doing some mind-reading of his own. This Blackwell guy, seemingly all easy and good-humored, was counting the minutes until he could declare the evening over. You could see it in his eyes. Worried. Definitely worried. You noticed such things in Zinck's line of work. He wondered whether Blackwell had told the cops everything he knew. This mind-reading stuff went only so far.

chapter eighteen

The mood in the audience had changed. People were growing more restless, more expectant. Nguyen Nhu Thanh was talking now about the re-education camps, his voice awed and hushed as he recalled incomprehensible horrors. "Eighty prisoners in a cell measuring twenty-two feet by eleven feet . . . no room even to lie down . . . fly larvae from the toilet hole getting into our ears and mouth . . . and constant deaths from dysentery, tuberculosis, malaria, malnutrition."

Chip McElroy was too excited to listen carefully, and the lecturer's dismal recitation was barely getting through to him (". . . and so desperate for food, all we can think about is our next miserable meal . . . forced and dangerous labor . . . felling trees, chained by ankle to the tree trunk . . . and our starvation rations cut if we failed to meet the norms . . .").

This was some crowd, Chip thought. It didn't matter what the little guy was saying (". . . and excruciating punishment for any infraction of the rules . . . solitary confinement in a stone 'coffin' for a week . . . chained in a completely dark cell for months . . . and hands and feet shackled so tightly as to cause gangrene . . ."). The only thing that mattered, Chip said to himself, was what was happening in this crowd. And something memorable was surely about to happen. Maybe they'd all be arrested (". . . and hands cut off, tendons of heels cut, for trying to escape"). He'd like to be arrested again.

Don't rush it, Chip cautioned himself (". . . and sentences added to sentences . . . five years, ten years, and more . . . and only very few people surviving these sentences, which are truly death sentences"). Let it play itself out, thought Chip, in its own time, in its own way. There'd be plenty of time to push things along. If things needed pushing.

The lecturer's recital was suddenly interrupted by a student from the center of the hall. "We've seen it all on TV, and one of our church groups gave testimony before Congress. It isn't that way at all. The camps are for rehabilitation, nothing else." Chip nodded vehemently in agreement.

Nguyen Nhu Thanh looked impassively in the direction of the student's voice. "You have been misinformed by your television reporters and your church groups. Perhaps they have been misinformed themselves. Or they wish to misinform you. I know the truth. I have lived it. In one case, a model prison was prepared especially for television. In another case, all but the healthiest prisoners were hidden from the cameras. False menus were posted. Evidence of overcrowding was eliminated. Pictures can be made to lie, even as words can."

The student persisted. "*You* are the one who is lying. The camps are *humanitarian*. They rehabilitate without trial. They heal without judicial condemnation." Again Chip nodded.

"Yes, that is the claim, and I can hardly accuse anyone of being more gullible than I. But if the camps are humanitarian, young man, I sincerely hope you will never receive such humanitarian treatment in your life. If you survived it, and were released — perhaps because your family bribed an official with everything in its possession, as mine did — you would never be treated as a full citizen. You could be re-arrested. Fear would sit at your table, false shame would walk with you in the street. Do you call this humanitarian?"

Chip was temporarily unsettled by the mention of family, and he was startled when a man immediately behind him began to shout at the lecturer.

"What does it matter? The camps are a thing of the past. Thousands of prisoners were amnestied in 1987 and 1988. You are living in the past, old man. This is 1990."

Nguyen Nhu Thanh chose his words with care. "It would be an error to conclude that re-education is over. The government has merely instituted a policy of 'consolidation' to disguise the reason for the detention of any prisoner. Why is it that the Hanoi government refuses to give information on the people who are still detained in re-eduation, or give the reasons for their detention? Why do they not tell how many camps are still in operation? Why do they not allow foreigners freely to visit the camps? Why was Amnesty International, as late as 1989, allowed to visit only one camp and meet only one prisoner? 'Re-education,' you must remember, was instituted immediately upon the North's military victory — even as Hanoi was speaking of 'reconciliation and concord.'"

He went on, seeming to gather strength. "And in the time between 1975 and now, tens of thousands of Vietnamese have gone into re-education. Many of them have died there. We are speaking not only of government officials and military persons from the South and deserters from the Viet Cong. But religious leaders, and journalists, and poets, and doctors. Even people who were guilty only of being college graduates or going abroad to study. Even people who were opposed, as I was, to the regimes allied with the Americans."

Chip was growing impatient. What was this old guy trying to prove, with his tiresome recital? "We are speaking of military officers who were against the invasion of Cambodia in 1978. And young people who were in the resistance struggles of 1978 and 1979. And disaffected people who were arrested in 1980, after refugees in the United States began to speak openly of the resistance."

Chip had his hand inside the pocket with the gun in it. He was more than impatient. He was ready to move.

• • •

Ossy Blackwell was ready for anything.

The lecturer was winding up his list. "And 10,000 people arrested in 1990 alone — in an 'anti-crime campaign,' it was said, but in truth in a political crackdown against the winds of revolution from Eastern Europe. And all of these people are in addition to the thousands killed outright when this regime began, while your anti-war people were still celebrating the end of the war. What kind of government is so savage to its own people? This is a government which cares only about itself, only about remaining in power. Its leaders have boasted, 'We have been worse than Pol Pot but the outside world knows nothing.'"

These last words were lost in a growing disturbance as three young Asians strode down the aisle to the front of the hall. They took up a position opposite the two Caucasian students with the scroll, who now jiggled the scroll up and down a few times as if on cue. Nguyen Nhu Thanh looked out nervously over the lectern.

One of the students with the scroll suddenly raised his free hand toward the audience. It was a delicate gesture, as if he were conducting a piece of music and wanted to hear more of the clarinet, perhaps, or of the viola. But the effect was as if all the brasses and drums had responded. From different parts of the hall came raucous hoots, and cat-calls, and a stomping of feet. Out into the aisles came half a dozen young people, several of them moving down the aisles toward the dais.

Ossy Blackwell rose and moved toward the lectern. "I see we're losing some of our audience. Let's give 'em a moment to leave. Or to be seated again." He nodded toward the side of the hall, and several more young people moved out into the aisles. "Let's have proper student decorum here," he said smiling. He knew there were no students in that second batch of people, and possibly none in the first batch.

When no one left the hall, Ossy spoke again into the microphone. "This is a public lecture, let me remind you. Anyone who isn't happy here can leave. The rest of you will act in a civil manner or you will be *asked* to leave." And then the Blackwell humor broke through. "Anyone who wants to stay for the question period is certainly welcome to do so." He smiled a broad smile, knowing it was as phony as a three-dollar bill, and nodded appreciatively at the scattered applause.

Without turning his back on the audience, Ossy moved to his seat and sat down again.

• • •

Marjorie's eyes were closed. She didn't care for controversy, and the past few minutes had been as unpleasant as any she could remember in this hall. People from the audience had shouted to the lecturer that the reforms instituted by Communist Party Chief Nguyen Van Linh (a.k.a. "Vietnam's Gorbachev") were completely transforming Vietnam. The lecturer replied that this was untrue. The reforms were minimal, largely for show. The hardliners had seized the day and Linh himself was virtually their captive, making pronouncements he had much earlier disavowed. In short, as Nguyen Nhu Thanh detailed it, Vietnam today was a place of vast oppression, vast corruption, vast misery. Unemployment was high. Morale was low. Bandits worked every major road. Prostitution was common. Nor would Linh's stepping down (by his own choice or not) be of any help. The *system* was not stepping down and the system was the real problem — the *Communist* system: totalitarian, bureaucratic, brutal, calcified, stifling.

Nguyen Nhu Thanh capped his response by saying that the only people who could believe in Vietnam's "renovation" and "openness" were cynical manipulators, or self-serving opportunists, or naïve fools, or agents of Hanoi. He was hissed from the audience.

Marjorie opened her mouth to hiss but no sound came. Her hatred of this little man was changing, growing more passive. She was committed to sitting in this seat and listening to him, but she no longer knew why.

"Keith, I want my knitting."

"Be quiet, Marjorie."

"But I just want to knit."

"Be *quiet.*"

The subject had shifted to refugees who were still leaving the country illegally in large numbers — unwilling to wait for any possible change to result from "renovation" and "openness." A student called loudly to the audience. "Why must we weep for these people who cannot accept the new egalitarian Vietnam? Why don't we weep instead for the impoverished country they leave behind — the country that America did so much to impoverish?" Applause greeted his comments.

Nguyen Nhu Thanh answered with resignation. "You do not ask me your question, but I will give you my answer. The refugees are not just the formerly wealthy. The refugees are also the destitute peasants and fishermen. Even the poor and uneducated can hate a system in which people must spy upon their neighbors, must forsake the religion of their forebears, must attend political meetings in every spare moment, and must be careful what they say or they will be marked for re-education or a New Economic Zone." He paused, and his grief was profound. "The egalitarian system of which you speak does not exist in the Socialist Republic of Vietnam. My countrymen are equal today only in the grave, and on this side of the grave only in their miserable and fearful lives." This was greeted with both applause and cat-calls. Ossy rose to his feet and the audience grew quiet again.

"With all respect," called a man from the balcony, "North Vietnam was right next to you. Why didn't you see what it was like? It was a police state. It was not paradise on earth. Half a million people had fled from there. Why didn't you use your eyes and ears?"

The little Vietnamese man paused for a long moment and the audience was fascinated by his motionless silence. Had something happened to his mind? Would he never speak again? Was this the crucial moment of the night they would long remember: the night when the little Vietnamese guy went over the edge, around the bend, clean out of his skull?

Nguyen Nhu Thanh had every eye upon him — the compassionate and the voyeuristic. And then he spoke. "The people who fled from North Vietnam were only . . . *refugees*. I did not believe them." Again he was silent. Every eye was still upon him.

"Please, my knitting," Marjorie whispered to Keith.

"*No*," said Keith. She reached across him. He elbowed her away.

Four rows back, Charlie Zinck gently nudged Hallie Cooper. "Your social worker seems to be having a bit of a problem there."

"Um," said Hallie.

And on stage, Ossy suddenly noticed the puddle of liquid at Nguyen Nhu Thanh's feet. Sweet Jesus, he had pissed in his pants! Or was it blood? Or some involuntary draining of intestinal fluids? Ossy moved quickly to the lectern and put his arm around the slender shoulders of this wounded man. Enough. The evening was over.

"We've been honored to have Nguyen Nhu Thanh with us tonight. This is a courageous and honorable man. We are greatly in his debt. Let us give him our thanks for being here with us, and let us now conclude the evening. We've already had many questions, which our guest has already addressed."

"No," interrupted the little Vietnamese. "I have final comments. Please. It is important to conclude properly."

Ossy stood with him as he continued.

"Vietnam is a small country. Poor. Far away. And many of its people only simple peasants. Why is it important? Because of *you*. Because so many of you, from this important and rich and energetic country, have allowed yourselves to be used. You have been manipulated. You have been misled and used." The audience was silent. "You have been misled by the journalists who are more interested in their careers than in the truth. You have been misled by the idealists who have never cared for the tarnish of truth. You have been misled by the Communists who have always concealed the truth, always hoping for even the smallest gain in power. If the treachery we call Communism is dying, as some would have us believe, we can only wonder what will be the next ideology to seduce the unthinking and the unscrupulous among you."

He was trembling now. With emotion? With despair? With illness? "But you are too great a people to be misled. You cannot continue to be used. You are good-hearted and naïve, and therefore dangerous. But there are too many lives at stake, all over the world, for you to be manipulated so easily."

The very feebleness of the little man's voice held the attention of all. Were they watching the last gasp of some dying animal? Again the thrill of being present at an extraordinary event. Why not? Some people died in the middle of a sentence. "There is much agony for me in all of this," he said. "To confess my part in deceiving you. To recall my beloved homeland now in slavery. And there is much agony for me in remembering my idyllic days in the Resistance. Those days were idyllic only because we were blind. We blinded ourselves. Your own anti-war people must be suffering a similar agony and I sympathize with them. They, too, were easily led and badly used. Some of them only wished an end to the war."

Marjorie Rupert looked at Keith wide-eyed, and breathed "Yes."

He stared stonily ahead.

"Your anti-war people have a difficult job now," continued Nguyen Nhu Thanh. "Some of them will simply continue along the same path. They are again on the wrong side in many places around the world. . . . They are still on the wrong side concerning Vietnam," and he nodded to the students holding up the scroll. "Hanoi is happy to see you still misled."

"But some of your anti-war people will learn from their past errors. To live with past errors is harder, I assure you, than to live in the jungle. . . . Your anti-war people would wish to see history frozen in time, and that cannot be. One learns from history. One *must* learn from history. One cannot have a temper tantrum with history." He paused for breath.

Chip McElroy was sweating. This little guy sounded just like Chip's father. Who the fuck did this guy think he was, lecturing at them like this? Chip would *never* let his father be right. *Never*. . . .

"I had no idea," Marjorie wailed softly. Her voice was audible for some distance around her, and heads turned toward her.

"Be *quiet*, Marjorie," snapped Keith. His voice, too, was heard by everyone sitting in nearby rows. On stage, Nguyen Nhu Thanh was momentarily distracted.

Four rows back, Hallie Cooper whispered to Zinck, "I had no idea Miles Aldrich was so *surly*."

"Miles Aldrich?" said Zinck, remembering his late-night telephone call with the elusive Dr. Aldrich.

Hallie nodded toward the man in the front row, who was now almost physically restraining the woman next to him, his hands reaching across her. "The social worker," Hallie said in bewildered explanation.

Zinck took a moment to get it. So the social worker who talked to Hallie after Anna McElroy's death — the social worker who seemed to have no answering machine but talked freely on the phone with Hallie about the dying Francis Minot — he was Miles Aldrich!

But Zinck himself had come upon Miles Aldrich in that crazy telephone call the other night when Jackie O. was favoring him with her favors (and her grousing). Zinck had placed the call to "Keith," the name in Orlov's pitifully empty address book, and the answering machine had promised that Dr. Miles Aldrich would return the call — as indeed he did, in the middle of the night, stepping cagily around Zinck's probing even as Zinck was stepping cagily around Aldrich's hesitations.

"Miles Aldrich!" Zinck said again. His eyes widened in stunned discovery. So there *was* a link between Minot and Orlov! They both knew Miles Aldrich. Then there could be a link between the death of Anna Carr McElroy and the death of Bernie Novinsky. . . . He couldn't quite grasp it yet, but he sent a glance of gratitude (and apology) to Hallie Cooper, who had apparently known it all along. Funny, she hadn't mentioned the name to him before, Zinck thought. Social worker, yes. Thanatologist, yes. A name to go with the job description, no. . . . But what was Miles Aldrich doing *here*? Why was he —?

Everyone heard the shots. Loud. Like nothing they'd ever heard before. And then came the screams, hysterical, out of control. And then the frantic movements as people ran wildly for the exits.

Very few, beyond those in the front row, saw that with the first shots Ossy Blackwell and Nguyen Nhu Thanh had dropped to the floor.

chapter nineteen

Marjorie Rupert leaped from her seat and stood quivering with shock. She turned to Keith, stunned. "*I* didn't do it! It wasn't *me*!"

Keith felt a surge of panic. "Marjorie, get control of yourself. Of course it wasn't you." He glanced around them.

"I didn't even *want* to, finally," Marjorie wailed loudly. She ran a hand distractedly through her wild hair.

"Of course you didn't. Now be quiet," said Keith. He grabbed her arm to pull her out of the path of the crowd.

"I didn't *do* it, I didn't *do* it," Marjorie repeated, standing her ground. Her face was drained of all color.

"Shut up, Marjorie." He gripped her arm tightly.

"I didn't *want* to do it. I *wouldn't* have done it. I *couldn't* have done it." There seemed to be no end to the recitation that poured from her.

"Be *quiet,* Marjorie," Keith shouted. He held both her arms now, and was digging his thumbs and fingers into her upper arms.

He could see that the crowd was out of control, scrambling madly to get out. But Marjorie, odd duck that she was, was standing there argung. "Take your hands off me," she said. "I didn't *do* it,

I tell you. I didn't even remember *how* to do it."

That was when Keith hit her, hard, across the side of her face. She looked at him then, really looked at him, and was finally silent. But her mouth hung upon and he could see new thoughts forming. He hit her again: another sharp whack to her head with the flat of his hand.

"Why are you hitting me?" Marjorie yelled. "You hate me. Why do you hate me? I tried, I tried. But I didn't want to do it."

That was when Keith clubbed her on the ear, with all his fury and frustration, and she staggered backward into an empty seat. A worm of blood began to crawl out of her nose.

She lifted her dazed head then, wiped her bloodied nose with the back of her hand, and stared at Keith. You're a . . . *monster*," she shouted above the noise of the crowd. And then, gathering her strength, she continued breathlessly. "You were supposed to *help* me. Why do you hit me? What did I do, that you have to hit me? Why do you . . ." She was caught in mid-sentence as Keith hit her again, hard, across the side of her head.

She was silent now and he stood menacingly over her. Any normal person would have shut up long before this, Keith thought. But Marjorie Rupert, he knew, had probably never been normal in the sad and lonely life she had led, and would probably never be normal in the short time remaining to her. All the others in Miller Theatre were trying to save their precious skins, pushing and shoving toward the exits or diving under the seats. Marjorie alone, it seemed to Keith, was trying to have a *discussion*, for crying out loud.

From the fourth row, Charlie Zinck saw the thanatologist arguing with the woman. *Arguing*? At a time like *this*? Zinck was not a huge fan of the social working profession, and it took only a moment for him to decide that *this* member of the profession was surely an Emotionally Disturbed Person. When he saw the thanatologist haul off and slug the woman, it took less than a moment for Zinck to decide that wherever else the police were needed, in this place of near-bedlam, someone was surely needed — and now — in the front row.

Trouble was, the people pushing and shoving their way to the exits had become an almost impenetrable mob. Zinck left bruises himself on some of the folks he shoved aside as he fought to reach

Aldrich and the lady being battered in the front row.

• • •

"I wouldn't have done it except for *you*," Marjorie wailed to Keith. "I *couldn't* have. Why do you turn against me? . . . Here, I don't want the gun any more. You can have it. I don't want *you* any more." She grabbed the knitting bag.

Jesus Christ, thought Keith. How did she get *that* again? And was she going to turn the gun over to him *now*? *Here*?

He reached out with both hands, grabbing her solidly around the throat. She would black out in a minute and he would disappear into the mindless mob around them. . . . He pressed his thumbs into her carotid arteries. He pressed harder.

He heard the shots and felt them. But that was the last he knew, except for some final millisecond of bafflement, or understanding, as he fell backward onto the floor.

Zinck heard the shots just as he reached the struggling pair. He saw Miles Aldrich collapse. Point-blank range. Who could miss? One of Aldrich's legs had hit Marjorie as he fell, and she had fallen on top of him, dizzy from what had been done to her and what she had done. She rested on him for a short moment as the life went out of him. And then she pulled away from him and vomited. Pieces of chicken, half-chewed noodles, bits of carrots, all swimming in a sour slime of soup, poured from Marjorie and joined the vital fluids spurting from Keith's dead body. She wiped her mouth with the back of the hand that still held Keith's gun.

Zinck grabbed the woman's right arm and twisted it until her gun dropped to the floor. In an instant, he had the cuff on her right wrist; in another instant, on her left. Holding her, he put a firm foot on top of the gun. She was heavy against him, but docile. He bent to retrieve the gun and tucked it into his belt. His own gun had never left its holster. Not in this mob. Every cop worried about hitting an "innocent civilian" in the rush to apprehend a possibly guilty one.

The woman sagged against him and he eased her with difficulty into a seat. "Thank you," she said. Her gratitude seemed strangely out of proportion to his efforts, he thought. . . . Unless she meant something he couldn't begin to understand.

Zinck looked into the crowd, and back to the fourth row, for Hallie Cooper. He didn't see her. Ah, but here she was, miraculously beside him, a little girl's horrified face on her as she contemplated the dead thanatologist with his guts still bubbling out of him. She put her hand on Zinck's arm, not tentatively but as if she knew exactly where to find solace. And he, not one to give a heap of solace on the average day, withdrew his arm to put it around her, draw her close, tell her without words that everything was fine. . . . Even when he knew it wasn't. He had just glanced up to the dais and had seen Ossy Blackwell and Nguyen Nhu Thanh lying near each other on the floor, surrounded now by Henry Barrkman, Steve Marino, and several other people who could have been students but weren't.

• • •

Forty feet away, about twelve rows back from the dais, Katie Borghese knew what she had seen — and what needed to be done. "Drop it!" she shouted, welcoming the familiar surge of adrenaline.

"Don't get excited," said Chip. "It's empty."

"I can count too. But drop it. *Now.*"

Chip stood his ground.

"It's either the gun on the floor, or your blood on the floor. Do yourself a favor. *Drop* it." Katie Borghese was approximately Chip's size and weight and age, and approximately five feet away from him. She had her gun on him in a steady Weaver stance. She saw his own gun dangling from his hand, pointing toward the floor.

She was in "plainclothes," which meant she was trying to look as unlike a policewoman as possible — in black leather jacket, black jeans, sneakers, a bright red sweater, a pink scarf. This also meant that she, as much as he, could be taken for the person who had fired those five shots. She flipped her badge out, on its heavy bead chain, but it was visible only from the front. She wasn't exactly worried, but she was aware of the problem.

But what was *this* guy's problem? He was grinning at her. "You're cute," he said.

"And you're dead, if you don't drop that revolver." She took an imperceptible step toward him, her weight not so much shifting from one foot to the other as gliding — as if on skates, in slow motion. Her eyes held his.

"You'd shoot me? Here?" He was facing her, his feet apart, a smile on his lips. "Yeah, you're cute."

Katie Borghese moved quickly. Turning slightly to her left and pivoting on her left foot, she snapped her right foot out to connect with Chip McElroy and then quickly drew her foot back to regain her balance. She would have preferred a groin shot, but the department tended to frown on it. Bad for public relations. A good kick in the solar plexus was usually better anyway. Indeed, Chip was now doubled over and clutching his mid-section and groaning. He had stopped smiling. And he had dropped the gun.

"I'll ask you again, Hot Shot. Who were you shooting at?" Katie Borghese asked.

"I can't . . . talk . . . now."

"You'll talk. And you'll talk *now*."

"I was . . . shooting . . . at the fucking wall," Chip gasped, trying to catch his breath.

"The *wall*? Why the *wall*?" She had the cuffs on him now. Two other cops had appeared and they kept their weapons on him while she finished hooking him up. A circle of onlookers watched, dumbstruck. This was an evening certain to be talked about later. In spite of all instincts telling them to flee, they knew they'd want later to have been there, seen it first-hand.

"Who's *with* you?" Katie Borghese demanded.

"I'm . . . alone," Chip groaned.

"Why were you shooting at the wall?"

He moaned. "I just wanted it to be . . . over."

"So you whip out a revolver and start a stampede. You're a real Hot Shot." She gave him a look of contempt. "He's cute," she said with disdain, into the crowd.

Into her radio she said, "Officer Borghese here. On the left side of the hall facing front. About half-way back. In the aisle. It's all over. Anyone wanna see the Adam Henry who fired the shots?"

She couldn't know that for some of those in the front of the hall, it was anything but over.

chapter twenty

Over the next ten days, some things fell quickly into place. And some didn't.

• • •

Henry Barrkman couldn't get over seeing Ossy Blackwell and Nguyen Nhu Thanh lying next to each other on the floor, completely unhurt and chuckling. Ossy had tried to explain, as he laughed, how he'd always been elated in Vietnam to be shot at and missed. Nguyen Nhu Thanh, who had often shot at the likes of Ossy Blackwell — and often missed — smiled in Henry Barrkman's direction, saying, "I have been similarly amused, on the battlefield." Henry had blinked, managing a smile in return.

• • •

Marjorie Rupert was taken to jail, of course. She spoke little. "He *used* me" was her repeated refrain. Questioned eighty-nine different ways about the gun, she said nothing. "And loaded with Glaser Safety Slugs," Zinck marveled. "They can goddam *Cuisinart* a person. Where does a woman with a nice clean job get to know about Glaser Safety Slugs?"

From the few questions she did answer, it emerged that Marjorie Rupert was alone in this world. No one cared that she was in jail, no one cared that she would probably be charged with murder, no one cared that she would soon be dead. (She *had* revealed that she was seeing Miles Aldrich on a professional basis.)

• • •

Charlie Zinck was coming to know a lot about Hallie Cooper — the size of her apartment, the color of her bedroom curtains, and the scent of her body after a shower. He was also coming to know the depths of her mind and heart as she was opening them to him. He was staggered by these multiple gifts. His ex-wife hadn't had a clue. Nor had Jackie O. (or various others). Nor had he — with his wife, or Jackie O., or the various others.

Late one night, as they lay quietly looking out at the Manhattan skyline, Hallie mused, "Marjorie Rupert and Francis Minot were a lot alike, weren't they? So completely alone. No wonder they needed that thanatologist. And my hunch is that he needed their aloneness."

The penny dropped for Zinck. After all, what had he noticed about Maurice Orlov but the aloneness of the man — no one to eat with, at the Chinese restaurant, and no one to laugh with, over the Joke-of-the-Day. But if Orlov and Minot and Rupert were connected to each other, maybe they were connected to any number of others under the "care" of Miles Aldrich. This hadn't made sense to Zinck until now. But a lot of things were making sense to him these days.

It didn't *quite* make sense, though. Here was this upstanding member of the helping professions. Maybe a bit on the Emotionally Disturbed side, but not so much that his practice suffered. One of his patients, Maurice Orlov, had probably pulled the trigger on Bernie Novinsky. But Orlov couldn't be questioned. Dead of a brain tumor. . . . Another patient, Francis Minot, had probably given the shove to Anna Carr McElroy. But Minot couldn't be quesioned. Dead of an unexpected intimacy with a string of subway cars at the Christopher Street station of the IRT. Uptown side. . . . But then there's this Marjorie Rupert, another patient, and she had blown this "helping professional" clean out of his socks. *Not* so clean. Very messy, in fact.

So if Miles K. Aldrich had been orchestrating something, with Orlov and Minot his oboe and flute, how come this second violin had turned against the conductor with a gutful of Glaser Safety Slugs? It *didn't* make sense.

Not yet. Maybe not ever. . . . There were plenty of murder cases like this. Never got figured out. Zinck was discovering yet again that however close he got to the criminal mind — observing it, analyzing it — there was always some wrinkle he could never have figured on. Maybe it was a wrinkle the murderer could never have figured on either.

"His apartment, Stevie boy," he said to Marino the next day. "And his records. We gotta be all over 'em, like cockroaches on your kitchen floor." But what were they looking for, and how would they know if they found it? Were Orlov and Minot and Rupert linked only by their aloneness? Were they *even* linked by their aloneness?

• • •

Miles Aldrich, too, had been alone in his life. In his death, nobody had yet come to sift through his belongings, cull them for mementoes.

With Zinck and Marino taking the place apart, the clippings turned up in half an hour, in a desk drawer holding little else. Marino held them up — two carefully trimmed columns, each with its upper-left corner gone, and each with a picture of Hallie Cooper looking out at the world with her clear eyes, her open smile. Zinck found it suddenly hard to breathe. Why the hell was Aldrich saving her columns? And why was one corner clipped off? He forced himself to take a deep breath. "Stevie, we gotta find out more about this guy."

The cards turned up in another half hour, in a fashionable little upholstered box on a bookshelf in Aldrich's well-furnished study. On each 3x5 card were the bare facts of Aldrich's patients — the name, address, and phone number; the name of the illness; the name of the referring physician. Maurice Orlov had a card. Francis Minot had a card. Marjorie Rupert had a card. . . . There were dates, too. One date was undoubtedly the date of the person's death. Orlov and Minot — and several hundred others — had such a date. Marjorie Rupert and twenty-odd others did not.

But nowhere among the effects of Miles K. Aldrich were there any further details on these people. No notebooks, no file folders. No hidden safes behind the tasteful artwork, no false-bottomed drawers in the bureaus. The guy didn't even have a computer. Whatever was on file concerning these people and their course of treatment had been stored in Aldrich's brain — and lost in an instant when the Glaser Safety Slugs tore the life out of him. Even his financial records were on these tiny cards. On the back of each card, a series of numbers indicated the patient's various visits — never many.

And then Steve noticed the other things on the cards: a checkmark on one, a dot on another, a corner clipped off here, a corner bent there.

Zinck needed some air. What he really needed, he knew, was more information about this Aldrich character and his patients. Quick in a hurry.

Back in the office, he called Steve Marino and Joanne Liu into his cubicle. "I want you two to go through these cards and get information on everyone who's still living. Right away. Drop everything else. I don't care how you get it — telephone is OK — but find out who these people are, how sick they are, what they thought of the late Dr. Aldrich, whether they were uncomfortable with him in any way, stuff like that. We'll probably want to get back to some of 'em. So keep it pleasant. Keep it open. There's gotta be some kinda pattern here. We need to know if it matches any pattern on these cards. We don't know what he was trying to tell us — or *not* tell us — with these markings. Maybe you'll get some ideas, as you go along."

"You think maybe it hasn't played itself out yet?" asked Steve. "Maybe more of these people are ready to go after someone, even if Aldrich isn't around any more?"

Charlie nodded. "It's a possibility." This Marino was one smart young cop; those pigeons were definitely an aberration. And Aldrich was one sweet piece of work. His Perps, if they acted, would not survive long enough to stand trial. And if they *didn't* act, because they had died in the meantime, Aldrich could always get a replacement.

"Should some of these people be under surveillance, do you think?" asked Joanne Liu.

"Yeah," Charlie Zinck responded slowly. "The problem is which ones. We don't have manpower to do 'em all." Another smart one, this copchick.

Don't worry yet, Zinck said to himself. Yeah, but you're *paid* to worry. But it's just a wild hunch. Yeah, but you're *paid* to get wild hunches.

On a hunch and in a hurry, he called Hallie at home, where she said she'd be working all day. "Do me a favor, honey? Don't go out anywhere. I mean *nowhere.* And don't answer your door. If you need anything, I can pick it up for you. . . . I'll tell you later."

Even as he celebrated the openness between them — treasured the trust he was getting from her and giving to her — he knew it would be a struggle later to tell her about this. And then he knew it wasn't just an unwillingness to frighten her. He knew suddenly, in his bones, that he wanted to take care of this woman, protect her, keep her safe and secure and comfortable and happy and laughing and unworried, for the rest of her life. He swallowed hard, on the grim thought that the rest of her life might be measured in days.

• • •

For her part, Hallie had her own information she was keeping for later. This morning, getting some groceries, she'd seen the man across the street, then in the grocery store, then back on the street again. He was lean and dark, his hair a little thin for his age, his eyes a bit too focused, his path a bit too direct. His gaze held Hallie's as he approached.

"You're Hallie Cooper, aren't you?" he had said. "Forgive me for intruding. I've been reading you for years. I just wanted to tell you I think you're great." And with that he turned, crossed the street, and walked off.

She would tell Charlie tonight, even though it would worry him. And she knew suddenly that she wanted only to make his life easy and sweet and happy, for as many years as they would have together. . . . Funny, all the advice to women about meeting men. Nobody ever said, "After a friend gets murdered, go to the police station and argue with anyone you find."

• • •

By late afternoon, Steve Marino and Joanne Liu had finished their phoning. Everyone on the list had been reachable at home. The two young cops walked Charlie Zinck through the high points, flipping pages and reading aloud from their notebooks.

"This one lives alone. His wife ran off with someone three years ago. Had to give up his job in August. Has his dinners with someone on his floor."

"This one is pretty much home-bound too. Gets out to the park when his daughter takes him. Does some repair jobs at home, little stuff, lamps and toasters, sometimes a TV set. Does his own cooking."

"Here's one who goes out a lot. For chemotherapy, mostly. With her sister, or her nephew, or the nephew's wife. Nice family, sounds like."

"Here's one who doesn't see any of his family. Doesn't see anyone except his doctor, and Aldrich."

And so it went, through all twenty-two of Aldrich's current clients, who were all dying.

"Did they sound sorry to hear about Aldrich?"

"You bet," Joanne answered.

"They liked what he was giving them?"

"The guy was a real life-saver to them," said Marino. "Well, you know what I mean."

"Go on," said Zinck. "Anyone *not* 100 per cent for him?"

"Not really," said Joanne. "But one man said — wait a minute, let me dig it out — yeah, he said, 'I never thought he was in it to *help* people. Not like the others I've known.'"

"He's known a lot of *thanatologists*?" Zinck was surprised.

"You know, that's just what I asked him," said Joanne. "What he meant was psychologists, psychiatrists, that kind of thing. Said he'd done a lot of that when he was younger. But all the social workers he's ever known were very kind people. Bleeding hearts, in fact.

His wife was a social worker. They really care about other people. He thought Aldrich didn't care about anyone but Aldrich."

"What gets me," said Steve, "is that some of these people don't see anyone but Aldrich. Except for maybe when some food gets delivered, or a nurse stops in. Some of them don't even have that."

"Mmmmm," said Zinck. "Not Marjorie Rupert, though. She saw students, teachers, deans. She was part of an *institution*."

"That doesn't say she wasn't alone," said Steve, his face serious.

"You bet," Joanne agreed, and to Zinck she said in an extravagant aside, "Any man who likes pigeons can't be all bad." She grinned.

"Will you stop with the pigeons," Steve protested. "That was ages ago."

"It will live in our memories forever," said Joanne. She had been a cop two years longer than Marino and took her pecking privileges very seriously.

"OK, you guys, knock it off," said Zinck, faking a cough to hide his laughter. Those pigeons would have eternal life, he thought, and Steve Marino along with them. . . . Reluctantly, he forced himself to leave the immortal pigeons and get back to the mortal humans he must now try to reduce to some broad categories: how sick, how alone, how mobile, how able to commit murder. He reached for his Gaviscon and in an uncharacteristic gesture he tilted the bottle to each of the young cops in turn, inviting them to join him. Each, very solemnly, took a couple of tablets and began to chew them, very thoughtfully.

Charlie Zinck got his large blackboard from behind a chair and rubbed it clear of a few traces of chalk. With a bravado he didn't feel, he said, "OK, let's find out whether we've got anything to worry about here."

chapter twenty-one

Steve Marino was on a surveillance. Since the guy he was watching hardly went out, there wasn't much to it — mostly trying not to fall asleep standing up. Relieved each day only by the appearance of Charlie Zinck for an hour or so, Steve spent a lot of time thinking about Bernie Novinsky. Not that he wanted to. He couldn't help himself.

Steve didn't have much experience with murder cases. The guys with thirty years on the job had seen hundreds of them. Some got solved and some didn't. You took it in stride, either way. But for Steve, with not even thirty years on this *earth*, every failure seemed monumental, looming as the certain pattern for the great, gray, unremittingly bleak future.

That's how Steve saw the Novinsky case: a failure of the most monumental proportions. The Perp in the case never got nabbed because he ran off and died. And in a related case the Perp never got nabbed because he ended up in front of, and underneath, and all over, a subway train. And while there was probably a third Perp behind the first two, *he* never got nabbed because some chemistry teacher did an experiment on his innards with a handful of Glaser Safety Slugs. Days like these, it didn't feel so hot to be a cop. What were they doing anyway — just keeping count of the bodies? That, yes, and doing a surveillance on someone who might become a fourth Perp. He snapped out of his reverie.

He had bought new handcuffs a few days ago at Jovino's downtown, hoping he wouldn't see anyone he knew. Later, stopping briefly at the station house, he was at pains to mention that his sister had finally located his cuffs. The guys ribbed him for a while — who'd he really lost 'em on? Ha, ha. A million laughs. But no sweat. In a few years, Steve consoled himself, *he* wouldn't be the butt of the jokes: he'd be ribbing the *younger* guys.

Yesterday, one of the older officers seemed especially glad to see him. "What's the name of that lady with the bazooms? On the Novinsky case. Came in one day with you, with her bazooms all hanging out and covered in jools."

Steve Marino shrugged. "Oh, you mean Kimberley, uh, Dayline. The jewels weren't real, you know." (He knew a thing or two.)

"Yeah, but what was *behind* 'em was. Dolly Parton, eat your heart out. She called you today."

"Oh yeah? What'd she want?"

"A dame like that calls you and you have to ask what she *wants*?"

"Come on, Willy, I don't have all day for this. I was just heading home. What'd she say? And why didn't you write it down, for Christ's sake, and not have to deliver the message to the entire squad room, for Christ's sake."

"What she said, Stevie boy, you're not gonna believe this."

"Will ya just —"

"OK, OK, she said — and this was the whole message — she said she didn't find your handcuffs but she had something else for you sometime, if you'd care to stop by for it."

"That was her message? You gotta be kidding."

"Would I kid you, Stevie boy?"

A smart guy wouldn't have taken bets on that one, and Steve Marino was basically pretty smart. But he got to thinking, in the days that followed. And he decided it was just possible that the fabulous woman had probably indeed called. So he decided he might just possibly give her a call sometime. Yes, perhaps indeed, he definitely thought he might. . . . So the Novinsky case, as they say, shouldn't be a total loss.

• • •

Two days later, the item made all the papers. In the paper where Hallie Cooper's face and words made the top of the first page of the second section, this brief news story made the bottom of the seventeenth page. No picture.

Ex-Congressman Escapes Assailant

Ex-Congressman Charles Ogden Hammond escaped injury yesterday afternoon when an off-duty policeman disarmed a man who was pointing a handgun at the former peace activist. Mr. Hammond was standing on the southwest corner of 57th Street and Eighth Avenue, waiting to cross the street, when Louis Gauthier, 56, asked him whether he was the former congressman.

Mr. Hammond acknowledged that he was, and Mr. Gauthier then took a loaded revolver from his pocket and put the muzzle against Mr. Hammond's chest. Before Mr. Gauthier could pull the trigger, however, New York City patrolman Steven G. Marino, who was in civilian clothes and standing nearby, stepped up to Mr. Gauthier and disarmed him.

Mr. Gauthier, who has been under treatment for a serious illness, collapsed on the sidewalk before the officer could question him. Mr. Gauthier was rushed to Roosevelt Hospital where he is in grave condition.

A leading figure in the peace movement of the Sixties and Seventies, Mr. Hammond represented the 43rd Congressional District of Manhattan for 16 years in the U.S. House of Representatives. After the American withdrawal from Indochina and the Communist takeover of South Vietnam, Laos, and Cambodia, Mr. Hammond came to believe that in adding his weight to the anti-war protests he had been on the wrong side of the Vietnam War issue. He wrote the controversial book "On the Wrong Side" about his conclusion that he had been misled and had misled others. Soon after publication of his book, he was defeated in his bid for re-election to Congress. He has recently been writing and lecturing on foreign policy issues. He had just participated in a seminar on the future of Asia, when the incident occurred.

• • •

Steve Marino couldn't get over it. "You know what he said to me, just before he passed out? He said, 'Go ahead, gimme life.' Whaddya think he meant? I mean there's life and there's *life*."

Charlie Zinck shrugged. He was looking triumphantly at the names on his blackboard — the names from Aldrich's cards. For some days now, two of Aldrich's clients had been under full surveillance. They were the only possible ones for what Zinck had in mind (and perhaps for what Aldrich had had in mind). They were the only ones who were sufficiently mobile and yet were completely isolated from all supportive human contact.

The men rarely left home. Then, suddenly, one of them left home for the hospital: a one-way trip, the doctors assured Zinck. And yesterday the other one made his move, fueled not so much by animal energy (he was a bag of bones at the time) as by a raw determination to get this last thing *right*, this only thing in his life that wouldn't be a failure, this one thing that would give his whole life meaning. He wouldn't have anyone to brag to, about it. But he'd never had anyone. Keith picked up on that right away.

• • •

It was over, wasn't it? Zinck convinced himself that Hallie's admirer, the other day, had been simply — an admirer. Well, he hadn't *quite* convinced himself, but he managed to convince Hallie. Then, to calm his nagging worries, he taught her how to check on anyone behind her, swiveling her head ninety degrees to right and left, as she walked. (He never told her about finding her columns in Aldrich's study.)

It was over, surely. But had there been others before Bernie Novinsky and Anna Carr McElroy, others who had tried to reopen the discussion about the Vietnam War, only to be killed by the loners that Aldrich had manipulated into murder? In one of their middle-of-the-night conversations, Hallie wondered about this with

Charlie Zinck. She could have been reading his mind, Zinck thought.

On another matter, he was certain she was reading his mind. She'd known, almost before he'd said a word, that what bothered him more than anything else was arriving at the front row an instant too late to keep Aldrich alive. Charlie had dreamed about this failure of his, awakening to the metallic taste of it.

Too late by what — ten seconds, fifteen? A crying shame is what it was. And he knew enough about the way the mind chooses its words to know that in some way he felt ashamed of himself and in some way, too, he felt like crying. She comforted him, treating him like the grown-up that he was, but also like the child that was still in him: "You did your best," she said, caressing his shoulder softly and then resting her head on it.

"But aren't brains and brawn supposed to solve things?" he asked. The stubborn kid in him was refusing to be comforted. "Luck isn't supposed to have anything to do with it. I mean, the Good Guy is supposed to win out because he's tough and he's smart, right? Aren't I tough? Aren't I smart?"

He sighed deeply, then, and suddenly the stubborn kid was gone. "*You*, marvelous woman, knew what it was about from the beginning. I should just shut up and be glad you dropped by. And I *am*. I am so *truly* glad."

"It's probably only on TV that the guy solves it brilliantly, all by himself," Hallie said. She raised herself onto one elbow and leaned into him. "And then he explains it to his girlfriend in the last seven minutes. Didn't you tell me that?" They both laughed.

She gave him a smile that could have been the grin of a proud ten-year-old or the tease of a grown woman, as she added, "But maybe he doesn't *have* to explain everything to her."

He hugged her. "I don't have to explain *anything* to you."

"Yes you do. You have to tell me, once again, how happy you are to be with me. Following which, I will tell you the same. And that should be all we need to discuss tonight." She let the blanket fall from her breast.

"You are some demanding woman," said Charlie, in an exaggerated rebuke. He kissed her gently. She returned his kiss with passion, and in the breathless and joyful moments that followed, they had no need for words.

• • •

On that same evening, Chip McElroy was alone in his rented room. He took another beer from the tiny fridge and banged the bottle down on the dingy piece of furniture that was his dining table, his desk, his bookshelf, his coat-rack.

A well-worn scrapbook lay open, amid the clutter. In recent days, he had gone often to this scrapbook. Seeing these clippings again was like being back with friends, being back in "The Movement."

Since he knew the clippings by heart, he wasn't so much reading them as making sure they were all still there. Here was the clip about the march on the Pentagon. A good picture of Chip — fist raised, smiling. Good of Anna, too. . . . And here was the clip about the first flag-burning in Central Park. Another good shot of Chip in the center of the action. . . . And here was the clip about Jane Fonda just back from Hanoi; Chip had introduced her. She had given him a hug afterward as she hurried to her next appearance. Anna hadn't liked her. Anna never liked the good-looking chicks. But things had been good between them in those days. He loved those days. He loved this scrapbook.

He loved being identified as the son of Richard McElroy, knowing that this really got to the old man. By some arrangement that could hardly be coincidence, Chip's name never appeared in the Terre Haute papers. Everywhere else in the U.S., Chip was described as the activist son of the well-known Hoosier entrepreneur. The old fart. The well-known Hoosier fart, Chip thought. Never did know what to make of Chip.

Chip's father had posted his son's bail — of course — even though he didn't begin to comprehend the whole episode. What sort of lunatic, for God's sake, tries to make a social comment by emptying a loaded revolver in a place full of people?

To Rick McElroy, his son's act was ridiculous, juvenile, self-indulgent. But Rick McElroy wouldn't allow *his* son to spend *weeks* in a holding facility with common *criminals*. Chip was relieved to be told he couldn't leave Manhattan while his case was pending. Rick McElroy, who had invited Chip back to Terre Haute, was also relieved.

Now, sitting in his apartment with his scrapbook, Chip had a brainstorm. I don't *need* to stay in Manhattan, he thought, I could fucking *disappear*! Grow a beard, gain fifty pounds, they'd never find me. Go South, good beer-drinking country all year 'round. Stiff his father for the bail money. The old fart would never miss it.

Chip put his scrapbook on the table and got up for another beer. When he sat down again, he held the book to him in a long agony of understanding. The only thing wrong with his escape plan was this book of yellowed clippings. A guy on the lam — a guy with a whole new identity — doesn't bring a goddam *scrapbook* with him.

Absurd, that's what it was! He'd heard of guys being married to their cars, or their jobs. But married to their scrapbooks? He laughed, then, great heaving bellowing guffaws that turned, quite unexpectedly, into sobs. The tears ran down Chip McElroy's face as he sobbed and gasped and rocked back and forth, holding his scrapbook tightly to his chest.

• • •

Late that night, in the tiny second bedroom of the fourth floor rear apartment rented by Mrs. Luerine Pemberton, a teenage boy was startled awake from something he'd been dreaming.

The gun that had killed Bernie Novinsky was never recovered by the police. Instead, it was in this tiny bedroom, wrapped in a T-shirt belonging to Mrs. Pemberton's grandson Joshua, and tucked deep under his mattress.

He took the gun out often, to look at it. He suspected (rightly) that he shouldn't tell his gramma about it. Best, too, not to show it to anyone else. Wouldn't want to get picked up by the cops and tortured until he confessed to a murder he hadn't done. He, Joshua Tyrone Pemberton, knew about these things.

He looked at the gun now, musing yet again about the murder he had witnessed. The one who did it, he was a sick old man and he ran funny. The one who got it, he was old too. Not as old as his gramma, thought Joshua, but old. (The concept of middle age was not known to Joshua.) The one who got it was surprised. The one who did it was determined, but he threw away a perfectly good gun as he ran away all funny.

Joshua often thought about why the one had shot the other. Maybe the one who had gotten himself shot was in possession of something that the sick man ached like a fiend in hell to have. And when the one who had gotten shot wasn't able to hold onto this thing any more, because he was dead, the sick man felt a lot better. Maybe *he* wouldn't have the thing the other man had, but the other man was dead on the sidewalk and wouldn't have it either.

Joshua wrapped the gun back in the T-shirt, and stowed it carefully under his mattress.

He knew he would think about these things again and again, over the years, about what it meant to take life, to lose life, to kill, to be killed.

Wouldn't it be funny, he thought, if maybe the sick man hadn't wanted to take anyone's life. Maybe he just wanted his own, but couldn't have it.

Joshua's teachers were always impressed with his imagination.

epilogue

Over the past dozen years, Hallie Cooper and Ossy Blackwell had become friends.

It began with their grieving together over Bernie and Anna. It continued with Hallie almost single-handedly putting Anna's book on the bestseller list by mentioning the book in several columns. It continued further with Ossy creating the Novinsky Lectures, each of which had focused on a controversial "trouble spot" — and none of which had (yet) involved further shootings.

Today the two were at a small Japanese restaurant on Columbus Avenue, sharing a sushi lunch and their concerns about the world after 9/11.

"That's why the next Novinsky lecture is about Vietnam," said Ossy.

"Oh?" said Hallie. "Why?" She was busy getting her chopsticks around a piece of California roll.

"Because I'm ornery," Ossy laughed. "I'll keep talking about Vietnam until I see people begin to understand it. And because we have a new enemy out there today in international terrorism, as evil and determined as the Communists were. We gotta get things straight about what went on during the Vietnam era — especially what went on here at home, where the war was really lost. We gotta understand what wars are for, and why we gotta stand up to the people who are out to destroy us." He worked at keeping a piece of eel in his chopsticks, first dropping it, then picking it up again, then dropping it again, finally getting it into his mouth. "See what I mean? I'm a stubborn son of a gun."

Hallie smiled. "So who've you got coming?"

"He makes documentaries. And he's done a knockout film on life today in Vietnam. It's pretty terrible. I mean the life there, not the documentary. And he has well and truly done his homework. So after we watch his film, he'll give us all his sources."

He smiled impishly. "I'll love dumping this on the students. They gotta learn that what sends 'em out marching has to be solid facts, not 'feel-good' feelings. It ain't enough to be self-righteous about what we feel. We gotta be *smart* in what we *think*, and *right* in what we *do*."

Hallie nodded solemnly. "So, give me some facts." She waved her chopsticks at their plates. "Good lunch, isn't it?"

"*Great* lunch. But help me out. This is too much for me." He pointed his chopsticks at the wooden platter in front of his plate. . . . "OK, facts. This guy is a walking encyclopedia on Vietnam. And he isn't like those Smith College alumnae who came back in 2001 raving that their trip was 'nothing short of fabulous.' The only thing this guy thinks is fabulous — unbelievable — is our denial about what happened there after we abandoned the South Vietnamese and they were overrun by the North."

"OK, facts," Hallie urged.

"You'll be attending, won't you, and writing about it?"

"Sure will."

"Bring your husband. I like that guy."

"So do I," she laughed.

"OK, facts. . . . Can you believe, they had to import *rice*, after Hanoi collectivized agriculture in all of 'unified' Vietnam! Things improved when collectivization was abandoned in 1986, and small-scale private enterprise was encouraged. But still the poverty level is 30% in rural Vietnam — and four-fifths of the country is rural."

Hallie was attentive, and Ossy went on. "Per capita, their Gross Domestic Product is right down there with Kenya, Bosnia, Cuba, and Azerbaijan. Not quite as bad as Ethiopia or North Korea, but not even as good as Mongolia or Zimbabwe. Any improvements in living standards are mostly in the private sector, which accounts for fewer than 1.5 million of their 40 million workers. *You* do the mathematics. The economy may have doubled in the past ten years — as some folks love saying — but things are pretty goddam dismal for the Vietnamese people."

Ossy's eyes narrowed. "Education isn't free (and it isn't compulsory). Health care is poor, especially if you were on the wrong side during the war. You lose a leg stepping on a leftover landmine — and not all of them are American mines — and you won't easily get a prosthesis if you were aligned with the South during the war. . . . And unemployment is high. Things are not good there, even with the new economic liberalization. A major part of their economy is the money sent back by refugees."

"What's the total population?"

"Just short of 80 million. In a place smaller than the two Dakotas, I might add. Fourteenth most populous nation in the world. And if you can believe it, tenth in the number of active troops — 484,000 in round figures. That's a higher percentage of the population than in China or the U.S."

Hallie was making notes and Ossy continued.

"Next, prostitution. Would you believe, more than 10,000 women are working as prostitutes in Ho Chi Minh City alone? And child prostitution is a problem throughout the country, because of the pervasive poverty. Malnutrition stunts the growth of 45% of all kids under the age of five. And 20,000 kids are 'street children.'"

"Not an easy place to live."

"Especially if you want to use your mind. Sure, their constitution provides for free speech. But don't try to criticize the Communist Party, which controls *everything* — or criticize the government leadership, which is drawn 100% from the Party. And don't even *think* of promoting a multiparty democracy, or a religion not on the government's approved list. If you're an artist, don't even *dream* of exhibiting anything that criticizes or ridicules the Party or the government."

Ossy shook his head. "One dissident just got a 15-year sentence. And their leading dissident, Tran Do by name, had his memoirs confiscated in 2001, the year before he died. He was a decorated veteran of the war, a general, and he had been head of the Party's ideology and culture department. But the Party expelled him in 1999 for suggesting that it ought to give up its monopoly on power. And he wasn't the only one to have his books confiscated and destroyed."

Ossy gave an unamused chuckle. "Even the *New York Times* carried this news, when Tran Do died. But most of the anti-war people aren't interested. They still travel there, without a second thought, to experience the 'exotic allure' of the place, and meet its 'cordial and welcoming' people. . . . I notice the travelers don't stay there, though."

"It wouldn't be my favorite place to live," said Hallie.

"You in particular — you'd go bonkers. For one thing, a free press simply doesn't exist there. A new survey shows only 26 of the 188 nations of the world with less freedom of the press than Vietnam. And, can you believe — sorry, I shouldn't be so amazed — a law passed by their National Assembly in 1999 gives anyone harmed by a news report the right to compensation even if the news report was *accurate*! That's not likely to encourage fearless truth-telling.... But interestingly, the National Assembly is beginning to tolerate some openness toward local grievances — about corruption, inefficiency, and the like. They still don't pass any law opposed by the Communist Party. But the new head of the Party, as of 2001, is considered a moderate. So who knows where things are moving, for these battered and aggrieved people."

"Toward a freer economy, wouldn't you think?"

"Hard to tell. The moderates want to head off popular unrest, so they want an expanding economy. But major privatization could cost millions of jobs and create a serious backlash against the government. . . .The hardliners, on the other hand, worry that if the state loosens its control over the economy, the Party's power over everything could be compromised. And power has always been any Communist Party's main concern. We'll see."

Ossy chewed for a minute. Then, "Plain and simple, Vietnam is one of the most oppressive places on earth. There's been some easing up. They don't maintain surveillance on *everyone*, these days. Or open *everyone*'s mail. Or enforce *everyone*'s denial of access to satellite TV. Or require *everyone* to register with the police when they spend a night away from home. But basically it's the same government that came to power in 1975 — the same government that executed 65,000 people outright, killed 250,000 in their gulag, and turned a million Vietnamese into boat people."

Ossy's face tightened. "Did you know that right after the fall of Saigon, teams of North Vietnamese questioned every last person in South Vietnam to ascertain their political beliefs? From this, the Communists knew who to send to prison, who to send to re-education, who to deport to a New Economic Zone. The Party cadres loved it. They got to seize the belongings of anyone caught trying to escape, just as Party officials up and down the ladder benefited a couple of years later when some 30,000 businesses in Saigon were nationalized or closed."

His face twisted into a deeper scowl. "That government has owned its people as if they were slaves. The 'exit fees' extorted from the boat people reached an estimated 2.5% of the GNP, one year. And the government sent thousands of Vietnamese workers to the Soviet Union and its satellites, in arrangements that were never revealed. It shouldn't come as a big surprise that some people — me included — think these workers were sent against their will, into precisely the kind of forced labor the Communists know so well."

He sighed. "Most Americans never cared about what happened there after we left."

"Maybe because they felt we had no right to be there in the first place," said Hallie.

"Then this lecturer will open their eyes. He quotes historians and policy-makers who think we were *absolutely* right to engage in that war. Our credibility as a major military power was at stake. If we hadn't — early on — tried to stop the Communist take-over of South Vietnam, we'd have encouraged the Communists to do whatever they wanted, anywhere in the world. As it was, they went on to some serious aggression anyway — Angola, Ethiopia, Afghanistan — thinking we'd stay out of their way. But if we'd stayed out of their way in Vietnam, things could have been much worse around the world, and worse for us, ultimately."

Hallie was thoughtful. "Of course, that doesn't address the view that we were in a war we couldn't win — that it wasn't so much *immoral* to be there, it was *foolish.* Will he talk to that point?"

Ossy had just guided a delicately wrapped spoonful of salmon roe into his mouth. He chewed briefly, gathering his thoughts. "He'll say that what's coming out now — not from everyone, but from a few careful researchers and re-thinkers — is that the war wasn't only *winnable*, it was already *won.* Well before the last of our troops left in '73, and maybe as early as the end of '70. Once we stopped counting bodies — remember 'search and destroy'? — and started securing the villages and hamlets of South Vietnam, it was all over for the Viet Cong. By early '71, they were finished, and without coming anywhere near their hope of a popular uprising in the South." He laughed, without mirth. "But who could seriously expect the hearts and minds of the South to be won by the Viet Cong, when the V.C. were kidnapping and murdering and coercing and terrorizing the South Vietnamese in every village and hamlet?"

His voice was rising. "But even with our turning real energy by the end of the Sixties to the 'pacification' and 'Vietnamization' aspects of the war — providing real security for the people of South Vietnam, and building up their military forces so they could handle things themselves (with some logistical and financial help from us) — even then, with real success growing in these efforts, the folks back home weren't getting the whole story. Maybe our reporters didn't understand that the war was more than a 'conventional' war. Maybe they didn't *want* to understand. Remember when Walter Cronkite proclaimed the Tet Offensive of '68 a disaster for us, and for the South Vietnamese? It was actually a disaster for the *North* Vietnamese. But the media always gave more coverage and credibility to the folks wanting to get us out of South Vietnam than to the folks wanting to get us into North Vietnam."

Hallie gave him a weak smile. "True, very true."

"Most recaps of the war don't even get into the later years. Our operations in Cambodia and Laos, for instance, in the early Seventies, brought terrible losses to the North Vietnamese. Our anti-war people were furious about these campaigns, despite the fact that international law allows a belligerent to take appropriate action whenever a neutral nation allows its territory to be used by the other belligerent. . . . And then the Easter Offensive of '72. It was such a disaster for the North they couldn't launch another major offensive for three whole years. The war really *was* over for the North. So what did they do? They turned most of their energies to the Paris negotiations — not relinquishing their attention to the anti-war movement, of course — and that's where we really lost it. The treaty signed in 1973 allowed the North to keep 160,000 troops in the South. What could we have been *thinking*? And after more than four years of negotiations! . . . Then, when the North almost immediately violated the Paris Accords in multiple ways — the Ho Chi Minh Trail had *traffic jams*, can you believe, from all the stuff and people they were putting into South Vietnam — even then we didn't respond as we had promised the South we would. Finally, a year or so later, when our Congress failed to vote the military and economic aid we had promised the South, the North saw their big chance and grabbed it. In a few short months, the South was fully conquered. We, in effect, had thrown South Vietnam overboard." He pounded the table with his fist, drawing the brief attention of two people at a nearby table. "Our failure wasn't military, it was *political*. . . . And I don't say that just 'cause I served there. . . . Still, it was the right political decision to *be* there. Some even think it was right to leave when we did because it kept us from losing our resolve for the Cold War of the Eighties. I don't know. I still think we shouldn't have left the way we did."

When Hallie made no reply, he continued. "And *that's* what's so important for us to see as we face this new enemy — with their suicide pilots and suicide bombers today, and their chemical and biological and nuclear weapons tomorrow. The America-haters (a lot of 'em in our own country) have called us everything they can think of, for retaliating against these new terrorists. We're 'jingoistic,' 'imperialistic,' 'egotistic,' 'arrogant,' 'rabidly nationalistic,' 'racist' — you name it. We're also 'genocidal,' even 'Nazis,' who deserved the attack of 9/11 because we're 'greedy,' and 'too rich,' and somehow 'terrorists' ourselves. Sounds like language from the Sixties and Seventies, doesn't it? . . . These 'peace-lovers' hate us for retaliating. Sometimes I think that the America-haters among us have as much hatred for our freedoms, our energy, our achievements, as the Islamic militants do. Or as the Communists did. We cannot let the peaceniks, and all their friends in the media and in Congress, give it away again. We're strong militarily. We've got to stay strong in every other way."

Ossy smiled. "I'm making a speech. I apologize." They ate quietly for a few moments. Then, "Hallie, let me ask you something. Where was your head during the Vietnam War? We've never talked about it."

"No, we haven't. It isn't easy for me to talk about. . . . I was in my first job, doing a lot of typing for senior people. I marched against the war partly because *they* did. But I wanted to bring the troops home because I was married to one of them. And then he came home. . . . To a hospital. . . . To die. . . . I was shattered, holding onto my life with great difficulty. The protests were a good place to take my anger. And then it was over. The protests, the war, and finally my grieving. . . ." She sighed, remembering the pain without quite feeling it. "It all seems a very long time ago."

"It *was* a long time ago," Ossy said softly. "I'm very sorry for your loss. I had no idea. . . . A lot of good men died. And a lot of lives here were in turmoil." He held his chopsticks at the ready, not for eating but for further comments. "War has a purpose, though. It stops the bullies from grabbing what they want, or destroying what they please. All this talk about 'learning to love,' and 'trying to understand' — going for a peace treaty even when we know it won't be honored — all of it overlooks the basic truth that when the good guys are prepared to fight, they either *prevent* a war or they *win* it."

"That's my thinking, too. It was certainly Bernie's thinking. He helped me to understand the Vietnam War — that we *couldn't* have opted out of it, and that we shouldn't have backed out of it so completely. And I finally understood why I was widowed. . . . He was enormously helpful to me, altogether, in my bereavement. He called me almost every day. We had lunch almost every week. He introduced me to all his colleagues. I think he saved my life." Again her sigh went deep. "I can't imagine getting to where I am now — in my mind, in my spirit — without Bernie."

Ossy smiled. "Quite a guy, that Bernie."

"You can't begin to know. Sure, I had other friends, Joan Novinsky among them. And mentors. And a support group. And a psychologist. But it was Bernie who was everything all in one. In addition to being the brother I never had, and the father I didn't have any longer. He was everything but a lover — we each went elsewhere for that. It wasn't until he died that I realized I wanted someone who would be all that Bernie had been, and more. And that's when I met Charlie. He thinks we fell in love at that lecture when the thanatologist was killed." She laughed. "So we owe it all to you."

Ossy bowed his head in mock acknowledgment. "Say, I just saw that photo exhibit you raved about — the one about the women of Afghanistan getting out from under the Taliban. I agree. Great pictures. Great captions. And I love it that she credits Anna's book with sending her there."

Hallie chuckled. "Charlie has an entirely different take on her. She had talked to the man waiting for Bernie, that awful night, and Charlie will never forget the day she sailed in to tell them about it. The entire squad room came to a halt. She was — uh — very well endowed and not very well clad. . . . Charlie says she probably doesn't give a hoot about politics in Afghanistan, she just doesn't like *burqas*."

"Ha! Don't knock it. Whatever gets people to take a better look at the world is OK. This documentary about Vietnam shows prostitutes delivering their goods right there on the street. Quite a film," he laughed. "It's not pornographic, though; the women are too beaten-down and ugly. . . . But I'm telling everyone about that scene. Get 'em into the tent, so to speak. I guess I don't need to do that with you," he laughed.

"No, I'll be there," said Hallie. "Although I'm always interested in how to get 'em into the tent. We writers are always working on that."

"We professors too," said Ossy. "Maureen tells me I'm just a showman, deep down. Sure, I love a good show — if you can sing the songs afterward, fine. But what are the songs *saying*? That's what I *really* care about."

"That was Bernie's thinking, too. Why not give 'em a good show, while you're trying to get your message across, he used to say. But the message was what he really cared about. And the message had to be *true*. And *important*."

"Here's to Bernie Novinsky," Ossy said, solemnly lifting his cup of Japanese tea.

"Here's to Bernie Novinsky," Hallie repeated, clinking teacups with him.

THE END

Printed in the United States
18346LVS00004B/196-219